Phyllis Wong

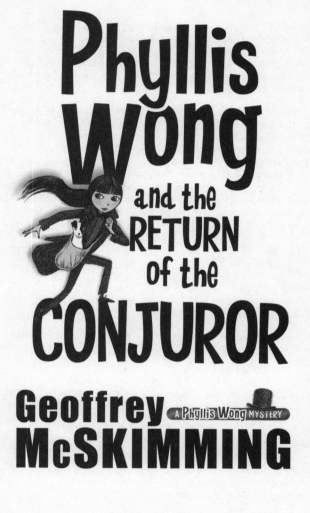

and the RETURN of the CONJUROR

Geoffrey McSKIMMING

A Phyllis Wong MYSTERY

ALLEN&UNWIN

SYDNEY · MELBOURNE · AUCKLAND · LONDON

Allen & Unwin
83 Alexander Street
Crows Nest NSW 2065
Australia
Phone: (61 2) 8425 0100
Email: info@allenandunwin.com
Web: www.allenandunwin.com

A Cataloguing-in-Publication entry is available from the National Library
of Australia – www.trove.nla.gov.au

ISBN 978 1 74331 837 9

p. 107, 136–37: quotation from 'Antigonish' by William Hughes Mearns

Cover and text design by Seymour Designs
Cover and internal illustrations by Peter Sheehan
Author photograph by Sue-Anne Webster
Set in 12/17 pt Sabon by Midland Typesetters, Australia
This book was printed in April 2014 at McPherson's Printing Group,
76 Nelson St, Maryborough, Victoria 3465, Australia
www.mcphersonsprinting.com.au

10 9 8 7 6 5 4 3 2 1

MIX
Paper from
responsible sources
FSC® C001695

The paper in this book is FSC® certified.
FSC® promotes environmentally responsible,
socially beneficial and economically viable
management of the world's forests.

For my conjuror, Sue-Anne Webster

Contents

PART ONE

PART TWO

PART THREE

'The only reason for time is so that everything doesn't happen at once.'

—Albert Einstein, physicist, 1879–1955

'There are Pockets of different strengths where you least expect them. In them you will find the greater magic. It is more marvellous than the sum parts of any duck.'

—Wallace Wong, magician, 1898–?
(from his journals)

'If your messenger find him not there, seek him i' th' other place yourself. But indeed, if you find him not within this month, you shall nose him as you go up the stair . . .'

—William Shakespeare, writer, 1564–1616
(from *Hamlet*, Act IV, Scene III)

PART ONE

Flames and futures

You do something to me . . .

On a crisp, dark, frosty night in December, as the last of the city lights were being turned off, a clear, melodious whistling was floating through the air like a thick, syrupy fog.

It was not a quickly whistled tune that floated along the almost deserted streets, but a slow, almost melancholy air. It rose and fell and sometimes it hovered on a single note, freezing that note and suspending it.

At times, the tune trembled, like a delicate cobweb vibrating in a steady breeze. At other times, it swooped down low, then shot up again to reach thin, high notes. But mostly, the whistling was strong and direct.

It had such strength in it that if anyone were to hear it they might think that the notes were here for good, never to dissolve away, as music always does.

It was a whistling with a purpose behind it.

It was the whistling of a man who had vanished . . .

Off to Thundermallow's

'Hey, Phyllis Wong! Where's the fire?'

Phyllis Wong was hurrying down the street, her school bag half slung across her back and her long black hair billowing behind her in the breeze. Her friend Clement, who had asked the question, was trying to keep up with her as she strode the pavement.

'What're you talking about?' Phyllis said over her shoulder.

'What's the rush?' Clement pushed his glasses back up his nose. His legs were shorter than hers and he was struggling to stay alongside her.

'There's no rush,' she said.

'Then how come you're leaving scorch marks on the sidewalk?'

She shook her head, as if to say, *you always exaggerate too much*, and kept powering on.

'I know what's wrong,' Clement said, puffing. 'You're narked. You always hurry like this when you're angry about something.'

Phyllis came to a corner and waited for the WALK light to turn green. She watched the cars and buses and taxis crawling along the avenue, but she was seeing something other than traffic.

Clement's phone rang and he pulled it out of his jeans pocket. 'Hi, Mum. On the way home. With Phyllis. I dunno. Yep. Uh-huh. No. I think I left it at home. You sure? I can't remember . . . yeah, I know. It's just a *coat*. Um, yeah. Okay.' He put the phone away and said, 'You're not the only one who's narked. Mum was checking up about my new coat. I think I must've left it at school.'

Phyllis shook her head again, as if to say, *you're always losing things.*

The lights changed and she strode onto the road, Clement running next to her.

'So, c'mon, Phyll, what's eating you?'

Phyllis knew he wouldn't let up, so she answered him. 'If there's one thing I can't stand, it's people trying to expose my tricks!'

'Ah,' said Clement. 'Leizel Cunbrus.'

Phyllis's dark eyes blazed at the sound of the girl's name. 'She's always trying to be smart. Every time I perform magic at school, she's there with her friends, saying smart things like "It's up your sleeve" or "I saw it under the deck" or "I bet you can't do it again with a different card!" She drives me nuts.'

'She's just jealous. You know things she doesn't. She hates that. She always wants to be the best at everything.'

'And she thinks she's so beautiful! She keeps telling her friends how beautiful she is—*ergh*. And if she says to me one more time "You're not a *real* magician, Phyllis Wong. A *real* magician has rabbits and doves!", I swear I'll take my wand and show her exactly what a real magician can do with it!'

'Yeah, well at least a real magician dresses properly. Unlike Leizel Cunbrus. A real magician would never wear jeans that show off her—'

'Ah, don't worry about it, Clem, I know what you mean. You're right. She's just jealous.'

'Ha! It's like the sidewalk's always throwing a party and inviting her jeans to come down and join in . . .'

Phyllis giggled then, and her eyes cleared. 'You're so observant,' she said to her friend.

'Learnt how to be from you,' he said. 'Like you always say, "The more you see, the less you'll stumble."'

'No, that's Wallace Wong, not me. I found it in one of his old journals. He was always writing things like that.'

'Wallace Wong, Conjuror of Wonder!' Clement said. Phyllis was often mentioning her great-grandfather. Before his mysterious disappearance while performing the Houdini sub-trunk illusion in Venezuela in 1936, Wallace Wong had been one of the most famous and successful and brilliant magicians in the world.

Phyllis looked at the time on her phone. Then she turned the corner and headed up a smaller street, one that was lined with tall, narrow buildings and older shops, many of which had been built more than a hundred years ago.

'Hey,' Clement said, keeping up with her. 'This isn't the way home. Where are you going?'

'To Thundermallow's,' she replied, walking quicker.

'Thundermallow's?' Clement repeated.

'There's a little something I need . . .'

'What's Thundermall—*oooof*!' He sprawled face-down on the sidewalk, having tripped on one of his untied shoelaces.

Phyllis stopped and turned, reaching down to help him. 'You all right?'

'Ouch. Yeah, I'm fine.' He sat up, rubbed his elbow and straightened his glasses, which fortunately hadn't shattered from the impact. He hoisted his backpack around his shoulders so that it sat squarely against his back again. 'I'll just bruise, that's all.' He took Phyllis's hand and she yanked him up. 'So what's Thundermallow's, then?'

'My favourite magic shop in all the world,' answered Phyllis Wong as she hurried off.

'Ah,' said Clement, raising his eyebrows.

'There it is,' she announced as they approached a dark old shopfront.

Clement looked up at the neatly painted sign hanging above the door:

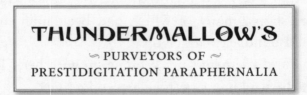

THUNDERMALLOW'S
~ PURVEYORS OF ~
PRESTIDIGITATION PARAPHERNALIA

'You come here often?' he asked Phyllis.

'Not as often as I'd like. Usually only when I need to find something special. Something I can't get from the internet or from other magic shops in town.'

She stopped in front of the windows—narrow-paned windows of pale green glass—and peered inside. Clement did likewise.

The display on the other side looked like it hadn't been changed in a long time. All of the apparatus behind the glass—tall copper cups with small red balls nested on their tops, decks of playing cards arranged in fan-like formations, several rubber skulls grinning vacantly out into the dying afternoon light, long black magic wands with silver tips, a yellow-and-red wrist-chopping guillotine, brightly painted silk cabinets, old magic books, large silks decorated with the grinning faces of mischievous imps and devils, assorted mysterious-looking tubes and boxes and velvet change bags—all of these things were covered with a fine layer of whitish, powdery dust.

Clement gave a shiver. 'Is this place still open?' he wondered. 'It looks like nobody's been here in years . . .'

'The window's always like that,' Phyllis told him. 'Has been ever since I can remember. Thundermallow's has been here forever.'

If *forever* had been *since 1907*, Phyllis's statement would have been perfectly accurate. That was the year the shop had opened, and it had always been owned by a Thundermallow. In fact, the founder of the business, Thurston Thundermallow, had known Wallace Wong way back in the early decades of the twentieth century. When he was starting out in magic, Wallace Wong used to buy many of his tricks from Thurston Thundermallow. Later, as Wallace became more and more famous, he used to commission Thurston Thundermallow to help him make new illusions. The two men worked closely and created many never-before-seen effects. Some of these illusions were so cleverly devised that even today, more than a century later, magicians do not know the secrets behind them.

'C'mon,' said Phyllis, opening the door.

Clement watched her disappear inside. He waited for a moment—for some reason he felt a bit strange about following her. It seemed like this was *her* world, and he felt apprehensive about intruding.

Then she poked her head out of the doorway and raised her eyebrows at him. 'You coming or not?' she grinned.

'Sure.' He smiled back at her, then pushed his glasses further up his nose and went in.

Inside Thundermallow's, everything was dim. The only light came from a series of shell-shaped lamps on the walls, and this light was spilling upwards in a soft, pale yellow glow. The walls, visible between towering black shelves, were covered in a dark purple, velvet-flocked wallpaper.

Both Phyllis and Clement blinked as their eyes adjusted to the gloom.

There was a sweet smell in here; a soft, honey-like fragrance pervaded the shop. It always eased Phyllis into a sense of quiet, eager anticipation when she came in. She never knew what she was going to find amongst all the old, dusty shelves that were lined with hundreds of neatly arranged dark green and purple cardboard boxes, all of which were labelled *Thundermallow's*, and all of which contained tricks and mechanisms and special gizmos that could only be found in a magic shop of serious reputation.

Clement's eyes grew wide as he beheld all of the shelves. Then, in one corner, he saw the special Disguises section. Quietly he read the signs there, whispering the words to himself: *'Hoodwink Your Friends—Real Van Dyke Beards!*, *Startling Sideburns!*, *Lifelike Goblin Ears!*, *Fangs You Very Much!*, *False Noses for Any Occasion!*, *Toupees to Amaze*, *Be INCOGNITO and the LIFE of the PARTY!*, *Scars, Scars, Scars!*, *Disguise the Limit!'*

Clement took a step towards Disguises. Suddenly a blurry, hairy streak shot out from one of the shelves by his arm. He quickly jumped back.

'Reeeeeeeoooooooowwwwwwwwwwwwwww-wwrrrrrrrrr!' came a blood-curdling squeal.

It echoed around Thundermallow's, and Phyllis and Clement both tensed. 'What the—?' whispered Clement, his heart beating hard.

'Don't worry,' Phyllis reassured him. 'It's just Madame Ergins.'

'H-huh?'

She pointed to a pair of steely-violet eyes that were glaring up at them from under a chair in the corner. Clement looked carefully and saw the very hairy, very annoyed, very *come one step closer and I'll claw you faster than you can blink* face of a grey Persian cat. 'Madame Ergins. She belongs to Mr Thundermallow,' Phyllis explained. 'She's why I never bring Daisy in here.'

11

'That I can understand,' Clement said, feeling his heartbeat returning to normal. 'It'd be World War III with fur!'

'Ah! Phyllis Wong! Welcome back to Thundermallow's!'

Phyllis and Clement turned. There, standing before a deep burgundy velvet curtain, was a shortish, plump gentleman with shining violet eyes (the same colour as Madame Ergins's, Clement observed). The top of the man's head was bald and pink and on the sides, above his ears, there sprouted a thick band of curly white hair. He was dressed in a smart three-piece suit of dark maroon, and the collar and cuffs of his coat were black velvet.

'Hello, Mr Thundermallow,' said Phyllis, giving him a big smile. He always looked so cheery, and every time she saw him again after not seeing him for a while, Phyllis got the feeling that he was the sort of person who never let the cares of the world bother one little curly white hair on the sides of his head.

'And how is my favourite young magician? The most practised prestidigitator, the cleverest conjuror, the legerdemainist most likely to learn the languishing, legendary secrets of our noble profession? *Hmm-yesindeed?*'

Phyllis blushed at all the compliments. 'I'm swell, thanks.'

'Ah-ha,' said Mr Thundermallow. 'Still speaking as though you're in one of your great-grandfather's movies, I see. You are a breath of the freshest air, always have been.' His eyes travelled beyond her shoulder. 'And who might this be? *Hmm-yesindeed?*'

Phyllis grabbed Clement's arm and brought him forward. 'This is my friend, Clem. I hope you don't mind me bringing him in . . .'

'Any friend of Phyllis Wong is welcome here.' The cheery man extended his pink hand. 'Aubrey Thundermallow. Pleased to make your acquaintance, Clem.'

Clement wiped his hand on the front of his sweater and then shook Aubrey Thundermallow's hand. 'Nice to meet you,' he said.

'I hear you've already chanced upon Madame Ergins,' said Mr Thundermallow, glimpsing the grumpy cat under the chair.

'He has,' said Phyllis.

'She nearly scratched my arm clean off,' Clement said.

Mr Thundermallow smiled. 'Ah. She's a good cat, really, under all that hair. She just gets a little temperamental now and then. Poor old thing, she's never been the same since she encountered the exploding mice.'

'The exploding mice?' repeated Phyllis.

'Oh, yes,' said Aubrey Thundermallow. 'Happened about ... *Hmm-yesindeed* ... four years ago, I believe. We'd just had a delivery of a whole lot of *novelties*.'

When he said *novelties*, he hunched his shoulders up close to his ears, raised his eyebrows and gave Phyllis and Clement a half-sideways look, the same sort of look a boy might give if he were just about to suggest doing something a little bit naughty.

'Boxes and boxes from the Blurtaceous Novelty Co. in Shanghai,' he continued. 'At that time the Blurtaceous Novelty Co. made the best things, the quality second-to-none. But apparently there was some unrest at the factory that we didn't know about ... seems like hundreds of workers were about to be laid off and they weren't at all happy about it, and apparently some of the more upset ones decided to take revenge on the Blurtaceous Novelty Co. so they switched around the mechanisms of some of the products.

'And of course, we had no idea this had happened. We opened up one of the boxes of what we thought were Blurtaceous Clockwork Mice—beautiful little spotted creatures made of tin, with whiskers that really twitched when the mice scuttled across the floor—and we wound them up, ooh, maybe about a dozen of them. *Hmm-yesindeed*. And then, just as they started scuttling around in circles and every

which way across the shop, one after another—
BOOM! KA-BAM! WHAPPOW!—they all blew
up, exploding all over the place. And poor Madame
Ergins, who up until that time had been a cat of
great and purring placidness, all at once became the
cat from the Underworld!'

'Weird,' said Phyllis.

'Well,' Aubrey Thundermallow went on, 'we
didn't know the *half* of it at the time. We unpacked
the other boxes and happily sold the rest of the
items. It was only a few months later that we
started hearing from customers whose exploding
cigars that they had given to their friends hadn't
exploded at all, but had started trying to scuttle up
their friends' nostrils in a twitching manner. Most
strange, and uncomfortable for their friends. We
had to give a lot of refunds. *Hmm-yesindeed.*'

Clement smirked.

Mr Thundermallow clapped his hands once and
rubbed his palms together. 'But enough chatter of
errant whimsicalities! What can I do for you today,
Phyllis?'

'Well,' she answered, 'I'm after something
special . . .'

'Special?' repeated Mr Thundermallow, leaning
closer.

Phyllis nodded. Then she looked across at Clem
and back to Mr Thundermallow. He immediately

understood, so he gave a quick wink and called out, 'Miss Hipwinkle? Would you kindly attend to this customer please?'

A short silence followed. Clement glanced at Phyllis and she smiled at him.

Then, from out of the shadows, there emerged a young woman with pale skin and jet-black hair and dark orchid-coloured lipstick. Her extra-long eyelashes were as dark as her hair, and her eyes were almost as black. 'Certainly, Mr Thundermallow,' said the young woman, her voice seeming to seep into the shop like thick honey sliding down the side of a honey pot. She turned her head—slowly, as though she were in a dream—and gave Clement a piercing look, her dark eyes big.

Clement couldn't help staring at her. There was something about the black dress she was wearing, and the languorous way she spoke, and those big unblinking eyes, that made her seem to be floating in the space before him. 'Um . . . erm . . . well, over there . . .' He turned his head towards Disguises, but kept his eyes firmly fixed on Miss Hipwinkle.

She watched him unblinkingly, as though she were trying to decide whether he should be allowed near the Disguises section and all the secrets it contained. Then her eyes seemed to become darker. She raised a pale hand, curled her index finger and beckoned him over.

Phyllis watched him following her, as though he were in a trance.

'So,' Mr Thundermallow said when they had left, 'something *special*, you mentioned?'

A new amazement

Phyllis nodded, smiling her inscrutable smile— a smile which always hinted that she knew that impossible things might be possible (a perfect smile for a conjuror to have). 'Yes, please. A little something special. To use in close-up. Something to startle and distract.'

'Ah!' Aubrey Thundermallow's violet eyes lit up. 'Something to *misdirect*?' he whispered.

'Exactly,' said Phyllis, still smiling. 'To misdirect.'

'I think I know just the very thing. *Hmm-yesindeed.*'

He went behind one of the counters, turned around and nimbly mounted a small stepladder. Phyllis watched as he reached up to one of the upper shelves that was crammed with dozens of the dark green and purple cardboard boxes with the *Thundermallow's* labels glued onto the ends. He moved his plump fingers across them, occasionally tapping one of the boxes as he muttered, '*Hmm-yesindeed . . .* now

I know I have them somewhere here . . . although for the life of me, I can't . . . let's see . . . it's been a while since we last sold these . . . ah, perhaps this one . . .'

Then he pulled out one of the boxes, and with it a propulsion of fine white dust that billowed like a tiny cloud of talcum powder. He descended the stepladder and placed the box on the counter. 'I think you will be *pleased*,' he announced in a hushed tone, brushing the dust from the box.

Phyllis placed her hands together, intertwining the thumb on one hand with the little finger on the other and curling her fingers around the backs of her hands. Her heart was beating with delicious anticipation.

Aubrey Thundermallow lifted the lid of the box, without letting Phyllis see what was inside. He quickly darted his hands in there, then withdrew them and took a step backwards, to be further away from her. What happened next was silent and astonishing.

He opened his left hand and, from the very centre of his palm, a brilliant blue light shot out. It dazzled Phyllis and she gasped out loud. 'Wow!'

He smiled at her, closed his hand, then opened it again. His palm was completely empty; the light had disappeared.

Phyllis would have said 'Wow!' again, but she was not one to repeat herself if she could help it.

Mr Thundermallow then slowly opened his right hand. Another brilliant blue beam of light shot out, shining into Phyllis's face.

She squinted at the brightness and started to giggle.

He closed his hand, then opened it again to show his palm empty and the light gone.

Whenever Phyllis was watching a master magician at work, she felt as though time had stopped. It was a feeling like she was floating, of being very still and motionless, of not being able to hear any sound around her at all. This was one of those times.

Aubrey Thundermallow now opened both hands, and two beams of the blue light speared towards her. He moved his hands in a circular motion (Phyllis thought how well this would go with music in a performance), then closed them, vanishing the lights.

He continued producing the lights from his palms: he made a single beam jump from his right hand to his left and back again, each time opening his palms wide to reveal them to be totally empty after the light had left them. He made the light jump to his forehead so that it looked like he had a third, blazing eye up there. He made it vanish from his forehead with a quick pass of his hand. And to finish, he put the light on the tip of his nose, wiggled his nose around and then said, 'Hey PRESTO *hmm-yesindeed*!' The light dissolved away quicker than a blink.

When he had concluded he asked, 'Was that special enough for you?'

'Oh, that was *brilliant*, Mr Thundermallow!' Phyllis had no idea how he had done that. She couldn't even begin to work it out, which was unusual, because Phyllis Wong knew so much about magic that she usually had an idea how a trick was being performed or what methods were behind it.

'Glad to be of entertainment,' he said, smiling. 'You just witnessed The Incandescent Blue Lights of Aurora, named after the ancient Roman goddess of the dawn.'

'It's really impressive. But it's not quite what I'm looking for.'

Mr Thundermallow gave a half-smile. 'Oh?' he said, a little surprised.

'No. Don't get me wrong, I loved every second of it, and I'll take the blue lights if I can afford them. But what I need that's special is for *outdoor* close-up. Something I can use in the playground at school.'

'Ah. I see, *hmm-yesindeed*. Yes, you're right, Phyllis Wong; daylight would all but drown out the brilliance of The Incandescent Blue Lights of Aurora. They'd be nothing but watery little piddle-ations of unimpressiveness. And we can't have *that*, not for someone as accomplished as your keen self, can we? No, most certainly we can not. Now, let me think . . . something to dazzle in the daylight . . . to distract and divert . . . to attract the attention away from—Ah!' All at once he stopped, and he clapped his hands together loudly. 'I believe I have just the thing!'

'R-*rr-r-rr-r-rr-r-rr-r-rr-r-rr-r-rr-r-rr-r-rr-r-rr-r-rr-r-rr-r-rr-r-rr-r-rr-r-rr-r-rr-r-rr-r-rr- r!*' Madame Ergins growled nervously from her Underworld beneath the chair.

And, once again, Phyllis waited expectantly as Mr Thundermallow mounted the stepladder and began searching his shelves . . .

✳

'So, what'd you buy, Phyll?' asked Clement as they made their way to their homes.

'Can't tell you. It's something I need for a trick I'm working on.'

Clement knew there was no point needling her to tell him—when it came to her conjuring, Phyllis Wong was incredibly secretive.

They walked along in silence as the evening shadows began to creep around the corners of the city blocks. Clement dropped back behind his friend and began fishing about in his Thundermallow's carry-bag. Phyllis watched the passers-by as she walked; she enjoyed studying people and wondering about their stories and where they were going, or where they had come from. She always had, ever since she was little.

'Well,' Clement said after a few moments, 'look what *I* bought. Don't turn around yet. Wait a sec . . . ouch! . . . okay, you can look!'

Phyllis turned around, and her jaw dropped.

There stood Clement, wearing a pair of spectacles with springy-out eyes (he had them on over his real glasses), a false pointy nose with a wart on it, a latex gory scar on his cheek, an enormous set of vampire fangs in his mouth, a bald-head wig with reddish hair sticking out at the sides and a fake black goatee beard and moustache.

'Whaddya think?' he asked, trying to smile in such a way that the fangs wouldn't fall out and the moustache wouldn't come loose.

Phyllis stifled a giggle. 'You look like you've been in an explosion in a joke factory!'

'Ha. Very funny. Hey, no one'll recognise me like this. I could go anywhere and they wouldn't know me. Not even my own mother!'

Phyllis shook her head. 'That's for sure. You could even get out of xylophone practice . . . your mum would die of a heart attack if she saw you like that. Or she'd put you up for adoption.'

'Ha. You are too, too droll.'

'Yes, I too, too am.' She laughed and he laughed too, quickly shoving the fangs back into his mouth when they started slipping out.

'So,' said Phyllis as they continued up the street, 'why'd you buy so much?'

'I've always been interested in disguises.'

'Oh, yeah? Since when?' Phyllis was smiling. 'All you've ever been interested in is your games or whatever new phone or webPad or computer's just come out.'

'Yeah, that too.' (Clement's parents owned one of the biggest appliance stores in the city, and when a new electronics item was released they often gave it to Clement to try out, so they could recommend it to their customers if it was any good.)

'So why the sudden interest in dressing up?'

'I don't know. I couldn't stop. She just kept showing me things, and they all looked like I should have them. Like I needed them, so that I can have a wide assortment in my disguises collection. You never know when a fake nose will come in handy, you know.'

'She's quite the salesgirl, that Miss Hipwinkle, isn't she?'

'She's cool. Hey, Phyll, did you see her lips? They were black!'

'They were dark purple. Yeah, I noticed. It was lipstick.'

'I knew that. And her eyes looked like she hadn't slept for eighteen months. And she was paler than a vanilla milkshake. She looked . . .'

'She looked like what, Clem?'

He thought for a moment, adjusting his fangs because he'd started to dribble while he'd been speaking. 'I dunno. She just looked cool, I guess.'

'She looked like it was her second time on Earth,' said Phyllis.

'Nah, you're wrong. Zombies don't have dark purple lips. Not in the games *I* play.'

'I'll bow to your extensive experience,' said Phyllis.

'Yep, I've battled 'em all. Every zombie game there is: *Attack of the Zombie Vampire Accountants*; *Zombies in Love*; *Muddled Zombies of Thistledrockit*—they wore kilts in that one; *Zombie Mission Implausible*; *Zombies A-Go-Go at the Astral Bloodbath Ballroom*; *Revenge of the Crumbling Zombies*; *Fire-spewing Zombies of Varaswani*; *Fifty Shades of Zombies*—that one was really weird—'

'Thank you, Clement, I get the message.'

'Yep, if there's anything you want to know about zombies, I'm your expert.'

They had arrived at the Wallace Wong Building, the small Art Deco apartment block that had been built in 1932 by Phyllis's great-grandfather. (The

Wallace Wong Building was only three storeys tall from the street, and was overshadowed by a phalanx of towering, gleaming skyscrapers. Despite many offers to buy the building, Phyllis's father, who owned it, had always resisted.) Phyllis and her father and her little dog Daisy lived on the top floor, in a big penthouse apartment above a floor of other flats, which in turn were on the floor above the ground-floor shops: Lowerblast's Antiques & Collectables Emporium and The Délicieux Café.

'Okay,' Phyllis said, 'I'll see you at school tomorrow.'

'Ergh,' grumbled Clement. He took out his fangs and shoved them in his pocket. 'Thanks for reminding me.' He pulled off his bald-head wig with the hair on the sides, and the springy-eye spectacles, and shoved them into his Thundermallow's bag (he forgot he still had on the false pointy nose and the scar and the goatee beard and moustache). 'Okay, see you tomorrow.'

He started up the sidewalk while Phyllis found her key to unlock the old glass-and-chromium front doors. Then he turned. 'Hey, Phyll, are you going to do your new magic tomorrow?'

'Wait and see,' she said, smiling her inscrutable smile. 'Wait and see what tomorrow brings . . .'

✳

That night, after dinner, Phyllis was lying on her bed, trying to concentrate on her homework, but thinking of other things.

Daisy was lying at the end of the bed with her little pink stomach on display. The brown-and-white miniature fox terrier always liked these times of the evening, when Phyllis had settled down and was still. Daisy was the sort of dog who believed it was her duty to keep a watchful eye on her best human friend, and sometimes, especially when Phyllis was in a darting-about-here-and-there mood, it became very tiring for the small dog to keep vigil.

Daisy watched sleepily as Phyllis pushed her homework out of the way and fanned out a deck of Bicycle cards across the bed instead. 'This is a great trick, Daisy girl,' Phyllis said quietly. 'I've been practising it and practising it and tomorrow I'll be all set to perform it. It'll be my special birthday present for my friend Selena. You remember her, she always wants to hold you and squeeze you whenever she meets up with us . . .'

Daisy made a tiny sound at the back of her throat—a sort of gargling sound, as though she had small marbles rolling around back there.

Phyllis reached into her Thundermallow's carry-bag. 'And now I've just got the very best thing to add to it,' she said, her eyes glowing. 'Something to finish it all off with a bang!'

Unforeseen outcomes

At lunchtime the next day, in a corner of the playground protected from the chilly breezes by a tall row of shingle oaks, Phyllis sat at one of the wooden outdoor tables, surrounded by her friends.

'This one's for you, Selena,' she said to the red-haired girl sitting next to her. 'Happy birthday.'

Selena smiled, and a mild ripple of excitement made her shudder. She loved it when her friend performed magic.

Clement, standing around with the others, had one eye on his phone (where he was battling a creature from the marshes of Abbyssnottia) and the other eye on Phyllis.

The young magician reached into her black velvet bag, the bag in which she always brought her tricks to school. 'Today it's a card trick,' she told everyone. 'Well, actually it's more than one. It's two card tricks I really like.' She turned to Selena. 'You ready?'

'Ready,' Selena answered.

'Swell,' said Phyllis. 'Prepare to be astounded, my dear friend! Now I want you to concentrate. I want you to clear your mind of everything—'

'Ha! That won't be hard,' came a loud voice from the back of the crowd. 'Selena's head isn't exactly Ideas Central!'

Everyone turned to see Leizel Cunbrus, who had arrived with three of her friends. They stood there with the sorts of expressions that implied that they were only there because they had nothing better to do at that particular moment.

'Shut it, Leizel,' said one of the boys standing nearby.

'Or what?' said Leizel. 'I can be here if I want. My parents pay the same school fees as yours, and I'm entitled to be wherever I want to be in the playground.'

'Yeah,' said one of her friends, the corner of her mouth lifting in a sneer.

'Yeah,' repeated another of her hanger-onners.

Phyllis took a deep breath. 'You're welcome to stay and watch,' she said. 'This is for Selena's birthday.'

'Couldn't you afford a *proper* present for her?' sneered Leizel Cunbrus.

Clement put his phone away. 'Are you going to heckle and spoil it for everyone?' he asked her.

Leizel sized him up from head to toe. Then she sniffed and said loudly to her friends, 'Some people should be put through the washing machine before they come to school.'

Clement looked down at his sweater and tried to wipe off the fresh orange juice stain that had ended up there earlier, while he'd been battling the swamp creatures from Abbyssnottia as he'd been drinking the juice and walking across the playground, which had caused him to bang into a fence post. He pushed his glasses further up his nose and blushed.

One of the bigger boys—a softly spoken boy named Gervase Fielding—said, 'Leizel, if you want to stay just keep quiet, okay?'

Leizel snitched up the corner of her mouth, waggled her head in a mimicking fashion and rolled her eyes at her friends. Like copies of her, they also rolled their eyes.

Everyone else turned back to Phyllis and Selena.

Phyllis took out a deck of blue-backed Bicycle cards from her velvet bag and opened the packet. 'Now, Selena,' she said as she took the cards out, 'just clear your mind and concentrate.'

'I'm concentrating,' said Selena. She hadn't let Leizel's taunts get to her—she was too excited at her special gift from Phyllis.

Phyllis spread the cards face-up so that Selena and all the spectators could see them. 'Observe. A complete deck, all different.'

'Uh-huh,' said Selena.

'Yeah, sure,' said Leizel under her breath, but loud enough for her cronies to hear her. Gervase Fielding shushed her and she shushed him back.

Phyllis closed the cards and turned them over. She spread the deck again. 'Now observe: all of the cards have blue backs, yes?'

'All of them,' Selena said after a moment.

'Now, my friend,' Phyllis went on, her voice low and inviting, 'as I spread them again, I want you to select a card. Choose it from anywhere in the deck, anywhere at all.'

Slowly Phyllis re-spread the deck with the blue backs visible.

'That one!' Selena put her finger on a card towards the end of the deck near Phyllis's left hand.

'Take it out,' said Phyllis. 'Look at it and memorise it. You can show it to the others if you want, but not to me.'

Selena took the selected card, turned it over so that Phyllis couldn't see its face, and showed it to the people closest to her. (Leizel tried to crane her neck to get a glimpse, but she was too far away.)

'Okay, is it memorised?' Phyllis asked.

'It is,' replied Selena.

'Now put it back into the deck, anywhere you want.' Phyllis held the spread deck out to Selena, and she slipped the card, still face-down, back in amongst the other cards, somewhere near the middle. Phyllis closed the deck and squared it, tapping the edges of the cards on the table.

'Now,' said Phyllis, 'what was your card?'

'You're the magician,' said Leizel, loudly. 'Why don't you tell her what it was?'

'Shut up, Leizel,' said Clement.

Phyllis ignored her. 'What was it, Selena?' she asked.

'The eight of clubs,' said Selena.

Some of the spectators nodded.

'The eight of clubs?' repeated Phyllis. 'Because it's your special day, and you're special, I'm going to make your card—the eight of clubs—special. Presto!' Phyllis waved her hand across the deck. 'Now look. Look at what's special!'

Slowly she spread the cards face-down across the table. Halfway along, Selena gave a gasp.

There, in the middle of all the blue-backed cards, a single red-backed card had appeared!

Phyllis smiled, and she zinged with the zingingness she always felt at the moment that someone had lost themselves in a trick.

'Take out the red card,' she said to Selena, 'and turn it over.'

Selena did so. It was the eight of clubs.

'Wow! How did that happen? How did it change?'

Some of the kids gave a small round of applause.

Leizel Cunbrus snorted, but she said nothing.

'Magic,' answered Phyllis Wong. 'But where there's a *little* magic, there's usually more . . .'

She took up the cards again. 'I want you to hold onto that card, Selena. Put it face-down on your palm and put your other hand on top of it. Keep it firmly on top of it, as though your hands are a safe and the eight of clubs is a valuable gem.'

Selena did so, sandwiching the card firmly between her palms.

Phyllis began slowly shuffling the deck, face-down. 'I'm going to ask you to choose another card now. Tell me to stop at any time.'

Selena watched her shuffling, then she said, 'Stop!'

Phyllis separated the deck where she'd been stopped, and held up one half of the deck in her left hand, displaying the card at the point where the shuffling had stopped. She took this card out. 'What's the card?' she asked.

'The five of hearts,' Selena answered.

'The five of hearts,' repeated Phyllis. She put it face-down on the top of the deck, which was now in her right hand. 'Now I have the five of hearts here. You have the—?'

'The eight of clubs,' said Selena, looking down at her hands, safe-keeping the card.

'I think not,' Phyllis said, smiling. 'Behold!'

She took the top card off the deck and turned it over. To everyone's astonishment, it was not the five of hearts. It was Selena's card, the eight of clubs!

'What?' said Selena.

'And what do you have?' Phyllis asked.

Tentatively, Selena took her hand off the card she'd been holding. She turned the red-backed card over. 'The five of hearts!' she exclaimed. 'But how? It changed in my hand! I never felt a thing!' She turned the card over and over and held it up to the sunlight and even gave it a small bend, but there was nothing tricky about it. It was just a normal playing card. A normal five of hearts.

'Man!' said Clement. 'That's one of the best tricks you've ever done!'

'Thanks, Phyll, that was great!' Selena gave her friend a tight, quick hug, and for a moment Phyllis knew what Daisy must feel like whenever Selena squeezed her.

Another small round of applause came from the crowd. Phyllis smiled.

'It's all fake,' declared Leizel, coming forward. 'She's got faked cards, anyone can tell! She's not doing real magic.'

'No,' said her friends.

'Go on,' Leizel dared Phyllis, 'I bet you can't make a rabbit appear out of my lunchbox!'

Her friends sniggered and looked defiantly at Phyllis.

'Real magic?' Phyllis said quietly. 'You want *real* magic?'

'Yeah,' said Leizel, 'but it's not going to happen here.'

'You think not?' Phyllis rose, and what happened next took place so fast that some of the kids gathered there didn't see it: Phyllis extended her arms, held out her hands with all her fingers spread wide apart, and two enormous bolts of bright yellow flame spewed from her fingers, flying across the table towards Leizel with a muffled air-parting *whooooooooooosh!*

And Leizel Cunbrus screamed loud enough to wake every zombie that Clement had ever encountered.

Burnt

'It is a most serious occurrence, Mr Wong. Most serious indeed.'

Harvey Wong, Phyllis's father, sat opposite Dr Ronald Bermschstäter, the headmaster at Phyllis's school. The headmaster stared across his desk angrily, his glasses perched on the very tip of his bulbous nose.

'I agree, Headmaster,' said Harvey Wong, nodding. 'I am very sorry this has happened. And so is Phyllis. I do apologise, most sincerely.'

'It's a matter of safety,' the headmaster continued. 'But more importantly, it's a matter of the school's reputation. Why, sir, if this gets out, we'll never attract the sorts of students who will proudly uphold Pritherlee College's traditions.'

Harvey Wong listened and noted in his head how the school's reputation was so important.

'No,' Ronald Bermschstäter went on, 'Pritherlee College is at the forefront of providing quality education in a safe, no-nonsense, *calm* environment. We have been doing it for one hundred and forty-seven years, and our motto—*Strive Sensibly; Rock No Boats*—has carried us through without blemish or the slightest hint of scandal.'

'Pritherlee College is a very fine school,' Harvey Wong said quietly. 'That's why I send Phyllis here.'

'Yes, a very fine school indeed. All I can say is, thank goodness that none of the students filmed the thing on their phones and posted it up on the interweb.'

'Net,' Harvey said.

'I beg your pardon?'

'Nothing, Dr Bermschstäter. Please, carry on.'

'Yes, thank goodness it hasn't gone out into the world. This sort of thing would go virus, I have no doubt about it.'

'Viral,' said Harvey Wong.

'Pardon?'

'Nothing, Dr Bermschstäter.'

'It's the last thing we want, grainy footage of a girl getting singed in her lunchbreak. And with the fire coming from another girl's digits . . . why, heavens above, the world would think we are turning out witches and the like. That's the stuff of storybooks, sir, not calm reality like we strive for here.'

'Indeed not.'

The headmaster's wide nostrils twitched, and he clenched his fists. 'And now I'm faced with the threat of legal action! The girl's parents are considering suing! The Cunbruses are most upset. They say Leizel's plaits will never be the same.'

'I'm very relieved it was only her plaits that were singed,' said Harvey Wong. 'Is Leizel all right apart from that?'

'Oh, she's very flustered. She's calling Phyllis a "little arsonist" every chance she gets; letting everyone know what's happened. I think I will have to make some sort of compensation to her and her parents before they take the story to the press . . .' He paused and looked at Harvey Wong above the top of his glasses, giving him a glare that seemed to say, *It's not in the school's budget to have to pay out on this sort of thing, you know . . .*

'Please,' Harvey said, reading the unspoken message in Dr Bermschstäter's glare, 'I would be only too ready to provide some sort of assistance. If you let me know what it takes, I will have my solicitors provide suitable compensation.'

Hearing this, Dr Ronald Bermschstäter sat back in his chair. 'A wise decision, Mr Wong,' he said. 'A good idea to not rock any boats any further.'

Harvey nodded. He gave the headmaster a measured smile.

'Now, regarding Phyllis.' Dr Bermschstäter leant forward, placing his wide elbows on his desk and clasping his hands so that his sausage-like fingers interlocked.

'As I said,' Harvey told him, 'Phyllis and I are both very sorry about what has happened. I will see to it that nothing of this sort will ever take place again.'

'Certainly it will not take place again.' Ronald Bermschstäter's sausage-fingers were turning red. 'It cannot be *allowed* to take place again, Mr Wong. And Phyllis needs to know that.'

'She will know that,' Harvey said. 'I will make sure of this.'

'I think the message needs to be a strong one. One that she will not forget in a hurry. And I think, in this case, in order for the message to have the *full* impact, I should take some action also.'

Harvey Wong felt his jaw muscles becoming tense. 'What are you suggesting, Dr Bermschstäter?'

The headmaster leant back in his chair and gave a smile. 'There is only one thing for it, Mr Wong. Phyllis must be taught a lesson.'

✳

'*Suspended?*' gasped Phyllis.

'That is what Dr Bermschstäter has decided,' her father told her.

'But he can't!'

Daisy, sitting in one of her beds on the living room floor in their apartment, heard the tone in Phyllis's voice. The mini foxy jumped out of the bed and sprang up onto the lounge next to Phyllis, putting her front paws on Phyllis's leg and peering up with her shiny brown eyes into Phyllis's face.

'But he can, Phyllis,' Harvey Wong said. 'He can, and he has. Effective from this afternoon.'

'What?'

'As of this afternoon, you are not allowed back at school for three weeks.'

'Three weeks? But Dad, school will have broken up by then!'

'I think that is the headmaster's intention. You won't be going back to Pritherlee College until next year.'

'That's screwy!' said Phyllis, using an expression she had picked up from one of her great-grandfather's movies.

'Screwy or not, that's the way it is.'

'But I'll miss the end-of-term concert! You know how hard I've been practising that new illusion with Daisy! It was going to be the first time she'd ever been levitated. Oh, Dad . . .'

'There's nothing I can do, Phyllis. It's the head-master's decision.'

Phyllis stroked the top of Daisy's head. 'That's so not fair.' She crossed her arms and stared straight ahead. 'Well at least I won't have any homework for the next three weeks.'

'Ah, but you will.'

'Huh?'

'Dr Bermschstäter said that he will arrange for your teachers to give Clement your homework. Clement will drop it in every day on his way home from school. He will then pick it up the next morning and take it back.'

Phyllis's jaw dropped open. This was totally not a good thing.

'And it all has to be completed,' said her father.

'Oh well, at least I'll get to see Clem,' she grumbled.

'No, you won't.'

She looked at him.

'No,' he said. 'I have arranged that Clem will leave your homework in the mailbox in the foyer. When you've done it, you'll put it back in the mailbox and he'll collect it every morning en route to school.'

Her jaw dropped open again.

Harvey Wong frowned. 'I am not happy about this, Phyll,' he said. 'I don't think the headmaster should be suspending you. I think he is being too harsh.'

'I'll say he is.'

'But I am also not happy with what you did. You know that you have a great responsibility with your magic. There are some things that you are performing with that might be dangerous, and you should show caution with these things. We have discussed this before. What on Earth possessed you to shoot fire at the Cunbrus girl?'

Phyllis thought for a few moments. Then she replied, 'It was an accident.'

'An accident?' Harvey stood and started pacing the room. 'An accident? How could it be an accident? You shot fire out of your hands!'

Phyllis squirmed; she couldn't explain how she did that, not even to her father. It was against the magicians' universal code, to reveal the secrets behind magic.

'Well?' Harvey questioned.

'It just went a bit wrong. It was something new I bought from Thundermallow's. I didn't think the flames would shoot as far. I only wanted to use it to have a big finish to the tricks I'd been doing for Selena. I guess I should've practised with it a bit more before I performed with it for the first time.'

Harvey stopped pacing. 'A bit wrong? Yes, it did go a bit wrong. You are very lucky, my girl, it didn't go a whole *lot* wrong! You could've seriously hurt somebody.'

'She was being a nuisance,' said Phyllis.

'*That is beside the point!* Nuisance or not, you do not have the right to set fire to people!'

'I just told you, it was an accident!'

'So did you mean to singe her plaits?' he asked. 'Was that your intention?'

'No! I just wanted to . . . to startle her. To make her back off a bit.'

'And now you are suspended,' her father said, shaking his head slowly. 'That is a shameful thing, Phyllis Wong. Never has a member of this family been suspended from their school.'

Phyllis stroked Daisy's ear—the ear that was not permanently folded down. 'I'm sorry. Really I am. I'll be more careful next time.'

'Next time will be a long time coming. Phyllis, I am also grounding you.'

'No! Ground me? But—'

'You will not be allowed to leave this building for the next three weeks. The only times I will allow you to go outside is to walk Daisy for her usual morning and afternoon outings. And then you will come straight back here again. Understood?'

Phyllis gave her father a wounded look.

'And there is another thing,' he continued. 'I do not want you doing any magic during the time of your suspension.'

'*What?*' she gasped loudly. Now she felt like she had been punched in the stomach.

Daisy gave a small yelp and hopped up onto her lap.

'You heard me,' said Harvey Wong. 'You will not practise any magic, you will not open a single conjuring book or a pack of cards, you will not pick up a wand or handle any coins for prestidigitation. And you will not go anywhere near Thundermallow's, do you understand?'

'But—'

'No arguments. This is what *I* have decided. There will be no magic for you for the next three weeks.'

'But Dad, if I can't do any magic, I'll—'

'You will not die, Phyllis Wong. You are being melodramatic now.'

'I wasn't going to say *die*. I was going to say *go crazy*.'

'That is still being melodramatic. You will not go crazy. It takes more than this to drive somebody crazy. Believe me—I work in the insurance business.' He looked at his daughter, but not harshly—he could never look harshly at her. Then he said, in a softer voice, 'I am sorry it has come to this, my girl. But you must trust me when I say to you that I am doing this for your own good.'

'Huh.' Phyllis made her lower lip tight so that it wouldn't tremble in front of him.

'And now,' said Harvey, making for the door, 'I will be in my study. I have some paperwork I must finish before tomorrow morning.' He stopped at the doorway and turned. 'Oh, and Phyllis?'

'Yes?'

'I hardly need to tell you that the basement of this building is strictly out of bounds for the next three weeks. Understood?'

Phyllis said nothing; she just looked at him, her dark eyes wide and incredulous.

It was only when he had left the room and shut the door behind him that she buried her face in Daisy's fur and let her bottom lip tremble.

Definition below

A few weeks earlier, Phyllis had come across a new word when she had been reading something for school: *mortified*. Now she knew exactly what it meant, and she felt that if anyone looked up the word *mortified* in the dictionary, they would see, as part of the definition, a photo of Phyllis Wong.

She felt a combination of being *embarrassed* (at the fact that she wouldn't be at school for the rest of term, and her absence would be a talking point for many of her friends, and probably a gossip point for Leizel Cunbrus and her hanger-onners); of being *ashamed* (that the dreadful climax of her tricks for Selena had gone so messily wrong) and of being *humiliated* (by being suspended and grounded and above all, by being forbidden to do any magic).

She felt *truly* mortified.

Never before had Harvey Wong prevented Phyllis from being what she was: a magician. Being a magician was as natural to her as breathing; it was something that she had been born with, and it had developed over the years as she had found new tricks and effects and illusions to add to her repertoire. (Her father had said to her on more than one occasion that he felt that her love of magic had come directly from her great-grandfather. He had also commented that she had the same smile as Wallace Wong, Conjuror of Wonder!)

Not being able to be with her magic was the most hurtful part of the whole thing.

The first week of her suspension/grounding/ forbiddance seemed to last a year. If it weren't for the company of Daisy, Phyllis felt she *would* have gone crazy. They would set out straight after breakfast for their morning walk, sometimes going to City Park (where there were the best smells for the small dog—Phyllis often thought that if smells were a rainbow, then the odours were always the brightest and most colourful and glowing for Daisy here in the park).

Other mornings they might walk along the streets, down towards the Tennis Centre and over to the river before heading on back to the Wallace Wong Building. Or they might wander along the ritzy avenues, early, before most of the commuters arrived for work. Here they would amble by what Phyllis's friend Minette Bulbolos (a professional belly dancer who lived in an apartment on the second floor of the Wallace Wong Building) called the 'zhooshy establishments': pricey jewellery stores like Duckworth's and Tiffany's; clothing outlets that always stocked the latest fashions from Paris and Milan and Port Moresby; trendy shops full of the latest must-have crazes like sheepskin boots and electric toothbrushes encrusted with emeralds, and sunglasses that were so expensive that you almost had to sell your grandmother to be able to afford them.

But wherever Phyllis and Daisy walked, Phyllis felt like part of her had been left back at the apartment. She stared vacantly at the shop windows, and watched quietly as Daisy snouted around in the park.

She felt strangely incomplete.

She did her homework. She found it every afternoon in the foyer mailbox after Clement had dropped it off. Clement always included a note with it, telling her the latest news and gossip—things like the fact that Dr Bermschstäter was going to fill Phyllis's spot in the concert by performing his recitation of ''Twas the Night before Christmas' (Clement had drawn a picture next to this of a boy looking like he was being strangled, with his tongue lolling out the side of his mouth and his eyes bulging); or that Clement had just got a new game that hadn't been released yet called *Zombies of Stratosphere 7 Grand Perm Auto!* (he had drawn a zombie next to this with a very weird-looking hairdo and five stars beside it); or that he had made a cat run away when the cat had seen him in his latest disguise (there was a drawing of a boy with a pair of bats' ears and a long, pointy chin, and a cat with its fur all zithery); or that Leizel Cunbrus was telling everyone that she was going to Chamonix-Mont-Blanc, France, for a skiing vacation as soon as school broke up (next to this fact he had drawn a boy being very sick into a bucket).

Clement had always been good at drawing and Phyllis looked forward to his daily updates in a groaning sort of way.

One of the good things about living in the Wallace Wong Building was that it had the ground-floor shops: The Délicieux Café and Lowerblast's Antiques & Collectables Emporium. Although her father had forbidden her from leaving the building (apart from when she was walking Daisy), Phyllis felt that it would be okay for her to visit these places in the afternoons before he got home from his office. She wasn't really *leaving* the building (even though, strictly speaking, to go into the café and the antiques shop she had to go out the front doors and then into the shops from the street). But she reasoned that it'd be all right.

Late one afternoon towards the end of the first week of her grounding, she and Daisy were sitting in The Délicieux Café, Phyllis with her homework spread out on her usual table by the window and Daisy with her paws spread out on her usual patch of the floor at Phyllis's feet.

'I 'ope you do nert spoil yer appetite fer yer dinner tonight, Phyllees.' Pascaline Ravissant, one of the café's owners, placed a chocolate milkshake and a slice of *Reine de Saba*, a chocolate almond cake that Phyllis especially liked, on the table next to her homework.

Daisy got up and placed her front paws on Phyllis's knee and tried to get her snout as close to the table—and the chocolate cake—as she could.

'I'll have room,' Phyllis said. She gave Pascaline a half-smile, and Daisy a half-push back down to the floor. 'Thanks.'

'*De rien*, my treasure.' Pascaline reached across and gently pushed a lock of Phyllis's long dark hair back over Phyllis's ear. 'So,' she said, 'you are coping all right wiz zis explosion frerm yer school, *oui*?'

Phyllis had a forkful of the cake halfway to her mouth. 'What explosion?' she asked.

'Why, you erf curse. You 'ave been exploded frerm school, 'ave you nert?'

Phyllis shut her eyes for a moment. 'Oh, you mean *expulsion*.'

'*Oui*,' said Pascaline. 'Zis is what I say, *non*?'

'I'm okay. It was an accident, what happened.'

'Ah!' Pascaline smoothed down her apron. 'I am sure it was. Zey are over-reacting, to explo . . .

to *expulse* you like zis. Zermtimes I wonder zat ze world has becerm far too serious. We live in ze ninny-state, *mon amie*. *Oui*, we certainly do.'

Phyllis smiled and ate her cake.

'Never you mind,' said Pascaline. 'Zree weeks? Whert ees zree weeks? Zey will go in a flush!'

Just then some more customers came into the café. Pascaline winked at Phyllis, excused herself, and went to show them to a table.

They might go in a flush, all right, Phyllis thought as she slurped the milkshake. *But I'll probably be flushed away with them . . .*

✷

Towards the end of the second week of the suspension/grounding/flushing-away of Phyllis Wong, she felt like she barely existed.

She missed her friends at school, she missed Clem and their walks and talks on the way home, she missed being able to have her life the way she knew it. Mostly she missed her magic. It hurt her, almost like someone was squeezing her tightly around her ribs, not to be able to rehearse her tricks and try out new magic effects.

If it hadn't been for little Daisy and her four-footed company, Phyllis was sure she would have faded away to a tiny ball of nothing.

The mini foxy sensed the sadness and frustration in her friend. On their walks, Daisy would trot as jauntily as she could to try to make Phyllis feel lighter and happier. And sometimes, when Phyllis saw the tiny terrier prancing along on her dainty paws, it was as though the heaviness on Phyllis's shoulders was lifted. But only for a few minutes. It always returned when she and Daisy went back to the Wallace Wong Building.

Then, on the Friday morning of the second week, after her father had left for his office, Phyllis made a decision.

'I have to do this, Daisy,' she said as she scooped the dog up and carried her towards the elevator.

Daisy snuggled into her arms—she loved being carried around.

'I know Dad said I couldn't,' Phyllis muttered, 'but if I don't, I'll explode.' She shut the apartment door and pressed the elevator button. 'And anyway, he doesn't have to find out, does he?'

'R-r-r-r-r-r-r.' Daisy made her quiet gargling-with-marbles sound.

They waited while the elevator lurched up from the ground floor. It was an old contraption—as old as the building—and it usually took a long time to get anywhere. Anywhere, that is, except for where Phyllis and Daisy were about to go.

Finally, after what seemed like months, it juddered to a stop. The beautiful wooden elevator doors, decorated with shooting stars and comets, slid open. Phyllis and Daisy entered the elevator. The doors slid shut again.

Phyllis hoisted Daisy under one arm. She reached into her pocket and withdrew a long, old, silver key. This she put into the keyhole that was next to the button for the basement. She turned the key once to the right and pressed the button.

The elevator shuddered with a loud clanging noise. Then it started dropping—fast!

'Keep your seats, please!' said Phyllis, using a saying from one of her great-grandfather's old movies. She often said this when the elevator was plunging to the basement.

Daisy clung on tightly.

Down they sped, and Phyllis and Daisy watched through the windows in the doors. The floor on which Minette Bulbolos and Chief Inspector Barry Inglis had their apartments blurred past. The shiny chromium balustrade of the stairs in the ground floor lobby glinted and then disappeared, sliding up and out of view.

Then there was a thump, and a huge juddering, and the elevator landed with a groan of metal and wood and aged machinery.

The doors slid open and, carefully, Phyllis stepped out into the darkness. Daisy wriggled under her arm.

Phyllis's hand fumbled across the wall opposite.

Her fingers found the light switch and she flicked it down. Instantaneously the cavernous basement was lit up by brilliant golden light shining down from the towering ceiling.

'Home,' Phyllis whispered to Daisy. 'Where we belong.'

She put Daisy down and the little dog ran down the stairs and into the enormous area below.

A little while ago, Phyllis's father had given her the key to this place—a place that contained what he told her was her legacy.* The entire basement was filled with all of the magical props and illusions, all of the costumes and backdrops, all of the countless, beautiful tricks and books and secrets of conjuring that had once belonged to her great-grandfather, Wallace Wong, Conjuror of Wonder!

Phyllis followed Daisy down the stairs and made her way to the area in the centre of the basement that she'd set up as her rehearsal space. Here, amid all the sawing-in-half cabinets and zig-zag boxes and gimmicked tables and sword baskets and guillotines and the shelves overflowing with silk handkerchiefs, oversized playing cards, magic wands, feather flower bouquets, artificial skulls and automated red imps and green goblins and other strange and sparkling amazements, there were a

---

* Find out more in *Phyllis Wong and the Forgotten Secrets of Mr Okyto*.

few old sofas and armchairs, and a big clear space where she could practise in front of some mirrors.

She went to one of the many tables and found her hat. It was her favourite top hat, and she always put it on whenever she retreated to her basement. It was a beautiful black silk hat, very old, that sprang from being pancake-flat to more than ten inches tall when she slapped the brim firmly against her opened hand.

She had found the top hat amongst the huge array of tricks and props and costumes. It wasn't the only top hat down here—she must have discovered more than a dozen when her father had given her the basement, and sometimes she'd find a few more tucked away in some dark corner of the place—but there was something special about this one. Something that made it feel different from all the others. What that something was, Phyllis didn't exactly know. It just felt right when she put it on.

Now she ran her sleeve over the opened hat and looked at it as though it were an old friend she hadn't seen in years. She smiled and plonked the hat on her head, pulling her fringe down over her forehead as she always did whenever she put the hat on. She never wore the hat when she performed magic for other people; only when she was here, alone with Daisy in the magic basement. Only Daisy had ever seen her wearing it.

Phyllis stood with her back straight and took a deep breath, letting the sweet smell of the dust and the talcum-like fragrance of all the old, wonderful things down here waft into her nostrils. Then she rubbed her hands together and said, 'Let's have some fun, Daisy!'

'Rerf!' said Daisy. She jumped up onto one of the sofas, turned around three times, settled down like a miniature Egyptian sphinx and started to lick her front paws.

Phyllis went to one of her magic tables at the edge of the cleared space. On this table, just as she had left it all the last time she'd been down here, were two long, silver metal tubes with gold-edged ends. Next to them were draped six beautiful silk handkerchiefs, three of them bright red and three of them bright yellow. And beside these was Volume I of *Grice's Encyclopedia of Silk Magic*, one of the many rare and original magic books that Phyllis had discovered in this enormous cache of conjuring.

'Now,' she said quietly to herself, 'let's see if we can master this Haunted Chimneys effect. Smoothness is of the essence, just like it says in the—'

'*RERF RERF RERF RERF RERF RERF RERF RERF RERF!*' Suddenly, like a bomb exploding on the sofa behind her, Daisy erupted in a barrage of barking.

The noise ricocheted around the magic basement, pinging loudly off the walls. Phyllis put her hands over her ears. 'Daisy, what's up?' she shouted above the barking.

The little dog continued yapping at the top of her lungs. She was on her paws now, and as Phyllis started towards her, she leapt off the sofa and ran straight between Phyllis's legs and off to a far corner of the basement near the old furnace, where some heavy, dusty, crimson-coloured velvet drapes hung across the brick wall.

Here Daisy stopped abruptly. She kept barking and yapping and now, as she lowered her front legs and put her snout closer to the floor, she began making another sound in between all the barking: a high-pitched whining, almost as if she were crying.

Phyllis followed her. 'What is it, girl?' she asked, but Daisy didn't look at her—she kept on barking and whining at the gloom in the corner.

'What's up, Daisy? What's there? Have you found a mouse again? Come on, don't worry. It won't hurt you.'

'*RERF ARF ARF ARF RERF RERF RERF ARF ARF ARF RERF RERF RERF RERF RERF ARF ARF ARF!*' Daisy was barking and whining even louder now, and she was also snarling at the velvet drapes.

Phyllis shook her head, trying to stop her ears ringing from all the noise. 'Stop it, Miss Daisy,' she said loudly. She frowned; Daisy didn't usually go on like this if she came across a mouse or a rat. She usually barked in a more threatening way if a rodent was anywhere about. She didn't sound threatening now. She sounded scared.

The small dog's fear took hold of Phyllis. She felt a chill run down her spine. Something was wrong. She felt her heart begin to pound.

'Daisy, come away from there,' she said, surprised that her voice was shaky.

Daisy lowered herself even more so that her pink belly was flat against the floor and her front paws were splayed out, extended towards the drapes.

'Daisy, come here!'

Daisy ignored the command. It was unlike her to do so. Instead, she stopped her barking and yapping, and the white and brown hairs along her spine hackled. She snarled, low and rumblingly, at the crimson drapes.

'*Grrrrrrrr - Rrrrrrrrrrr - Grrrrrrrrr - Rrrrrrrrrrrrr . . .*'

'Come on,' Phyllis said, her heart beating even faster. 'I think it's time we were going.' She went to pick Daisy up.

'*RERF ARF ARF ARF RERF RERF RERF ARF ARF ARF RERF RERF RERF RERF RERF*

ARF ARF ARF!' Daisy erupted again, and Phyllis jumped back. She saw how distorted Daisy's eyes were, the same way they became distorted whenever there was a thunderstorm about. Daisy always looked disfigured with terror at those times, and this was the look she had now.

Only now, there wasn't any thunder. The old crimson drapes billowed, and Phyllis's insides felt like they had been yanked away from her.

'Daisy! It's time to go!'

'The time to go has arrived,' came a voice from the other side of the drapes.

They were flung aside with a heavy *whooooosh!*

'*RERF ARF ARF ARF RERF RERF RERF ARF ARF ARF RERF RERF RERF RERF RERF ARF ARF ARF!*'

'The time is here,' said the man standing before them, his eyes throbbing with a bright green glow. 'The time is here and I have come!'

Whirl of wonder

Phyllis Wong froze.

Daisy's snarling grew louder, and deeper, and her eyes looked not like the eyes of a dog, but those of a wolf, wild and fiery and ready to strike!

Phyllis felt her heart pounding, and her mouth was suddenly dry. She couldn't move as she stared at the man standing against the wall. She knew he shouldn't be here—no one but she and her father and Daisy should ever come down here.

Then, as she stared, and as her terror immobilised her, freezing her to the spot, making her dizzy with dread, a strange thing happened. The air around her became filled with tiny molecules of light, minuscule balls of brightness that danced and swirled and twirled between her and the man.

It was as if time had almost stopped in those moments.

It was as if those moments were meant to linger longer than any moments should, so that Phyllis could see the man properly.

He did not move. He looked at her, and his eyes glowed brightly, green and garish—not just his irises, but the *whites* of his eyes also. Phyllis had seen these kinds of eyes before, and her skin was all at once flooded with goosebumps.

The man was tall and slender and not very old. His dark, glossy-black hair was slicked back and short. He had a long, fine nose, a thin, neat moustache and high, angular cheekbones. His ears were small and (Phyllis blinked as she looked at them) almost pointed on the tops.

He was dressed immaculately, in a midnight-blue silk tail coat with the tails extending down to behind his knees, a white low-cut waistcoat, a white wing-collared shirt and a white silk bow tie. His crisp trousers were of the same midnight-blue silk as his tail coat, and he wore pointed black shoes which had been polished to a brilliant shine.

The man had a calm, quizzical expression as he studied Phyllis. He seemed to be trying to focus in on her, for the greenness in his eyes brightened and then faded, and brightened and faded again, and again and again.

As Phyllis watched his eyes brighten and fade, she noticed something else about his face—something beyond his features: she saw, *really* saw, his expression. His face was not angry or harsh or, she thought, likely to turn quickly from one emotion to another. She sensed that he was not likely to flare up in any sort of uncontrollable rage or rampage. There was a calmness here. He had a gentle face, the face of someone who knew delight and excitement, and who relished these things.

When Phyllis realised this, her heart began to pound less, and her breathing became more natural.

Daisy was still on guard, however. Her snout low to the floor, she gave another guttural volley of warning to the stranger: '*Grrrrrrr-Rrrrrrrrrrr-Grrrrrrrrr-Rrrrrrrrrrrrr* . . .'

'Steady, girl,' Phyllis said quietly. Slowly she crouched down next to Daisy and stroked the top of her head, between her ears. She didn't take her eyes off the man. 'Steady on.'

The man looked down at her and her dog, and a smile slowly emerged, a smile that lifted the corners of his mouth like a gentle breeze lifting the wings of a butterfly.

And Phyllis gasped! That smile. She'd seen it before. She'd seen it when she'd been watching old movies with her father and Daisy in their beautiful home cinema inside their apartment. She'd seen it when she'd looked at the old posters that were hanging upstairs. She'd seen it whenever she looked in the mirror when she was in a happy, planning frame of mind . . .

Her heart rushed with a dizzy-making burst of confusion and warmth and incredulity, but she steadied herself as she patted Daisy's head, and she managed somehow to find her voice. Tentatively, she uttered, 'G-great-grandfather?'

The man stepped forward and the dancing molecules of light melted away into nothing. He crouched down before her and Daisy. He looked into Phyllis's eyes, and the greenness in his began to fade.

'So that *is* who you are,' he said, his voice deep and resonant, as though it were coming from a long way away.

'I'm Phyllis Wong,' she said to him. 'And this is Daisy.'

'I am most pleased to make your acquaintance,' he said, his smile growing wider. 'I am, indeed, your great-grandfather. I am Wallace Wong. I have returned.'

He extended his hand and took Phyllis's, then shook it softly. 'Phyllis,' he repeated. He stood, and she rose with him. 'Daughter of Harvey. Harvey, son of Roy. Roy, of course, being my son.'

Phyllis nodded.

'*Arf arf arf!*'

Wallace let go of Phyllis's hand and scooped Daisy up. He held her close to his chest, looking into her small face. 'Hello, Daisy, friend and companion of Phyllis,' he said to her.

She peered at him with her big brown eyes. Then she made a soft gargling sound and gave his hand a quick lick.

He laughed, and the sound of his laugh made Phyllis smile so widely that she felt her ears stretching.

'It is a good thing to be here again,' said Wallace Wong, Conjuror of Wonder!

❋

'This is screwy,' Phyllis said.

'Ha! Screwy it is,' Wallace said, laughing.

'But how?' said Phyllis. 'How can you be here? You disappeared, way back in 1936! You were doing the Houdini sub-trunk illusion on stage in Venezuela! You vanished without trace—no one ever saw you again!'

She looked at him, studying his face, which had hardly any wrinkles. And she could see a youthful twinkle in his eyes. 'And how come you aren't old? You don't look any older than Dad!'

'I do not age, Phyllis. I am lucky in that respect. I am the same age I was when I left,' he told her.

Phyllis squinted, and an idea shot into her mind. 'Hey . . . how do I know that you *are* you? That you're not just someone *pretending* to be Wallace Wong? Oh, man, I bet I know what's happening!' She started walking around the rehearsal area, looking at the ceiling and behind all the cabinets and boxes and tables. 'I bet Clem's put cameras in here and he's hired you to dress up and pretend you're Wallace Wong, and he's filming it all and he's going to put it on that *Pranked* show on TV . . . what a little wise guy!'

The man watched as she went from place to place, peering in the cupboards and under the Mirage Tables and behind the billiard ball racks and silk production cabinets and beneath the life-size mechanical Bengal tiger with the bared teeth and the glinting eyes in the corner.

'Okay, Mr Knucklebrains,' Phyllis called out, 'where're your little cameras?'

Daisy watched her as well, from the comfort of the man's arms.

'Come on, Clement,' Phyllis called. 'You're not fooling anyone, you know . . .'

'I like that hat,' said the man. 'Always have. It was one of my favourites.'

Phyllis stopped her searching. She turned to him, unsure. He was still smiling at her, and was gently scratching Daisy behind her ear.

'Take it off,' he told her, 'and look inside. Underneath the leather band near the brim.'

Phyllis squinted at him again. Slowly she took off the top hat and inverted it. She turned down the band and peered into the hat.

'See?' he said. 'There is my name: *Wallace Wong.* And the date and place: *January 1926. Paris.*'

Phyllis saw all of this, written in a neat script in blue ink on the back of the leather band.

'I bought that one,' he went on, 'when I was in that beautiful city, performing at the Théâtre du Châtelet. Oh, Phyllis, that is a marvellous theatre, the Théâtre du Châtelet . . . so grand and vast and so full of beauty! One of the greatest music halls in the world. I played for a month there, to nearly two thousand people at every performance. I was the headline act, I am proud to say. Ah, that was a superb engagement . . . and those *dancing girls* who performed before my spot!' He sighed wistfully, his eyes gleaming. 'Ah, yes, the dancing girls who could kick so high and flutter those feathers with more finesse than the most elegant of ostriches . . .' He blinked and gave a little cough. 'But that, my great-granddaughter, was a long time ago. And yet not such a long time ago, the way I Transit.'

Phyllis stared at him. She folded the band into place once again inside the hat and put the topper back on her head. Then she held her hands together, intertwining the thumb on one hand with the little finger on her other, and folding her fingers around the backs of both hands. And she studied him carefully.

He looked exactly like the Wallace Wong whom she and her father and Daisy watched in the old movies he had made in Hollywood, way back in the 1930s. He was the spitting image of the Wallace Wong who was depicted in the dozens of magic posters that were in frames in their apartment cinema and in the long rear hallway of their home. And he was identical to the Wallace Wong she had seen so many times in the black-and-white and sepia-tinted pictures in the family photo albums.

He saw her scrutinising him and he asked, 'You still are not sure?'

'I don't know,' she answered slowly.

'Perhaps this will help to convince you.' He put Daisy down and walked into the centre of the rehearsal space. Here he stopped before her and smiled. Then he lifted his head and pushed his shoulders back and spread his arms wide, holding his hands palm-upwards to the ceiling.

And Phyllis gasped.

Slowly his feet left the rug beneath them, and the man began to float. Up he went, silently and smoothly, still holding his arms out wide, still with his palms facing upwards.

Every pore of Phyllis's skin became riddled with goosebumps. Her jaw dropped open and her eyes widened.

The man levitated to six feet in the air and stopped. He looked down at Phyllis, and his eyes shone brightly, still glowing that strange green.

Phyllis knew what was going to happen next, but she'd never imagined how breathtaking it would be.

The man kept his arms outstretched and now he brought his hands together, palm against palm in front of him. Then, slowly, still suspended in the air, he began to twirl. Round and round he went, picking up speed, twirling and spinning faster and faster, until all Phyllis could see was a whirlwind-blur of midnight-blue and white.

She watched, hardly able to breathe.

Daisy also watched, startled, her head cocked to the side.

Now the man was twirling so fast that the midnight-blue and white became a smudged noth-ingness of colour: a blend of spinning, swiftly swishing confusion.

Until it vanished completely, and the man was gone!

Phyllis gasped again, this time loudly. Daisy barked once and looked at Phyllis as if to say, *Where? Where did he go? That shouldn't have happened . . .*

'Oh boy,' Phyllis muttered, her breathing coming fast and shallow. 'The Whirling Whirlwind Disappearance! The famous Whirling Whirlwind Disappearance of Wallace Wong! Wallace Wong's most celebrated trick, Daisy! No one else could ever perform that but him. People tried to copy it, but nobody could ever find the secret.' She let out a whistle and shook her head. 'Daisy, my darling, we just saw the greatest trick he ever did!'

'*One* of the greatest,' came the man's voice from behind her.

She turned to see him coming out of the shadows, his hair tousled and sticking up (it reminded Phyllis of the times Clement had experimented with hair gel to make himself look cool—every effort had been spectacularly unsuccessful).

'I can't believe I saw that!' Phyllis exclaimed.

'Ah, but you did,' he said. 'Now do you believe that I am me?'

She nodded vigorously. 'I'm sorry I doubted you.' She rushed to him and gave him a huge hug.

'That is perfectly understandable, Phyllis. This must all be a shock for you.'

She stepped back and said, 'Please! Teach me how to do that? Please? I'd love to know how to do that!'

'If I teach it to anybody, it will be to you. I know your passion. I have observed it in you.'

Phyllis's eyes went big.

'Yes,' he said. 'This is not my first visit here. I have been returning every now and then. I have been aware of your magic, Phyllis. It pleases me very much, I must say.'

'Returning?' she said. She put her hand to her head. 'Oh, brother, I'm getting dizzy with all of this. It's doing my head in. First, your greatest illusion, and now . . . What do you mean, *returning*?'

'Come, Phyllis.' He took her by the hand. 'It is time you heard the story of your great-grandfather.'

Unfolding

He led her to the sofa, lifted the tails of his coat, and together he and Phyllis sat, with Daisy sphinxing in between them.

'I am a Transiter, Phyllis,' he said softly. 'I move through Time.'

'A . . . *Transiter*?' Phyllis's eyes grew bigger. A faded memory from a recent incident rushed into her mind. She blinked and took a deep breath. 'Go on,' she said to Wallace Wong. 'Tell me how.'

'You do not seem surprised?' he said, smiling.

She shook her head slowly. 'I've been aware that this could be possible,' she told him. 'I've . . . I've *found* things. Down here, in all your props and effects.'

'Ah.' He gazed at her proudly.

'And,' she continued, 'I've been thinking about it. Ever since there was some strange stuff going down in the city. But I only ever half-believed that it could happen. And I started to think I was just going nuts.'

'No, my dear girl, you are not nuts. I am not nuts. It *is* possible. I am here. It is as real as the effort of the steadfast lobster in the maelstrom of the sandy vortex.'

Phyllis gave him a strange look.

'Oh, I know what I mean,' he said, a bit flustered. He cleared his throat. 'This Transiting—being able to move from Time to Time—is how I disappeared in Venezuela in 1936, when I was performing the Houdini sub-trunk illusion. I had found the Pocket I needed, and I was able, at last, to commence my Transits.'

Phyllis raised her eyebrows. 'Pocket?' she repeated.

'Yes, Phyllis. Allow me to tell you all about this. Sit back, listen, focus on my words, for what you will hear will need all your concentration . . .

'When I was a young magician,' Wallace began, his voice deep and soft, 'about your age, in fact, I was totally devoted to my magic. I breathed conjuring, I lived every moment thinking about my next trick and how I would perform it. I was constantly rehearsing and, if I were unable to be in the theatre or in my rehearsal space, I would still always be practising—always manipulating with coins or cards or matches or whatever I had at hand—and doing it everywhere, on trams and subway cars and while I was walking along the street or through the gardens of the city. Magic was my world, Phyllis—totally and wonderfully and all-consumingly!

'What I loved about it the most was the pleasure that comes from being able, for the briefest of times, to transport someone; to allow them to become completely amazed. That moment you get when your magic is working elegantly, smoothly, and you see in your audience's faces the exact moment of delight, of the *incredible*, of them being tricked and filled with the wonder of the *inexplicable*!'

'Oh, I love that too,' Phyllis said, beaming. 'It's the best feeling ever!'

Daisy gave her hand a gentle lick.

'Apart from having this one snuggling up to you,' she added, tickling the terrier's ear.

'Yes,' Wallace Wong said. 'It is a wonderful feeling, the moment of the magic. When you have your audience, to use a robust cliché, in the palm of your hand!' He closed his eyes and put his head back on the sofa. 'Only a prestidigitator can know the thrill of it.'

Phyllis put her head back on the sofa too, and her top hat was pushed forward, so that everything went dark. She took the hat off and placed it in her lap.

'And, Phyllis, this thrill and this love of the world of our magic grew. It grew every day. The more I learnt, the more I loved the mystery and the marvels of our profession. Mystery and magic became my life.

'And then, a brilliant young scientist named Albert Einstein began publishing his theories. He was coming up with all sorts of new ideas, ideas which pushed the boundaries of how people had thought up until that time. I started reading about his ideas in the newspapers and in scientific journals, and I became intrigued by the kinds of things he was suggesting. I came to realise that there were different types of mysteries in the world . . . mysteries that were even bigger than those I was creating in my magic.'

Bigger, thought Phyllis.

'I wanted to know more about those mysteries, Phyllis. I wanted to know the bigger things. I subscribed to more and more science journals and magazines, and I started attending lectures on all manner of scientific topics . . . things ranging from relativity to new ideas of Time. Einstein opened up the whole concept of the Fourth Dimension to me.'

'The Fourth Dimension?' she repeated.

Wallace opened his eyes and gave her a look of glowing wisdom, the likes of which she had never seen before. 'Yes, great-granddaughter. Einstein introduced his great theory, his Theory of General Relativity. That was in 1915, and I was a little older than you are now. This beautiful, blazingly brilliant theory, to put it in a nutshell of wonder, proposes that our universe has four dimensions. The first three of these we know as Space; and the fourth is known as *Spacetime*. That is the dimension where Time and Space are linked; where Time is totally dependent on Space.'

Phyllis concentrated hard on what he was saying, trying to focus clearly on every word and where they might be leading.

'To give you a simple example,' he went on, 'imagine this: Einstein said that if two people were to witness the same event—say, a ball dropping from the top of a tall building—well, these two people might perceive the event of the ball dropping happening *at two different times*, depending upon how far away they are from the ball dropping.'

'Huh?' She frowned.

'It's dependent on *distance*, my dear. And on the *Time* it takes for light to travel through Space. You see, light always travels at the same speed . . . a constant speed, a *finite* speed. Therefore, someone who is watching the ball dropping from somewhere further away than another person who is watching the same thing from a closer place will perceive that the ball had dropped *later* in Time. But the ball is actually dropping at the *same instant* in Time.'

Phyllis shook her head slowly. This would take a lot of getting used to, she thought.

'And so Einstein put it to us,' said Wallace Wong, 'that Time is dependent on Space. Oh, my dear Phyllis, that is just the beginning. We also know that Space *curves*. And Time, being dependent on Space the way it is, becomes curved as well.'

He stopped and noticed that Phyllis was biting her lip, and he saw deep creases furrowing across her forehead.

'Ah, great-granddaughter, there is much more to all of this. Much more that I shall not go into now.' He patted her hand. 'Too much information at one time is worse than the hidden ear of a pig,' he intoned mysteriously.

Phyllis gave him another strange look.

'I know what I mean,' he said, clearing his throat again.

'Okay,' Phyllis said. 'So Einstein came up with this theory—'

'Blazingly brilliant it is!'

'—and it's because of this theory that you're able to Transit?'

'Precisely.'

'But how? How? I mean, *knowing* something doesn't mean that you can actually *do* it. Does it? Anyone can learn about playing the piano, or the xylophone like my friend Clem, but just because they know how to do it doesn't mean they *can* do it, does it?'

Wallace Wong took a deep breath. He beamed at his great-granddaughter, and his eyes blazed proudly. 'I knew you would be the next one,' he said quietly. 'I knew your way of thinking would be right.'

Phyllis was looking extremely puzzled.

He patted her hand again. 'You are perfectly correct, Phyllis. Knowing about something does not mean you are able to do it. You can know all the theory about writing a story or a piece of music, or you can know exactly where to hit the ball in a game of golf, but it doesn't mean you will write a marvellous book or a symphony or get a hole-in-one. No, my dear girl, I delved deeper. I made some further discoveries. Some further discoveries of my own.'

His voice had dropped lower, quieter; it flowed (Phyllis thought) like a river beneath a dark, cloudless sky.

She felt her heart beating more quickly. Daisy, who had been grooming her front paws with her pointy, pink tongue, stopped her licking and looked up at the Conjuror of Wonder.

'I discovered the Pockets,' said Wallace Wong. 'The places that have enabled me to Transit.'

Phyllis went totally still. She clasped her hands in her interlocking-of-thumb-and-little-finger formation and looked at him.

'I discovered,' he told her, 'that all through this vast world of ours, there are what I have come to call the Pockets—places invisible to most people, places that are so aligned along the planet's rind that if you are able to access them, you will be able to Transit. Not only Transit from one Time to another, but also from one *place* to the next!'

Phyllis gasped. 'What, you mean you can go to the other side of the world, into any Time you want?'

'If you know what you are doing,' he answered. 'And if you have the necessary objects with you.'

'And you've been using these . . . Pockets . . . to Transit all this time? Since that night in 1936?'

'I have. My constant journey. Only recently have I started coming back, to your Time. But then I go again. I am always moving.'

'But why?'

'Why?'

'Why do you stay away for so long?'

'Ah. There is something I am looking for, Phyllis.'

Phyllis heard his voice go softer when he told her that. It was as though he had spoken to her from behind a silky screen. 'What?' she asked.

He smiled—a slightly weary smile, she thought. 'Ah,' he said gently. 'The Time will come when I will divulge what that is to you. But that Time is not the Time of nowness, my dear.'

Phyllis unclasped her hands and stroked Daisy's folded-over ear thoughtfully.

'And I like to keep moving. Always to stay on the go. In my search, I find that I need to keep moving about.'

'Don't you ever get lonely when you're away?' she asked Wallace Wong.

'No, great-granddaughter. Never! How can I feel loneliness when I can be, at any Time, surrounded by crowds, or when I find myself propelled into new cities or places where there is much to discover in my searchings? No, Phyllis, loneliness is something I do not taste. To dwell on loneliness would be like living with one hand tied behind an aardvark's back.'

She gave him another look.

'I know what I am meaning,' he said quickly.

It was then that Phyllis observed that his eyes were no longer glowing that strange green. 'Your eyes,' she commented, peering at them.

He smiled. 'Not pulsating any more?' he asked. 'The bright green has left them?'

'Uh-huh. They look normal.'

'That is because I have settled,' he told her. 'It is a hazard of Transiting the way I do, Phyllis. Sometimes I do not Transit very smoothly. When that happens, my eyes are affected in the green way, and sometimes also the way I speak and the way I move is affected. It is as if, when this happens,

I am struggling to communicate from behind a thick, swirling curtain of matter. When I arrive in my new Time destination, it sometimes takes me a while to re-align myself; to settle again.'

'Do you Transit smoothly very much?'

He screwed up his nose, and the ends of his neat moustache pointed upwards. 'I wish I could say I did. But the truth is, like a man who constantly gets seasick when on a ship, I suffer from the forces of the Transiting. For a little while at least. The smoothness of the journey and the amount of discombobulation suffered by a Transiter depends on the sort of Pocket the Transiter has entered.'

'Discombobulation?' Phyllis repeated, intrigued by the word.

'Giddiness,' explained Wallace Wong, smiling. 'Wonkiness. Judderaciousness. *Whoops-a-daisy-ness*, for want of a better term.'

Daisy, who had started falling asleep in the deep comfort of the old sofa, looked up at the sound of her name. Phyllis stroked the back of her head, and the little dog lowered her snout so that it was between her paws, gave a small marble-gargling sound and closed her eyes again.

'Some Transiters fare better in their journeys than others,' Wallace went on.

Phyllis looked at him, and he answered her question before she had the chance to ask it.

'Yes, great-granddaughter, there are *other* Transiters. Others who have stumbled upon the Pockets. Others who, for one reason or another and sometimes for very dubious reasons, have become my fellow wayfarers.' He frowned. 'Some use the Pockets for procurement, Phyllis. Some *misuse* the Pockets of Time.'

Phyllis clasped her hands again, this time tightly, and rested them on the top of her hat in her lap. 'How many other Transiters are there?'

'That I do not know. Every now and then I come across someone who is in Transit. Sometimes that person is easy to identify—they may not be Transiting smoothly, and I can detect it in their eyes or in their manner of movement or speech. Other times, it is difficult to identify the Transiter. Especially if they are not suffering any ill-effects from their journey through a Pocket.'

'You keep talking about these Pockets,' Phyllis said, turning on the sofa so she was directly facing Wallace. 'What are they?'

'Do you really want to know?' he asked.

'Yes!' The answer shot out of her so loudly that Daisy opened her eyes and gave a short, sharp yap.

Wallace Wong laughed. 'Then, know you shall. But, my dear girl, you must keep this knowledge to yourself. You must try never to reveal what I am about to tell you to another soul. Only if you think it absolutely essential must you share the knowledge. We cannot have too many people cluttering up the Pockets.'

'I'm a magician,' she said, smiling. 'I've had a bit of practice in keeping secrets.'

He winked at her. 'Which is one of the reasons why I am about to reveal some of the *greatest* secrets there are to you.'

He stood and smoothed down his sticking-up hair (but he missed the hair on the top of his head, which still looked like forty thousand volts of electricity had just passed through him). Then he went to one of the tall cupboards behind the sofas and started looking for something.

'It is nice to see that you have kept things, by and large, how I left them,' he muttered over his shoulder. 'It is good when the order of things remains. At least somewhere . . . ah! Here it is!'

Phyllis watched as he slid out a set of five square blackboard slates and a stick of chalk. She recognised the slates as Thayer's Famous 'Dr Q' Spirit Slates—props used for mind-reading tricks back in the 1930s.

'For today,' Wallace said as he came back to the sofa with them, 'we will not use these for the Spirit Slate Writing Mystery. I merely want them to write on.' He winked at her, raised the tails of his coat, and sat beside her and Daisy.

'Now concentrate, Phyllis, for the information I am about to impart will be of great use to you if you are to—'

He stopped and looked at her. Something had occurred to him, something that he had not anticipated. Sharing the secrets was one thing, but . . . *living* them . . .

The seconds ticked by, silently, stretchingly, in that enormous basement filled with secret things, as he considered this.

Finally Phyllis spoke. 'If I'm to *what*?'

'Phyllis, my dear girl,' said Wallace. 'I think you possess what it takes. I know how you perceive things. But I want to ask you something, and I want you to think carefully, to remember as hard as you can. If you are able to find a memory such as this, then it will all be possible.'

Phyllis's heart was beating quicker. She wasn't sure what he meant. 'Ask me,' she said.

Wallace Wong reached across and held her hand. 'Have you ever, in all your life, been in a situation, or a place, where you have thought that the bounds of your reality have shifted at all? Where things have seemed to become—even for the briefest of an instant—a sort of dream? Where you have glimpsed a different place to that where you were at that particular point in Time? And where this different place, this sort of dream, has been *almost real*? Think,' said Wallace Wong. 'Remember. Recall. Cast yourself into your past memories . . .'

Phyllis shut her eyes and concentrated. She cast her mind back, far back, as far back as she could remember.

A different place. A sort of dream. An instant. Where the bounds of reality had shifted . . .

She turned the phrases over in her head, letting them mingle with her memory, letting them ride her thoughts as though they were cresting the waves of her mind. Then, slowly, as if a soft light was being shone on a scene on a stage somewhere, she saw something in the darkness behind her eyelids . . .

. . . a moment that had happened when she was younger. A moment that she had all but forgotten about; that she had never recalled until now.

'Yes,' she answered, opening her eyes and staring wide-eyed at her great-grandfather. 'There was a time. There was a moment. When I was little.'

Wallace Wong smiled. 'Tell me,' he whispered.

Daisy gave a soft, feathery snore between them.

'I must've been about five or six,' said Phyllis. 'Dad had taken me to visit an old lady he was doing some business for. We went to her house—a big old place. We were inside, in this big sitting room, and Dad was going through all this paperwork with her and I was sitting on the floor, playing with her cat.'

Phyllis could almost see the scene before her as she was describing it.

'And the cat was rolling over on the rug and I was tickling its tummy—and then, really suddenly, it rolled over, almost snapped back at me, like a furry rubber band. And it scratched me. It hissed and scratched me, *slash*, right across the inside of my wrist! It drew blood.

'Dark red on my wrist, bright, quick. But I didn't cry out. No, because in the very same moment the blood appeared there, I saw something. Out of the corner of my eye.'

'What did you see?' asked Wallace, leaning towards her.

'It . . . it was as if a mist had spread in front of me, and through the mist I saw rooftops, lots of rooftops. It was like I was looking out from the window of a high-floor room somewhere. The rooftops weren't modern—there weren't any skyscrapers or anything. They were all tiled, the rooftops, dark tiles and steep, and there were little chimneys sticking up at all these strange angles. And the windows under the rooftops that I could see were all narrow, with small panes of glass . . . and the sky in the distance was all sort of cloudy and orange, and I could see some sort of tower there . . .'

Her voice trailed off, and she blinked heavily.

'Had you ever seen this place before?'

Phyllis shook her head. 'It was nowhere I'd ever seen.' She bit her lip, then she remembered another detail. 'I was only young, but for some reason I thought it was Paris.'

'Ah. And you had never been there.'

'Never.'

'What happened then?' asked Wallace.

'Then, after I don't know how long—it can't have been more than a few moments, but it seemed to be longer because I can still see the scene clearly, now that it's come back to me—I saw the blood on my wrist again, and I cried out. And Dad came over and scooped me up and put his handkerchief around my arm, and the cat had run away somewhere.'

Wallace Wong looked like he was about to erupt with uncontainable happiness. 'You have been shown,' he said, holding her hand firmly. 'You have the awareness.'

Phyllis blinked again. 'Huh?'

'You have the openness. You had it in that moment. You have the gift. And so, my great-granddaughter, I will ask you: would you like to become a Transiter?'

She gasped. From somewhere inside her, it was as if a brilliant golden ball had emerged instantaneously and was bouncing wildly around within her ribcage.

'Did Houdini ever get in a milk bottle?' she blurted.

'Ah, strange man, that Houdini,' said Wallace Wong. 'He wore the most peculiar socks—'

'Yes! Yes, yes, yes, yes!' Phyllis jumped to her feet, unable to stay still. 'I want to become a Transiter!'

Daisy woke up, leapt off the sofa and started dancing around Phyllis's ankles, springing up and running around the young prestidigitator.

'Then,' said Wallace Wong, clearly delighted at her response, 'I shall reveal to you the Pockets.'

Pockets revealed

Phyllis knelt on the rug in front of the sofa, waiting. Daisy, opting for somewhere more comfortable, jumped back up onto the sofa, next to Wallace Wong, and snuggled down by Phyllis's black hat.

Wallace picked up one of the Thayer's black-board slates and the stick of chalk. 'Now, my dear girl,' he said quietly, 'I have, in the course of my Transits, so far found that there are four sorts of Pockets. Some of these Pockets are big—very big—and others are smaller. The bigger Pockets, I have been finding, allow one to move great distances, not only through Time, but also through the world. Right across to the other side of the planet, even. The smaller Pockets are little more than blemishes, or tiny holes perhaps, or even *dimples*, in the fabric of Time. Through these smaller Pockets one can only Transit to the same place that one has left, but to that same place at another point in Time.'

Phyllis listened carefully. 'How do you know what sort of Pocket you're entering?' she asked.

'Ah.' Wallace Wong was about to write on the first slate, but he stopped, the chalk poised in mid-air. 'Oftentimes, you do not. The only time you can hope to know what sort of Pocket you enter is if you have entered that Pocket at that location before. And even then, things change. Time, you see, is a never-ending oscillation . . . of *uncertainty*. But, I have found that usually, if you Transit through the same Pocket more than once, you will have the same sort of experience. The *Time* where you end up is dependent on something different . . .'

He smiled and winked at her. Then, as Daisy began to snore feather-quietly next to him, he put the chalk to the blackboard slate and wrote. Phyllis saw his hand moving elegantly across the slate.

When he had finished he turned the slate around and presented it to her. With her heart beating loudly, she took it from him and read the single word he had written in his beautiful flowing script:

Anamygduleon

'Anamygduleon,' she read aloud.

'The Anamygduleon,' Wallace told her, 'is the most powerful Pocket I have so far discovered. It was the type of Pocket I disappeared into in Venezuela in 1936; beneath that stage, in that theatre, I found my first Anamygduleon! Anamygduleons are

89

huge, Phyllis, my dear, and they are the hardest to Transit through. I am thinking, as I go about my searching, that Anamygduleons lead you to places where events of enormous depth and meaning for the world have taken place. Places where there is great historical resonance. Where things still reverberate, like the trembling sounds of a bell after it has been rung. Places where Time has had, and still has, a precarious and shaky hold.'

Phyllis was scarcely breathing as she listened to her great-grandfather and stared at the word in front of her.

'And I find,' he continued, 'that on those rare occasions when I Transit through an Anamygduleon, my eyes and my speech and my movements take ages and ages to become re-equilibrialised. Until I return to normal, I am as giddy as a drunken crab with its shell filled with custard.'

Phyllis glanced up from the slate.

'Oh, I know what I am meaning,' he said quickly. 'Now, for the second type of Pocket.' He put his chalk to the next slate and once again he wrote.

When he'd finished, he handed the slate to Phyllis. Once more she read the word he had written, neatly and with a flourish:

Andruseon

'The Andruseon,' Wallace said, 'is another big Pocket. Not as vast, or with such strength, as the Anamygduleon, but big enough in its own right. I still suffer from Transitaciousness when I go through an Andruseon, but the effects are not as severe as when I use the Anamygduleons. I have found that an Andruseon Pocket will enable me to Transit a long distance in both Space and Time.'

'How far?' Phyllis asked.

'Ah, my dear, it all depends on where you are trying to go. And, as I mentioned before, that all depends on what objects you have with you.'

Phyllis put the second slate on the floor, next to the first. She watched as Wallace wrote on the next small blackboard.

'And so they get smaller, these Pockets,' he said, turning the slate around and handing it to her. There, before her eyes, was the word:

Anvugheon

'I find that I do much of my Transiting through Anvugheon Pockets,' Wallace informed her. 'I think that perhaps that is because there are more of them around. Anvugheons are quick passages, Phyllis. Not much turbulence or fuss by the time you get to the other end. Smooth is the flow through an Anvugheon, and that is the way I like it.'

'So,' Phyllis said, 'you can't Transit as far through an Anvugheon as you can through an Anamygduleon or an Andruseon?'

'That is correct. But an Anvugheon is very useful, nonetheless. Say, for example, if I have left my wallet somewhere and I discover the loss a few days later. An Anvugheon Pocket will enable me to return swiftly to the place where my forgetfulness occurred.'

'Wow.' Phyllis's mind started racing away with all the possibilities. To be able to return to a Time and place where something had gone wrong . . .

'And the fourth Pocket,' said Wallace Wong. He had written on the fourth slate and he leant down and gave it to Phyllis.

She turned it around and saw the word:

Anaumbryon

'An Anaumbryon is the simplest of the Pockets I have so far encountered,' Wallace said. 'I like to think of it as a blemish on the skin of Time, a place where one can slip through easily and come back again, just as easily. Whenever I have Transited through an Anaumbryon, I have always ended up in the exact same spot from where I had left, and the Time difference is minimal—sometimes only an hour before I had left. Sometimes, Phyllis, I go to the same place only *minutes* before I had left!'

'This is fantastic,' Phyllis muttered.

'Ah, that is so. That is how it seems. But I have been doing it now for nearly a century, so to me it has become a way of life. A way of being.' He smiled, and Phyllis saw a great peacefulness and calm in his face. 'I love the way I am being, Phyllis, my dear. I will love this way of being all the way until I find that for which I am searching . . .'

Phyllis raised her eyebrows, hoping that he would elaborate on the thing that he was searching for. But he merely smiled more widely at her and shook his head slowly. 'It is not the nowness for that,' he told her gently. 'I will tell you when the nowness is ready.'

'Hmm,' she said. She smiled back at him— the same smile that had travelled down between them through the generations. Then she thought of something. 'Great-grandfather?'

'Yes, my dear?'

'How do you know what the names for the Pockets are? Did *you* come up with the names? Or are there signposts or something when you come across a Pocket that tell you what it is?'

'No, no signposts. In fact, there is nothing to even tell you that a Pocket is there before you. But I find that I can often detect it because of my *awareness* . . . the same sort of awareness that you had when the cat scratched you at that lady's house.'

He nodded. 'The awareness is necessary to be able to know where the Pockets are.'

'So you did name them?'

'I did. They are merely names I invented to categorise each type of Pocket.' He gave a small chuckle. 'I have found, Phyllis, that the clearer your head is, especially when you are engaged in something so mind-stretching as Transiting, the easier it will be. I just thought that if I could give the Pockets names, I could get things clearer in my own head, and at least keep that part of the Transiting a little less confused.'

Phyllis looked at the four slates spread before her. 'So how did you come up with the names?'

'Ah. It was simple. The middle part of each name is just something I already knew. A term from geology, to do with rocks. Or a word for a small cupboard or store-room. And then I merely split another word—a magical word, if you like—and put it at either end of the middle part.'

Phyllis had been re-reading each Pocket name as he had been explaining this to her. She looked up at him.

On the fifth slate he wrote a simple word:

Anon

'Anon,' said Phyllis.

'Such a beautiful word, when you stop to think

about it. *Soon.*' He stared up to the high ceiling of the basement. 'So many possibilities, if only we know where to seek them . . .'

Phyllis looked at all the slates on the floor in front of her. She read each name again, savouring each one of them as though they were her favourite chocolate confections that she was eating at The Délicieux Café. Anamygduleon. Andruseon. Anvugheon. Anaumbryon.

The Pockets of Wallace Wong.

She looked up and caught him smiling at her. 'And now,' he announced, rising to his feet (and being careful not to wake Daisy), 'shall we go?'

Phyllis stood. Her legs were shaky, and she took several deep breaths to try to steady herself. 'Let's do it!' she whispered.

'Now I shall show you *how* it is done. Where would you like to go?' he asked her, taking her hand.

'I want to go where you go. Anywhere you want to show me!'

'Hmm,' hmmed Wallace Wong. He studied her face for a moment. 'You like History, yes?'

'Sure.' It was one of Phyllis's favourite subjects at school, and she had even come first in it last year.

'All righty.' He let go of her hand and went off to one of the rows of shelves near to the stairs. 'Most important: one needs to have something from the place one intends to visit. Some sort of object that came from that place. It acts, so I believe, as a sort of guiding signal. Some sort of *passport*, if you like.'

Phyllis watched as he started rummaging around in the boxes and amongst the cylinders and silk production cabinets on the shelves. 'What are you looking for?' she asked. 'Where are we going to Transit?'

'You'll see. Just be patient, my dear. Patience is a golden whisker that can never be twiddled.'

This time he didn't even turn around as he sensed the look that Phyllis was giving him. 'I know what I am meaning,' he muttered.

Phyllis smiled. Her legs were still shaking a bit, but she didn't feel scared—just exhilarated by the possibility of *anon*.

While Wallace continued rummaging around for his object, Phyllis remembered something that Clement had said to her after they had visited Thundermallow's, when he was decked out in his jumble of disguises. 'I could go anywhere and they wouldn't know me, not even my own mother,' he had announced excitedly.

Now, those very words took on a whole new meaning. Phyllis Wong realised that she could go anywhere and no one would ever know her. And she didn't need cheap and strange disguises for that to happen. For some reason, she found that prospect exciting.

'Ah! Found it!' Wallace came back to her.

Daisy opened one eye, checked that Phyllis and he were still there, and then closed her eye again, returning to her happy dreams of tigers who needed chasing and rounding up.

'What've you got?' Phyllis asked her great-grandfather, trying to see what he was concealing in his palm.

He held out his hand and opened his fingers. Phyllis saw a small object: a lapis lazuli stone that had been carved in the shape of a beetle.

'A scarab,' said Wallace. 'It's from Egypt, from the Khan el-Khalili, the biggest *souk* in Cairo.'

'*Souk?*' repeated Phyllis.

'The bazaar. The biggest bazaar district in Cairo. The man who sold it to me told me that it was ancient, over four thousand years old, and so I paid a lot of money for it. That was back in 1930, when I went to Egypt to buy some fabrics and furniture I could use in an act I'd designed— *Prestidigitations of the Pyramids!*' He turned the scarab over and frowned. 'I've always wanted to find out its exact age. Hopefully we shall be able to Transit back to when it was made.'

He handed her the scarab. Her palm was glistening.

'Ready?' he asked, his eyes gleaming.

'Yep.' She curled her fingers around the scarab. 'Oh, what about Daisy?'

Wallace glanced over at the small dog sleeping by Phyllis's top hat. Her chest was rising and falling so gently that he had to watch her for a few moments to see if she was still breathing. 'Oh, I think we should leave her be. Let us follow the robust cliché and let the sleeping pup lie, yes? Besides, when we return, she will still be there. In fact, she will only have slept for a few seconds, no matter how long we are away.'

'Wow,' said Phyllis.

'So,' Wallace said, taking her by her hand again. 'Off to Cairo?'

'Off to Cairo.' Phyllis was tingling all over, and she could feel her stomach becoming strangely lighter.

He led her to the stairs and positioned her so that she was standing in front of him. 'Hold on tightly to the scarab,' he told her. 'Do not let it go, no matter what happens.'

'Okay.'

'Now,' he said, peering ahead, 'look carefully. Up there. Concentrate hard on what will emerge, and divest yourself of all other thoughts. Think of nothing.'

Phyllis looked at the dimness on the stairs in

front of her. She half-closed her eyes and tried to empty her mind and her memory and her imagination of everything that had been in there.

'Ah!' she gasped. 'I see . . . it's . . .'

'Your first Pocket,' whispered her great-grandfather. He held her shoulders firmly.

'My first TimePocket,' Phyllis said.

'Let us move forward.'

Together, slowly, flowingly, they moved ahead.

Phyllis almost stopped breathing as they stepped towards what appeared to be a cavity, blurred around the edges with a faint green glow, and twinkling with out-of-focus beads of brightness. Beyond it was a dense darkness, through which no light shone.

'Steady, my dear,' said Wallace Wong.

Now they were right on the threshold of this deep, dark place. The twinkling beads of brightness were above them and beside them. Things were getting blurrier. Things were becoming thick . . .

'Oh, yes, Phyllis,' came Wallace's voice in her ear, muffled and drawn-out and deep like a ship's horn, 'I almost forgot. There is one thing more I have not told you!'

'What?' she yelled as a huge roar of wind engulfed them.

'The Pockets are always hidden on staircases!'

Bizarre bazaar

Everything stretched before her, as though all that existed, and all that had ever existed, was being pulled and twisted and extended—wobblingly, ever-onwards, into the distance of all Times jumbled.

Phyllis shut her eyes as the blurriness whizzed past her and her great-grandfather. But even with her eyelids closed, scrunched tight, she detected changes in the lightness through which she and Wallace were Transiting: now everything was dark, pitch-black, and then things seemed to be lightening, glowing brighter, before fading down to dimness again.

She could feel Wallace's hands gripping her shoulders as she and he moved forward. Forward *and* backward, she thought, as she felt her hair whipping around her shoulders and into his face. She heard him gasping, half-coughing, as he copped a mouthful of her long, dark locks, and she sensed him moving his head quickly to one side to try to avoid another mouthful.

And she heard something else: a soft, vibrating, high *hum*. It travelled with them as they sped along, swooping all around them, gently cocooning her with its reassuring tone. Phyllis had heard a similar sound sometimes when she had caught ferries, late at night in the city, when she'd been coming home with her father after an excursion to the amusement park by the wharves. She had always imagined, whenever she'd heard that sound on the ferries as they glided across the harbour, that it was the sound made by invisible wings in the cool night air . . .

Her stomach lurched, as if it were a single solitary sock trapped in a spin dryer, flinging around on full cycle. Phyllis gulped, as she felt something rise up in her throat. She felt like she was about to be sick. She pushed the thing back down, and took a deep breath, opening her mouth wide. But that wasn't the best thing to do; the wind shot into her mouth like an invisible cannonball, and her cheeks blew out into balloons of fleshiness, and her whole face felt like it was being flattened against an unseen wall. Struggling, she managed to get her mouth closed again. She wouldn't try that any time she was Transiting, she decided.

But it did manage to keep whatever was rising from her stomach at bay, and she found that, if she concentrated and breathed steadily through her nostrils, she could manage some sort of control over her insides.

She could feel nothing beneath her feet, or anywhere around her, except for Wallace's hands on her shoulders. She felt weightless, and tiny, and she felt like she was being warped—squeezed and pulled and whirled, all at the same time. She was giddy and zingly and a bit nauseous. She was a bit scared. But above all, she was excited. It was an excitement she had never felt; an excitement that seemed to electrify her, that almost made her forget who she was and where she had come from. It was an extraordinary sensation.

Presently she sensed that they were slowing down. The lightness and darkness and glowingness began to even out, until a steady, soft brightness warmed her closed eyelids. She felt her stomach settling, and Wallace's grip on her shoulders relaxing. Her hair had stopped billowing about in all directions. And she felt something firm beneath her shoes.

'We're here,' Wallace said in her ear. 'We have arrived.'

Phyllis opened her eyes. Wallace turned her around to face him and let go of her shoulders. He squinted and looked her quickly up and down. 'Ah, you seem dandy,' he said, smiling. 'Please, open your eyes wide for me.'

She did so, making herself look suddenly surprised.

He laughed, and then he pinched her cheek (she pulled away at that). 'You have Transited well,' he said to her. 'I detect no signs of turbulence coming from within.'

'Oh, you should be glad you weren't my stomach,' Phyllis said. 'I felt like I was going to throw up back there.'

'But you did not. You came through. With flying colours, great-granddaughter. I am very proud of you.'

Phyllis saw the greenness creeping back into his eyes. He put his hand to his forehead and shook his head. 'Yes,' he said, 'I am glad to see that you do not succumb to Transitaciousness as I do. It is reassuring to know that it does not run in the family.'

He straightened up his midnight-blue tail coat and pulled down his waistcoat. Then he did something that made Phyllis giggle: he extended his right leg straight out, to the side, and gave it a vigorous shake. He lowered his leg and repeated the action with his left leg. Then he lowered that leg and rubbed his hands together in a business-like fashion. 'That was an Andruseon, I am sure of it.'

'Ah,' Phyllis said.

'If it were a lesser Pocket, I would probably not

be feeling so much of these effects,' Wallace added. 'Now, the scarab?'

Phyllis opened her fingers and handed the scarab to him.

'Thank you, my dear.'

'You're welcome,' she said. Then, for the first time, she began to become aware of where they were. It was as if a heavy veil was being lifted, and sounds and smells and light started seeping all around her . . .

Phyllis and her great-grandfather were standing at the top of a tall, but not enormous, slightly dusty marble staircase. They were overlooking a vast maze of market stalls and awnings—some of them brightly striped, others tatty and faded by the sun. For as far as she could see, under the awnings and between the crowds of people, there were benches and tables and shop counters, piled with all manner of merchandise: heavy carpets and rugs; gleaming copper lanterns, old tarnished lamps and fancy coloured-glass lightshades; mountains of ancient, leather-bound books; antique crystal chandeliers; birdcages imprisoning beautiful scarlet and yellow-and-blue macaws and other bright green-and-orange parrots; vast bins full to the brim with rich and intensely coloured spices—cumin, turmeric, paprika, saffron; big tubs and bowls filled with fish and crabs and lobsters; piles of papyrus sheets, decorated for the tourist market with paintings of the pyramids and the Nile and scenes from the ancient *Book of the Dead*; ornate glass hookahs and water pipes; and other, strange-looking objects that Phyllis had never seen before.

Above everything, towering and spearing elegantly upwards, was a series of beautiful stone arches which fed into a network of huge, vaulted ceilings that, here and there, were opened to the skies. The ceilings appeared to stretch on for miles. Phyllis gasped as she beheld the bold, mighty archways . . . they beckoned her mind towards higher places, places that she had never contemplated, places suggesting the promise of mystery and the unknown . . .

She brought her gaze down to earth again. Between the stalls and shops were small alcoves where a few tables and chairs had been set up. Men were sitting at some of these tables, smoking hookahs and playing dominoes, or drinking glasses of what looked like tar-black tea. Most of the men were dressed in the traditional *galabiyya*—the long, flowing, cool cotton garment popular in Egypt. Phyllis had seen pictures of these garments when she had done a project for school a few years ago.

The sounds of the *souk* were now all around her: shouting coming from a far corner; loud conversations near the foot of the staircase; some high-pitched music wafting through from a quarter over to the right. Angry voices swelled from somewhere, then disappeared as quickly as they had started; she heard laughter—deep, hearty laughter of maybe a dozen people. They all sounded like men.

Snortings, too, she heard, and loud, deep bellowings. She saw, by a big marble archway, about two dozen camels, kneeling by a wall. Phyllis smiled as she realised how Daisy knelt in almost exactly the same way as these larger, placid-looking beasts who were busy chewing their cuds or spitting at hapless tourists who were passing by too close to them.

Phyllis took a deep breath. The bazaar smelled of all things: the spices, including the pungent aroma of cloves; the dust; the heat coming off the animals and the ground; the sweat and the sickly sweet perfumes which were also on sale (the perfumes, not the sweat, were for sale—although, as Phyllis beheld the vast array of offerings here at the Khan el-Khalili, she wouldn't have been surprised if you *could* buy small bottles of human perspiration. It seemed that everything under the sun was available here for a price).

She put her hand on the cool marble balustrade of the stairs, and she saw that it was impregnated with a fine and beautiful design of mosaic work—bright blue lapis lazuli diamond shapes and vivid golden stones forming a snake-scale pattern that ran along the length of the balustrade. She smiled and ran a finger across the stones.

'This is a beautiful TimePocket, to use your word,' Wallace said. 'I am glad you had such a one for your first experience. Take it from me, Phyllis, they are not all as pleasant as this. Why, sometimes I have emerged onto such ramshackle and putrid stairs that they look like they have been brought forth from the final days of the Earth . . .' He shuddered and shook his head at the memory.

Phyllis was tingling. She had always been fascinated with Egypt, and now here she was, standing on a beautiful staircase in the heart of the Khan el-Khalili. She was smiling so much her ears were sticking out.

Wallace asked, 'Do you know the poem "Antigonish"?'

Phyllis thought for a moment. 'I don't think so.'

'Goes like this:

'*Yesterday, upon the stair,*
I met a man who wasn't there
He wasn't there again today
I wish, I wish he'd go away . . .'

'Oh, yes,' said Phyllis. 'We read it at school. I like it. It's weird. I never really knew exactly what it's about—whether it's about someone strange or if it's just nonsense. I think that's why I like it.'

'That's just the beginning of the poem,' Wallace said. 'I know the man who wrote it. William Mearns. A gentle chap. He's a Transiter too, you know.'

Phyllis looked at him.

He gave her a wink. 'Oh, you might be surprised who Transits, my dear. All sorts of people. I'm sure you're bound to come across some surprises . . . but now, let's find out about this.' He held the scarab between his thumb and first finger and passed his other hand across it. When he took his hand away, the scarab had disappeared.

Phyllis giggled. She raised an eyebrow. 'Right or left?' she asked.

'Try your left,' replied Wallace Wong.

Phyllis felt behind her left ear. Sure enough, there was the scarab. She took it and gave it back to him. 'You're the only magician who's ever been known to disappear something and make it reappear behind someone's ear without you having to take it from them,' she said. 'How?'

'How is not now,' Wallace said, his green eyes gleaming secretively. 'I shall reveal this to you, all in the goodness of the Time to come. But for now, I need to find a newspaper. Come, my dear girl.'

He started down the steps, two at a time, and Phyllis followed close behind. As they jostled past other people on the lower steps, Phyllis asked, 'What do you need a newspaper for?'

'To find out what Time we have arrived at.'

They came to the base of the staircase and squeezed into the alleyway ahead, past all sorts of people: vendors carrying trays of sweets, with heavy samovars full of hot tea hanging from their shoulders; men and women laden with carpets and boxes and all sorts of paraphernalia as they hurried to get to their stalls and shops; and tourists, dressed in all types of clothing from all parts of the world. Phyllis observed that many of the tourists were dressed in Western-style clothes and seemed well attired, in fashions that suggested a Time from not so long ago.

'Ah!' exclaimed Wallace, stopping, and putting his hand out to stop Phyllis also. 'Over there. See, those men having coffee and eating dates at that little café? The fat man wearing the red fez has a paper.' He turned to Phyllis. 'My dear, pop over there and try to see what the date is on the front page.'

'Sure,' said Phyllis.

'And try to be inconspicuous. Do not draw any attention to yourself if you can at all help it.'

'Okeydokey. I'll be back in a flash.'

She darted through the crowds, zigzagging in and out and being careful not to bump into anyone.

She neared the man with the newspaper. He was sitting on a wooden chair while his friends were having a loud discussion in Arabic.

Unfortunately, because he was reading the inside of the paper, he had the front page lowered, so Phyllis couldn't get a good glimpse of the paper's banner.

She thought quickly. She approached his chair and then, when she was right in front of him, she knelt and pretended to tie up her shoelace, all the while looking up through her fringe.

After a few seconds she came bounding back to her great-grandfather. 'May 20th, 1927,' she said excitedly.

'Nineteen twenty-seven,' Wallace repeated. His greenness throbbed and his mouth curled disdainfully. 'Far from ancient! The scoundrel!' He held the scarab between his fingers, and stared daggers at it. 'He told me this was from the Time of the pharaohs! He assured me it was thousands of years old. He charged me a hundred pounds for it—a lot of money back then—here today—Phyllis. We have returned to the Time it was made—1927! Oh, wait till I get my hands on him! Come!' And off he hurried, up a side alley, the tails of his coat flying out behind him.

'But how do you know where to find this guy?' She ran to keep up with him.

'Well, Time is on our side here. You see, the vendors at the Khan el-Khalili tend to pass their sites down from generation to generation. It is a time-honoured tradition to be a seller at the most important markets in Cairo—indeed in all of Egypt and all of Africa. A stall at the Khan el-Khalili nearly always stays in the same family for hundreds of years. And it nearly always remains in the same location inside the bazaar.'

Phyllis side-stepped a puddle of some revolting-smelling purplish-brown liquid and tried to stay alongside Wallace as he darted into a smaller passageway. Her shoes smacked loudly against the cobblestones.

'And,' he added, his voice rising, 'fortunately for me, I have a very good memory for locations. Now, this way!'

She was starting to feel the heat now, as she hurried along—a dry heat which hit against her face and arms, but didn't cling to her or make her feel awash with perspiration. She realised that they had come out from the undercover, vaulted, arched section of the bazaar and were now in an outside space.

'Ah-ha!' announced Wallace Wong, stopping at the end of the passageway. He put his hand out and Phyllis also stopped.

Ahead was a small courtyard, in the centre of

which was a circular fountain. Wallace extended his arm and pointed to a small, darkened opening in the wall at the rear of the courtyard, behind the fountain. In front of this opening was a trestle table, upon which resided several dusty glass-and-mahogany display cabinets and a tall pile of old-looking, weathered sheets of papyrus and parchment. 'There it is,' he said quietly, his teeth flashing in the sunlight. 'That's where the rotter resides!'

He grabbed Phyllis's hand and marched across the courtyard, around the fountain and to the darkened opening with the table out the front. Phyllis half-hopped and half-ran to stay next to him.

'Hello? *Iwy em hotep?*' called Wallace, loudly. 'That's *hello* in the old Egyptian,' he said as an aside to Phyllis.

'Ah-ha,' she said, still holding his hand.

They waited for a few moments. Here in the open-air courtyard, it was quieter than elsewhere in the Khan el-Khalili. Phyllis and her youthful great-grandfather were the only people in this quarter.

There was no response from the darkened place in the wall. A small, warm breeze blew a scrap of paper across the courtyard, and the paper *ticker-ticker-ticker*ed across the cobblestones.

'*Iwy em hotep?*' Wallace called again. He let go of Phyllis's hand and with his knuckles he rapped loudly on the tabletop. 'Is anybody there?'

112

Phyllis saw something in the darkness. A small movement. A deep brown curtain was pulled lazily aside, and out from behind the curtain, emerging from the gloom in the wall, came a large, bristly man wearing a long, striped *galabiyya* and a squat mulberry-coloured fez with a black tassel. Phyllis detected the strong smell of aniseed coming off the man's clothing.

'*Iwy em hotep*,' said the man, in a gravelly voice. He looked carefully at Wallace, up and down at his immaculate silk suit, and then he addressed him in English: 'Welcome in Egypt. How can I be of assistance to you, my friend?'

Wallace held out his hand, the scarab resting on his opened palm. 'I bought this from you for a hundred pounds,' he said in a steady, courteous tone. 'You told me that it was ancient. But it is not. It is new. It was made, quite possibly, only yesterday.'

The man raised his heavy, coarse, black eyebrows and inspected the scarab in Wallace's hand. He shook his head. 'No, my friend, you are mistaken. That is ancient. It is from the time of the pharaohs. It is thousands of years old.'

'No, my friend,' retorted Wallace. 'It is not. It is a modern copy. A fake. You have hoodwinked me, by Houdini! And I desire to have my money back.'

The man lowered the black hairy rooftop of his brows, and a scowl began to creep across his fat lips

(Phyllis thought they resembled a pair of cuddling, bloated tadpoles). 'Why,' he asked, 'should I give you money? Why? I have never laid my eyes upon you before in my lifetime!'

Wallace gazed at him steadily and thought. Then he said, as another aside to Phyllis, 'He may be a scoundrel, but at this moment he speaks the truth. I bought the scarab from him in 1930, nearly three years after we are meeting today. And that was the first time I ever encountered him.'

'Ah,' said Phyllis.

'Sometimes,' Wallace added, 'the truth becomes as wibbly-wobbly as the jellied eel on the escalators of disparity.'

She raised her eyebrows and looked at him.

'Oh, I know what—'

The bristly man stepped around the table, moving closer to Wallace and Phyllis. 'I have never seen you before, yet you come here seeking money from me? You dare to *demand* that I give you money?'

'Well,' said Wallace, stepping back and taking Phyllis's hand again, keeping her well away from the bristly man and his aniseed odour, 'I do, erm, yes, I *did*, but things may not be as simple as they appear. Perhaps I should just—'

'Perhaps you should just meet my brothers,' said the man, his voice becoming more gravelly and deeper.

'No, no,' Wallace protested, retreating with Phyllis. 'I don't think they'd want to meet us. I think we'll just make ourselves—'

'Oh, yes, they will want to meet you. Husain!' called the man. 'Hosni! Hafiz! Hakim! Keith!'

From the gloom behind the deep brown curtain, five enormous, unshaved men spilled forth. Like their bristly brother, they all wore striped *galabiyyas* that smelled of aniseed. It looked like a whiskers convention had suddenly appeared.

The five enormous men gathered around Wallace and Phyllis. 'This man,' snarled the bristly one, 'demands that I give him money, yet he is a stranger to me. I think we should give him something for his'—the bristly man's eyes shone angrily—'*impertinence*!'

There was the sound of scraping metal, sharp and squealingly high-pitched, as each of the five brothers swiftly withdrew a long silver scimitar from a scabbard he wore on his hip. Each of the brothers pointed his curved, sharp weapon at Wallace and Phyllis.

'W.W.!' Phyllis gasped, her legs going instantaneously trembly. 'What do we do?'

'I think,' Wallace whispered, 'it's time for our exit.' He looked upwards and his green-tinged eyes widened as a look of amazement spread across his face. 'Heavens above! Is that a *roc*? Swooping

115

down, returning to the Khan el-Khalili to bring good fortune to those on whose marketplace it descends?'

All six of the brothers looked at each other, then, remembering the legend that foretold the return of the great bird in the great marketplace, they all looked up, in the direction of Wallace's amazement.

'Let's take it on the lam!' Wallace hissed urgently, grabbing Phyllis's hand tighter and pulling her away from the mass of sweaty bristliness. They ran as fast as they could, past the fountain and out into a wider part of the open-air bazaar.

'They escape!' cried the first brother.

'He has tricked us!' snarled another.

'After them!' shouted one of the others.

Wallace and Phyllis pelted through the alleyway ahead and came out into a big sunlit courtyard lined with small stalls. 'This way!' Wallace urged, pulling Phyllis across the courtyard.

The brothers were in close pursuit, their heavy feet echoing through the cobblestoned alleyway as they gained on Phyllis and her great-grandfather.

'See!' shouted the first brother as the two magicians ran into the centre of the courtyard. 'There they are! Surround them!'

The brothers nodded and grunted and, with their scimitars held aloft, they started spreading out, running towards the edges of the courtyard.

Phyllis could see that they would soon have the area surrounded. 'What'll we do?' she yelled, her mouth dry and her heart bursting against her ribs.

Wallace slowed his pace as he took in all that was around them. 'Ah-ha!' he exclaimed, spying something. 'Quickly, before they get to the other side of the yard! As long as they can't see us from the rear, this might just work. A little move I picked up in my picture *Neddy and the Nightshirt*. Just do as I do, my dear, and stay close!'

'Okay,' gulped Phyllis.

The Conjuror of Wonder started running again, holding Phyllis's hand and pulling her close to him, in the direction of a small, bright yellow truck that had driven in at the eastern edge of the courtyard and which was now travelling straight through the middle. It was moving at a swift speed, bumping and jerking across the uneven stone pavers.

'What?' yelled Phyllis—Wallace was leading her directly into the truck's path, towards a crashing head-on collision!

'Quickly!' he urged.

The bristly men saw what was happening, and they slowed their paces, wondering what was going on.

Wallace didn't slow down, but, rather, he began to run more quickly. Straight towards the oncoming vehicle. Phyllis wanted to stop, to pull up suddenly, but she couldn't—Wallace's grip was too strong.

Then, just in the last moments before he and Phyllis were to be hit by the truck, Wallace pulled his great-granddaughter to the side.

What happened in the next moment happened so quickly that it seemed truly magical. In the instant that Wallace and Phyllis were hidden from their attackers by the truck, Wallace, with no break in his speed, turned around, turning Phyllis with him, so that they were now facing the same direction in which the truck was heading. Then, hidden by the truck, he and Phyllis ran peltingly fast alongside it as it disappeared into a laneway at the western side of the courtyard.

His timing was perfect.

To the angry scimitar-wielding brothers it looked as if Wallace and Phyllis had disappeared without a trace!

'What devilry is this?' bellowed one of the brothers, his whiskers standing on end with rage.

'They are gone!' declared another, lowering his scimitar sulkily.

'Arrrr,' seethed another brother, the one named Keith.

As soon as Wallace and Phyllis were in the laneway, they veered off, up a narrow side passage, and the truck squeezed onwards, clattering and bumping away.

Wallace slowed down, and Phyllis did likewise. Together, they huffed and puffed and leant against the wall.

When Phyllis had got her breath back, she said, panting, 'Th-that was brilliant! You were amazing, W.W.!'

'W.W.,' repeated Wallace. 'I like that.'

Phyllis pulled her hair back, holding it like she was going to tie it in a ponytail. 'Man, I hope we don't come across those guys again. They meant business!'

'Yes. Funny business,' puffed W.W.

'*I'll show YOU funny business!*' came a snarl from the end of the laneway.

Phyllis and W.W. turned to see one of the brothers blocking the entrance, his scimitar brandished high above his huge head. It was Keith, the meanest-looking of all the brothers in his family!

'Die, dogs of deceit!' he bellowed, running at Phyllis and W.W. with a murderous expression on his hairy face.

Wallace grabbed Phyllis and they took off up the laneway. 'Ahead!' Wallace urged. 'Look! Stairs! Phyllis, do you have something from home?'

'Huh?' she gasped, running hard next to him.

'Something from the basement? Something to hold on to?'

Keith was gaining on them, his footsteps coming

after them like battering rams crashing against a fortress door.

Phyllis fumbled around in her coat pocket as she kept running. Her fingers brushed across some chocolate wrappers and what felt like a bus ticket and a scrunchy for her hair and some rubber bands and a packet of breath mints and then—a small ball, one of the red, sparkly balls she used when she rehearsed her cups and balls routines.

'Yes!' she exclaimed.

They were at the foot of the stairs. Wallace grabbed her and pushed her up. 'Hold it, hold it now. There is a Pocket here, I see it! Ascend, my great-granddaughter, run quickly up, to the sixteenth step. It begins there. I am right behind—'

'AAAAAAARRRRRRRGGGGGGHHHHH!' Keith's bellow was so loud, Phyllis thought it was right in her ear. She heard the cold, lightning-like *swiiiiiiiiish* of the scimitar blade.

There was no time to turn and look. Wallace was behind her; she could sense him there.

The heavy battering-ram footsteps were right behind him, relentlessly rising on the stairway.

She bounded up the steps, the sweat flying off her brow, running down into her eyes, almost blinding her with its saltiness.

Swiiiiiiiiiiiiiiiiiiish came the blade's hiss again.

She heard Wallace make a noise—a harsh noise, a startled noise. Once she had heard Daisy make a noise like that when she had cut the pad of her paw on a piece of broken glass . . .

'Do . . . not . . . *stop*,' Wallace urged, his words breathy and strange.

'W.W., are you—?' she began over her shoulder.

'Thirteen, fourteen, fifteen,' she heard him counting, gasping.

Phyllis felt his hand on her shoulder.

She pelted towards the sixteenth step and saw the dimness and the encrustations of brightness bordering the blackness beyond.

Swiiiiiiiiiiiiiiiiiiiiiiiiiiiiiiiiiiiiiish came the blade.

There was a cry, and a falling sound, and then the soft, high, vibrating hum.

And the thick, stretching, whizzing blurriness of the Pocket engulfed her.

PART TWO

Almost legendary

Settling the secret

Phyllis stumbled forward, her hair flying back behind her, her fingers clasped tightly around the red sparkly ball.

The soft, vibrating humming lowered and grew softer. The wind, which had been whipping all about her and blowing her cheeks out like over-inflated balloons, was subsiding. The darkness was melting away and everything was becoming lighter on the other side of her closed eyelids. The lurching, urgent, precariously rising feeling in her stomach started to disappear, and she became aware of things slowing . . . slowing . . . slowing down.

She opened her eyes and there were dancing molecules of light all around her. And then she saw Daisy. Her little dog was still fast asleep, next to her top hat on the sofa.

'I'm back,' Phyllis whispered, her heart beating wildly. She ran down the stairs into the centre of her magic-filled basement. And she stopped.

W.W.! Where is he? Her pounding heart

skipped a beat and she wheeled around, looking back up the stairs for him.

But the flight of stairs was nothing more than that; the bright ceiling lights were shining down onto the gleaming marble steps and presenting Phyllis with a vision of emptiness.

She shook her head. Thoughts started crashing through her mind, like dodgem cars out of control. What had just happened? Had she really been at the Khan el-Khalili? Had W.W. escaped the wrathful scimitar of murderous Keith? How long had she been gone? What—?

She opened her hand and saw the red ball. It was damp with perspiration. She took a deep breath, pocketed the ball, clasped her hands (her thumb encircling her little finger) and began to reflect.

Then she noticed something. A sheet of notepaper, folded in half, on the sofa next to Daisy. Quickly she went across the rug and picked up the notepaper. Daisy opened one eye, saw Phyllis, and made her marble-gargling-at-the-back-of-her-throat sound.

Phyllis sat next to her, giving her a long rub on her back as she unfolded the paper. Daisy moved closer to Phyllis and snuggled against her leg.

At the top of the paper, in neatly fashioned swirly writing, was a raised blue monogram and title:

Underneath it, flowing elegantly down the page, was her great-grandfather's handwriting. Phyllis's hands were trembling as she began reading.

My dear great-granddaughter,
You have now had your first experience of the biggest magic I have known—that of Transiting. Congratulations! I trust and hope that it will not be your last venture forth.

You will find this note but not me, for I have been and gone already. Like I told you, I find it difficult to stay in the one spot for too long. I have to be searching . . .

'He must've got back before me,' Phyllis muttered. 'He must be okay.' Her heart settled a little at the thought of that, and she read on:

But do not fear, Phyllis. I am certain that one day or night we shall Transit together again. In the meantime, I entrust the secrets to you. Like the secrets to your conjuring, they are to be held in confidence. Only Transit with others you can trust, and only if you feel it is absolutely necessary. And even then, if you do decide to share the knowledge of Transiting, you must be very careful. Your good judgement is paramount. As I told you, we cannot have too many Transiters cluttering up our paths.

The more Transiters there are, the fewer Transiting routes will be available. Sometimes it might be very difficult to find a Pocket, especially if other Transiters are going forth.

Now, before I leave, I want to share with you this further important advice:

Never Transit for selfish reasons, my dear girl. Never Transit for your own personal gain. Curiosity is one thing—a sign of your vibrant self—and it is perfectly acceptable to venture forth to discover things. That is what I am doing, or am trying to do. But never Transit for your own profit. Selfishness never leads to good.

Never attempt to change the course of Time or the events of what humankind calls History. To do so will upset the everlasting equilibrium of eternity.

'The everlasting equilibrium of eternity,' Phyllis repeated, reading it aloud quietly. She thought about that for a few moments. Then she finished reading the letter:

Remember the Pockets, and if you should discover any information about the Pockets that I have not shared with you (for I may not have discovered it myself), be sure to leave me a note, or a sign, or something. Hide any messages down here in our basement. No one else will find them if you are discreet.

Be the best magician you can be, Phyllis, and always entertain your audiences. And Transit well, my clever and magical great-granddaughter. Transit wisely, and carefully, and leave no trace to upset the ways of the past or the future. Hear more than you tell. Remember that there is a time to investigate things and a time to look at the clouds. And be as inconspicuous as the warm marshmallow that is dropped into the deepest well.

Oh, I know what I mean.

With love from your great-grandfather and fellow Transiter,

W.W.

When Phyllis had finished reading the letter, she was filled with a sensation she had never known before. It was a calmness that seemed to be cocooned by a warm excitement. She closed her eyes and put her hand gently on Daisy's head, and she let herself settle.

After a while she folded the letter carefully. She got up (being careful not to disturb her four-pawed friend) and went to one of the tall cupboards near the Bengal tiger. Here she found an old leather-bound journal. She'd originally found this journal some months earlier, and immediately she'd liked it for its aged, sweetly smelling covers and the fact that its thick, marble-edged pages had never been written in. It was a handy size—it would fit easily into the pockets of most of the coats she wore—and it had a thin leather cord that was sewn onto the back cover and which was long enough to wrap around the journal and tie at the front. Phyllis had decided, when she had discovered the journal, that she would save it to be used for something really special.

Now she knew exactly what she'd use it for. It would be her Transiting journal.

She went and sat on the rug in front of the sofa, surrounded by the blackboard slates. With a steady smile, she untied the cord, opened the journal and tucked W.W.'s letter into the back of it. Then she flipped to the front of the book and started writing down the names of the Pockets her great-grandfather had revealed to her, transcribing each name from the slates, slowly and with great care.

As she wrote, she kept thinking of her great-grandfather. She wondered when she would meet him again—she really, really wanted to. There were so many things she wanted to ask him. She didn't know it, but her eyes—the whites *and* irises—were glowing bright green.

✹

During the next week—the last week of her suspension/grounding/forbiddance—Phyllis spent most of her time thinking.

She had the biggest secret of her life to keep; a secret far greater than any of the secrets behind any of her magic tricks. She had a great responsibility to guard the knowledge of Transiting, and she understood that she shouldn't take that responsibility lightly. Somehow she felt that she should only Transit when she needed to, or when she had a huge desire to do so. She didn't want the privilege to become a commonplace thing, like turning on the TV or phoning Clement or any of her other friends whenever she felt like it.

She decided that she would only Transit when the Time was right. And she had a hunch that she'd know when those Times would be.

With this new knowledge, Phyllis felt a sort of inner strength, and she felt a ripple of excitement whenever she thought about what might be to come . . .

✹

'Suffering sciatica!' Phyllis exclaimed as she saw Clement coming to meet her in City Park. It was the first time she and Daisy had met up with him since Phyllis's isolation had ended. 'What on Earth's happened to you?'

He was hurrying, and when he hurried, he sometimes hobbled a little (it was because of an injury he'd got recently involving a streetsweeping machine, and it was barely noticeable).

'Huh?' he puffed, slinging off his backpack and plonking himself down on the grass next to her and Daisy, near the statue of an unremembered politician carrying a weasel which they often met by.

'Your face,' said Phyllis.

'I have no idea what you're talking about,' Clement said.

Daisy jumped over into his lap and licked his hand. 'Hey, Deebs,' he said, twiddling her ears.

'Don't act wise,' said Phyllis. 'It doesn't suit you.'

'Oh,' said Clement, as though he was suddenly remembering something. He pushed his glasses up his nose and grinned at Phyllis.

Phyllis just shook her head slowly. She looked at all the warts that covered his face like blotchy polka dots on a handkerchief: three on his left cheek, two on his right, one in the centre of his chin, five across his forehead and a big, full one on the tip of his nose. 'Are you contagious?' she asked, trying to shift away a little without offending him.

'No. Are you?'

'I'm not the one who looks like a hatful of peanuts. What's with all the lumps?'

'Aaaah.' He wiggled his eyebrows. 'Like 'em?'

'Clem! How could anyone like *warts*?'

'They're not warts, they're *protuberances*.'

'What?'

'They're protuberances.' He reached into the pocket of his coat and fished around for something. 'That's what Miss Hipwinkle calls them, and she's an expert on such things.'

Phyllis squinted closely. 'They're not *real*?'

Clement handed her an empty plastic packet with a label on it. Phyllis read out loud, '"FLESHIES— Protuberances for All Occasions! As Used by Stage Actors and Professional Detectives!" Oh, brother!'

'They're the best you can get,' Clement told her proudly. 'Really thin latex, the perfect match for skin. They can stay on for days if you want.'

'How long have you had yours on?'

'About a week.' He lay back on the grass and put his hands behind his head. 'I can't get 'em off, actually.'

'What?'

'I can't get 'em off. You're supposed to stick them on with spirit gum, but Miss Hipwinkle had

133

sold out and she told me to come back in two weeks when they'd have a new order in. But I couldn't wait that long, so I used some glue I found at home.'

Phyllis shook her head again. 'And it was super glue, yes?'

'Yep. I couldn't read the tube, it had all this gunk on it. Mum's not very happy, but the doctor said if I shower three times a day regularly, with lots of steam from the water, the glue'll gradually dissolve away. But you know the best part?'

'What?'

'Mum's not sending me to xylophone lessons until they're off. She doesn't want the teacher thinking I'm diseased.' He rolled over onto one elbow, pulled a distorted face and said, in a slurry voice, 'Feast your eyes! Glut your soul on my accursed ugliness!'

Phyllis laughed. 'You're priceless,' she said.

'I am indeed. And I can get a double seat all to myself on the bus,' he added. 'No one wants to sit next to me!'

'Surprised, I am not.' Phyllis gave him a sideways look. 'So, how *is* Miss Hipwinkle?'

Clement rolled onto his back again. 'She's cool. More to the point, how are you? What've you been doing these last few weeks?'

'Oh, you know . . . this and that.'

'This and that?' he repeated. Normally Phyllis

couldn't wait to tell him what she'd been up to. 'What sort of this and that?'

'Oh, Daisy and I walked'—Daisy gave a small yap at the sound of her name—'and I did all that homework. Thanks for collecting it and dropping it off, by the way.'

'Any time. It was stupid of Bermschstäter to suspend you like that. It was only an accident.'

'They happen,' Phyllis shrugged.

'Leizel Cunbrus will have another think before she heckles you again.' Clement smirked. 'She's a twerp.'

Phyllis smiled . . . now, the thought of Leizel Cunbrus didn't bother her at all. 'Hey, Clem? Have you got your webPad with you?'

'Yep.' He rolled over and undid the zip on his backpack, then up-ended it onto the grass. Everything spilled out in a heap: his webPad; a new boxed set of *A Zombie Place to Die, Parts 1–6*; his laptop; a half-eaten cheese sandwich squashed in plastic wrap; a blackened, mouldy banana; some coins; a fake grey beard; his dented glasses case; the latest copy of *Game for Life* magazine and a catalogue from Thundermallow's. Phyllis recognised the catalogue, having just received hers in the post the day before.

She watched as Clement pulled the webPad from the pile of his everyday distractions. *It's no wonder he's always losing things, or having things break on him*, she thought.

'Got it,' he said. 'It's the latest one; they're not releasing it until the week after next, just before Christmas.' He turned it on and immediately the screen lit up brightly.

'Can you look something up for me?' Phyllis asked.

'What?'

'A poem.'

'Yergh.' He gave a mock shudder. 'We're on vacation, Phyll . . .'

'It's called "Antigonish". I know the beginning of it but I want to read the whole thing.'

He looked at her, then typed the name in as she spelt it out. 'Here it is.'

Phyllis moved next to him and together they read the poem:

Yesterday, upon the stair,
I met a man who wasn't there
He wasn't there again today
I wish, I wish he'd go away . . .

When I came home last night at three
The man was waiting there for me
But when I looked around the hall
I couldn't see him there at all!

Go away, go away, don't you come back
*   any more!*
Go away, go away, and please don't slam
*   the door . . .*

Last night I saw upon the stair
A little man who wasn't there
He wasn't there again today
Oh, how I wish he'd go away . . .

Clement looked at her. 'What's it mean?' he asked.

She smiled at him. 'Who knows?'

'Maybe it's about a zombie.' He nodded as he considered this. 'Whatever, it's weird.'

'Ha! C'mon, Mr Warty, let's get some chocolate!'

'Brilliant idea! Good to have you back, Phyllis Wong.' He started stuffing everything into his backpack again.

'Good to be back,' she said, smiling. And indeed it was.

Going places

'Now, Phyll, there's something I have to tell you.'
Phyllis and her father were just settling down to dinner in the Art Deco dining room of their apartment. Phyllis, about to be seated, froze, half-sitting and half-standing over her chair. She always went cold inside whenever her father announced that he had something to tell her.

'Yeeeees?' she asked warily.

Harvey Wong took his seat and smiled at her. He gestured for her to continue her journey towards the chair. She took a deep breath and sat.

'It's nothing, really,' her father said, helping himself to a large serve of green beans and broccoli from the bowl in the centre of the table. 'I have to go away for a little while, that's all.'

Phyllis spooned out some steaming potato gratin onto her plate. 'Where to?'

'Hong Kong. There's a big deal being finalised out there. Normally I'd send one of the vice presidents of the company over to finish it off, but this one's a bit too delicate. So I'm going myself.'

'You said *I*, not *we*,' said Phyllis.

Harvey placed the serving spoon back into the bowl and poured some sauce over the filet mignon on his plate. 'I did. I'm afraid you'll have to stay here. I'll only be gone for three days. It won't take long.'

'Why can't I come?' she asked.

'I'm leaving tomorrow morning. It's all very sudden. There was barely enough time to arrange my trip, let alone arrange for you as well. Not to mention getting Daisy taken care of with a minder. I'm sorry, my girl. It's the way it has to be.'

'So,' said Phyllis, helping herself to the greens, 'the Deebs and I are staying here by ourselves?' There was eagerness in her voice.

'No, you're not.'

Phyllis stopped, the spoon poised mid-air. 'Why not?'

'You're not old enough. You know that.'

'But it's only three days. I'd be fine. And there's Chief Inspector Inglis and Minette Bulbolos downstairs, and the Ravissants at the café. They'd make sure I was okay.'

'I'm sure they would. Nevertheless, you are still too young to be by yourself.'

'Daisy would be with me.'

'Phyll. There's no changing it.'

'So what happens?' Phyllis shovelled the beans and broccoli onto her plate next to the potatoes and the filet mignon and stared gloomily at them.

'I've arranged for you and Daisy to stay with Minette. She is more than happy to—'

'Please don't say *babysit*. I'm not a baby.'

'It was not the word that I was going to use, Phyllis. She is more than happy to have you for company.'

Phyllis said nothing, but continued staring at her dinner.

'It'll be fine,' Harvey told her. 'You like Minette, after all.'

That was true: Minette Bulbolos was bold and bright and colourful and she always had time to spend with Phyllis. She had a regular belly dancing spot at the Baubles of Baalbek Nightclub in the swanky theatre district. She lived in one of the apartments on the floor below Phyllis's penthouse apartment, opposite another of Phyllis's friends, Chief Inspector Barry Inglis of the Metropolitan Police Force.

'And,' Harvey continued, 'I'll know you're safe with her. I won't have to worry about you too much while I'm gone . . . I know where you'll be.'

Phyllis looked up through her fringe at her father. Had he said that last part with any extra meaning

140

to it, other than what it sounded like? She looked down at her dinner again and speared up some of the potatoes and stuffed them into her mouth.

'Daisy and I would be fine here,' she muttered as she chewed. 'Minette could come up and check on us . . . And the Inspector is just a floor and a phone call away.'

In response, her father just stared at her. She knew that stare. She'd seen it often enough.

'Okay,' she conceded at last. 'Minette's it is.'

❋

On her second afternoon at Minette's, there was a change of plan.

Phyllis and Minette were sitting cross-legged on the Persian rug in Minette's living room. Phyllis had been showing Minette a new rising card trick, and Minette had been watching, totally absorbed, while Daisy had been licking her stomach (Daisy's stomach, not Minette's), when the phone had rung.

'Do you mind if I get that?' asked Minette, a little miffed that the call had come right in the middle of Phyllis's trick. 'It might be a gig.'

'Go ahead,' said Phyllis. 'Magic always waits.'

'Thank you, my *habibi*.' Minette gave her a dazzling smile and sprang up to take the call.

Phyllis leant back against the old, comfortable, over-stuffed sofa and waited. She looked up at the bright green and crimson silk drapes and the long ostrich plumes arranged across the curtain rail above the windows. They reminded her of the Khan el-Khalili and her trip with W.W., and she smiled secretively.

After a minute or so, Minette put the phone down and came back to join Phyllis and Daisy. 'I am so sorry about this, Phyllis, my *habibi*,' she said. 'Tonight our arrangement has to be altered a little.'

'What do you mean?' asked Phyllis.

Daisy stopped her licking and cocked her head, listening.

'Well,' explained the glamorous woman, 'a last-minute spanner is in the works. My friend Nina was filling in for me at the Baubles of Baalbek, but she has come down with the most awful case of knobbliness—'

'Knobbliness?'

'Yes, my sweet. It is a little affliction that artistes such as Nina and myself sometimes get. Little red knobs of puffiness come up all over our skin sometimes. I haven't had it happen for a long time, but poor Nina . . .' She heaved her shoulders and sighed loudly, fluttering her dark and heavy eyelashes. 'She is allergic to the new feathers she got for her big number "Take Me or Leave Me but Please Spare the Custard". They have made her erupt in horrid red knobs all over her shoulders and arms . . . she looks like one of those little rubber knobbly things that the people who work in post offices sometimes put on their thumbs when they are doing things with their thumbs that they need the little rubber knobbly things on for . . . ah, but I am wafting around like a butterfly in the breeze, aren't I?'

Phyllis smiled. 'So how are things altered for us?'

'Ah.' Minette patted Daisy's head. 'Well, tonight I will have to go and do Nina's spots at the nightclub. It means I will be gone from about seven-thirty to eleven-thirty.'

'Great!' Phyllis exclaimed. 'So I get to see the Baubles of Baalbek?'

'Erm . . . no.'

'No?'

'Phyllis, my darling, it is no place for a girl of your age. They do not let people under the age of eighteen in there. I would love to take you with me, but rules are rules.'

'But rules can be broken.' Phyllis gave Minette a challenging look. 'If we didn't bend the rules or break 'em, why, nothing new or exciting might ever happen!'

'Ah, you are wise and perceptive and very, very correct. But I am afraid that in this case, these rules cannot be distorted. I am sorry, Phyllis, but you won't be able to come with me.'

143

Phyllis frowned. 'Dad goes to Hong Kong, you go to the nightclub. It seems I can't go anywhere at the moment . . .' She stopped and thought. Then she gave a barely noticeable smile as she realised that that was the furthest thing from the truth she could have said.

'Don't fret, pet,' said Minette. 'It will only be for a few hours.' She stood and went to the phone. 'I will call our friend Barry Inglis and arrange for him to take charge of you during my performance. He is very obliging.'

While Minette dialled Barry's number, Phyllis picked up her cards in their box. She held the box in her hand and watched as a single card emerged slowly up out of the deck. One card separating itself from all the rest. She observed it rising higher and higher; then she took it away from the deck and let her smile appear fully.

✳

'Tonight?' repeated Chief Inspector Barry Inglis of the Fine Arts and Antiques Squad of the Metropolitan Police Force.

'Only for a few hours, while I'm working,' came Minette's voice over the phone.

'Oh, good lord, Minette. Ordinarily I'd say yes—Miss Wong is never a bother, of course—but . . . well, tonight's a bit tricky.'

'Ha! I am sure Phyllis will have no problem with trickiness.'

The Chief Inspector sighed, and looked out his office window across City Park, towards the Wallace Wong Building. 'That's not the sort of trickiness I meant. No, I mean I have to go to an auction tonight.'

'Oh, yes?' asked Minette, interested. She was always trying to find out more about Barry Inglis's private life.

'For work,' Barry told her. 'There's an item being auctioned we've had our eye on for some time. I need to be present.'

'I see. Well, you can still be present, and you can have a friend to keep you company.'

'What?'

'You can take Phyllis. Then bring her back here afterwards and I should be home around the time you return. Or maybe a little later, but she will be safe with you.'

'Of course she will be, but . . . an auction? She'll be bored out of her brain.'

He heard Minette laugh—it was like a light tinkling down the line. 'She is very intelligent, Chief Inspector. She will not be bored. She always finds things to see, and an auction is always exciting.'

Barry put his feet up on his desk, accidentally knocking over a small mountain of files and papers.

'I know very well how intelligent she is,' he said gruffly. 'But—'

'So, she'll be brilliant company tonight. Thank you, Barry, you've helped me beautifully. You are the best neighbour.'

'But—'

'Are you coming home before the auction, or going straight from the office?'

'Going straight from . . . but—'

'Then I shall bring Phyllis to you there, shall we say six p.m.?'

Barry ran a hand through his sandy-coloured hair. 'But the auction doesn't start until eight . . .'

'Then you shall both have time for a splendid dinner out somewhere.'

'Oh, heavens above, I—'

'Thank you, Barry, you are a dear, dear man!'

And Barry heard the phone go dead.

He looked at the receiver in his hand, as though he wanted to say something to it that a Chief Inspector with the Fine Arts and Antiques Squad probably shouldn't say while he was in the office. But he said nothing, replacing the receiver on the phone instead and wondering at how things always seem to go hiccupy when you least expect it.

Bard times

'A First Folio?' said Phyllis.

'A First Folio,' said Barry Inglis.

He had brought her to one of his regular eating establishments—a small, inexpensive diner, conveniently located near to Police Headquarters, by City Park—and he and the young prestidigitator were sitting in one of the big oak booths that were padded with slippery red vinyl cushions as they waited for their dinner to be served.

'What's a First Folio?' Phyllis asked.

Next to Phyllis, Daisy appeared out of Phyllis's shoulder bag on the seat. She put her front paws on the table, poked her snout this way and that on the tabletop and had a hurried sniff for crumbs of any sort. Phyllis pulled her down and gently pushed her into the shoulder bag again.

'She shouldn't be near the table,' Barry Inglis said.

'So arrest me.' Phyllis smiled at him and he gave a sort of *this is going to be one of those evenings* grimace. 'So . . . what *is* a First Folio?'

Barry thrummed the fingers of his right hand on the table. 'It's a book. A very old and valuable book. It was printed in 1623, and it's an almost complete volume of the works of William Shakespeare.' He stopped thrumming and said to Phyllis, 'Have you studied any of William Shakespeare's plays or poetry at school yet, Miss Wong?'

'No, not yet. But I've heard of him. *Romeo and Juliet, Hamlet, Macbeth, A Midsummer Night's Dream*, right?'

'Right. Just four of the thirty-six or so plays he wrote, yes. And all of those thirty-six plays are contained in the First Folio, which is being auctioned a little after eight o'clock tonight at The House of Wendlebury's auction rooms. Which is where we're headed.'

'Are you going to bid on it, Chief Inspector?'

'Me? Good heavens, no. Not on my salary. No, this is far and away beyond my price range. We are attending purely out of professional interest.'

'How much do you reckon it'll go for?' Phyllis asked.

'Hard to say. Millions to be sure, but just how *many* millions . . . well, it all depends on how fierce the bidding will be. I imagine there'll be bidders from all over the world, from private individuals to libraries and all sorts of places. There aren't that many First Folios around any more.' He stopped and looked down at his hands, frowning.

'What's wrong?' Phyllis asked.

He looked up at her. 'Ah. It's what I just said. I should have said, there aren't that many First Folios around any more, *or so we thought*. Recently things seem to have changed.'

'How?'

He looked over towards the kitchen, trying to see if their order was on its way and also sussing out the joint (as he liked to think of it); he didn't want anyone overhearing what he was saying to Phyllis. When he saw that their meals weren't yet coming and that there were no eavesdroppers nearby, he told her: 'It used to be that a First Folio hardly ever came onto the market. I've been going back through the records, and I discovered that last century there were only four sales or auctions of First Folios worldwide. And two of those transactions were of the same copy. But lately—in the last six months or so—we've become aware that there have been no fewer than *eleven* First Folios going up for auction.'

'Eleven?'

'That is correct. And all of them have been genuine, and all of them have been complete, in their original leather bindings.'

Phyllis interlocked her left-hand thumb with her right-hand pinkie and clasped her hands together on the table. 'How many copies of it were printed in 16 . . . what was it?'

'Sixteen twenty-three. We believe only seven hundred and fifty copies were published. But not many have survived over the centuries. At the last count, it's thought that only two hundred and twenty-eight copies still exist. At least that's how many are accounted for, in libraries and in private collections. But that was before these last eleven copies turned up so quickly. Eleven First Folios in six months! And there's the wonder of the thing, Miss Wong. And it's a wonder that smells a little fishy . . .'

'Do you think someone's making forgeries of them?'

Barry Inglis nodded at her. 'That would seem to be the most likely reason behind the fishiness. But the problem with that theory is that each of these eleven Folios has been tested by experts from the art world and from The House of Wendlebury's Auctioneers. And every copy has been printed on authentic paper—high quality rag paper that was brought to England from France, which was what they did in the early seventeenth century. What's more, the experts have tested the ink as well, and it's definitely ink that was made at the time the paper was made. So we have to discount the forgery angle.'

'Maybe someone just found a box of them?' suggested Phyllis. 'And they're selling them off one at a time?'

'That would be highly unlikely,' said Barry, frowning. 'I thought of that myself, but the chances of eleven First Folios surviving somewhere in a box, with the right climate conditions, and without being exposed to rats or dampness and mould or fires or whatever, is very small. Incredibly small. No, there's something not right about all of it, and I need to try to—ah-ha, here we are!'

He sat back as a gum-chewing waitress placed their meals before them: a hamburger for Phyllis and an enormous steak with fries, coleslaw, pickles and fried onions for Barry.

'Thank you,' Barry said to the waitress, who gave a quick chew and hurried off. 'Enjoy, Miss Wong. I've been eating here for years and I've never once had food poisoning or the collywobbles. Now that's high praise indeed, if you ask me—which of course you didn't, but I wanted to share it with you anyway.'

And Phyllis giggled as she watched him tucking heartily into his steak and onions.

❋

Chief Inspector Barry Inglis had been often enough to the auction rooms at The House of Wendlebury's, the largest and most prestigious sales room in the city for rare and valuable antiques, artworks, books and manuscripts. It was all part of his job and, while he didn't actually look forward to going there, he did find that he enjoyed the thrill and the sudden rush of excitement that usually came when each auction was in full swing, especially when the bidding seemed to be going crazy.

For Phyllis, though, it was her first visit to the place. Barry led her (and Daisy in her shoulder bag) up the stairs of the regal-looking building. He flashed his ID card at the doorman and the door was opened immediately. Phyllis noticed the doorman smiling at Barry as they entered; she also noticed how his smile instantly disappeared, like a flash-vanish effect she sometimes used in some of her tricks, when he saw her.

Great, she thought. *Another place that doesn't like kids.* Nevertheless, in she went, unchallenged, with Barry.

'Through here, Miss Wong.' The Chief Inspector ushered her into a big room which had many rows of red and gold chairs laid out, like in a theatre auditorium. All around the walls of this room, arranged on tall gold-painted wooden easels, were about twenty paintings—large, gilt-framed, dark canvases of country scenes and women and men wearing clothing that was fashionable at least three hundred years ago or earlier.

'Tonight they're also auctioning those artworks,' Barry told her. 'This place always auctions the biggies ... I've seen Rembrandts, Van Goghs, Turners, Ploegs and Picassos go under the hammer in here.' He gave a mild shudder at the thought of the last Picasso painting he had been involved with, and Phyllis saw this.

'Like the *Weeping Walrus*?' she asked.

'Now, that is a case that I prefer not to dwell on,' Barry said. 'I still get squirly when I think about it. Here, let's sit up near the back. That way we can see what's happening.'

They found a couple of seats close to the aisle and sat, Phyllis putting her bag on an empty chair between her and Barry. Daisy poked her snout out of the bag and blinked her dark brown eyes at all the bright lights in the room.

'No, Daisy girl,' Phyllis whispered, pushing her back into the bag. 'You have to stay invisible while we're here.'

Daisy gave a soft purring sort of sound (for a dog, she had quite a few qualities normally found in cats) and ducked her head back into the dark warmth of the bag.

'Yes,' said Barry. 'Best that she remains undetected. Wendlebury's is a bit stuffy when it comes to—'

All at once a man was in the aisle next to Phyllis's seat. He was tall and youngish and had a shiny flop of blond hair carefully arranged to fall across his forehead and almost conceal one of his eyes. On the lapel of his black coat he wore an enamel badge that said *Wendlebury's*, and underneath that, *Siiimon*. 'Excuse me, little girl,' he said in a voice that was dripping with sneeringness. 'Do you have an animal in that bag?'

Phyllis shot the floppy-haired man a glare—she hated being called a little girl.

Barry saw the look she gave him, and he pulled the sort of face he would have pulled if someone had just cracked an egg on the top of his head and let the yolk run down his face.

'An animal?' Phyllis said to Floppy Hair.

'Yes. I saw something. A squirrel or something. Or a rabbit.'

'A *what*?' asked Phyllis loudly.

Barry spoke up in his best policeman's voice. 'I can assure you that my friend has no squirrel or rabbit anywhere in the vicinity of this location.'

The man's lips turned down. 'I distinctly saw something partially emerge from the top of her bag. Animals are strictly forbidden here at The House of Wendlebury's.'

Barry looked at Phyllis. She was giving Floppy Hair a steely stare.

Barry shifted in his seat. *This could get tricky,* he thought. *If Miss Wong is asked to leave, then I'll have to go with her, and I'll miss out on the auction.*

Phyllis looked at Barry, and he thought he detected a very tiny twinkle in her eye. She turned back to Floppy Hair and said, in a sweet voice that Barry had never heard her use: 'If you're so sure, would you like to look inside my bag?'

'That's exactly what I plan to do,' the man said, leaning over.

Phyllis pulled the bag up from the seat next to her and put it onto her lap. Smiling, she opened the top of the bag and held it wide.

The man peered down into the dark recesses of the shoulder bag. He stood there, looking for a few seconds, and his face clouded with annoyance. All he could see inside the bag was a pack of playing cards, a small coin purse, a half-eaten candy bar in its wrapper, a cell phone, some yellow rubber bands and a couple of red sponge balls.

And that was it.

Barry, intrigued by the expression on the man's face, also leant over and looked inside. His eyebrows shot up, but he quickly lowered them and remembered to remain composed, as a Chief Inspector should always appear.

He leant back and said to the floppy-haired man, 'So, where's the furry suspect then?'

Siiimon straightened and looked down his nose at them. He opened his mouth and was about to utter something—from his expression Phyllis thought he was going to squeak at them—but he thought better of it. He closed his mouth, gave a tight-lipped smile, and said, 'Do pardon me. I hope you enjoy tonight's auction.'

'Thank you, Siiimon,' said Barry, reading his name badge. 'I'm sure we will.'

'Good evening.' Siiimon turned on the heel of his expensive shoe and wafted away to the front of the room.

'So where is she?' Barry asked Phyllis out of the side of his mouth as he watched Siiimon chatting to someone near the auctioneer's desk.

Phyllis gave Barry her inscrutable smile. 'Watch this.' She shut the bag again and re-opened it. Out popped Daisy's snout, and Phyllis quickly pushed her back inside.

Barry gave her a *now how on Earth did you do that but I shouldn't even ask because I know you're not going to tell me* look.

'It's an old trick,' Phyllis confided. 'I adapted my bag so it works like a change bag.'

'It changes things, all right. It changed little Daisy into nothing!'

'Yep. That's the idea, Chief Inspector.'

'I have made the observation in the past, Miss

Wong, and I will make it again: you are brilliant and astonishing.'

'Why, thank you, Chief Inspector. I'm just a magician, that's all.'

Barry nodded and took out a folded-over auction catalogue from the inside pocket of his coat. He opened it and studied it quietly.

Phyllis watched as the room began to fill up. She loved studying people and observing every little thing about them, and tonight she had a wealth of subjects. All sorts of people were arriving: old people, beautifully dressed in expensive clothes and with their white or silver hair perfectly set; younger people with serious expressions and designer jeans and leather and suede jackets; people who looked like they knew all there was to know about art and precious things; some men with neatly clipped beards and some other men with bigger, bushier bird's-nest beards and elbow patches on their Harris Tweed coats; small groups of elegant women dripping with pearls and diamonds and other sparkling gems; a cluster of muscly men in tight shirts who walked like they had feathers for feet and who spoke in light, sing-song voices; fat people, thin people, short people, tall.

Phyllis wondered what all these people would be bidding on, and who might be the successful buyer of the First Folio. She could feel a sense of anticipation and excitement growing in the room as all those around her took their seats.

Some of the feather-footed, muscly men came and sat in the row in front of Phyllis, Daisy and Barry. One of the men opened his auction catalogue and started making notes in it. Phyllis put her bag on the seat between her and Barry again and leant forward a bit, trying to see what the man was writing—she guessed he might be making notes about what he was going to bid on. She smiled when she saw that he was jotting something down on the page that had photos of the First Folio on it.

Across the aisle a youngish woman came and sat. Phyllis was aware of her as she moved into her chair—she seemed to glide into it smoothly, silently. Out of the corner of her eye, Phyllis glanced at the woman. She was dressed mostly in black: a black, fur-trimmed coat which she was taking off and draping back across her chair; a black shirt with a dark purple waistcoat; black, slim-fit trousers and black knee-high boots of shiny leather. Her shirt had a deep mauve ruffle collar, and her hair was long and dark and curly—not tight curls, but willowy curls, free and flowing. The curls fell across one side of her face, down onto her cheek.

Phyllis was never one to pay too much attention

to hairstyles or fashion (these things were not the reasons why she enjoyed studying people), but she couldn't help but admire the woman's curls, and she found herself wondering what it would be like to have hair like that instead of the straight hair she herself had.

On the woman's fingers were an assortment of gold rings: bright, gleaming yellow and rose gold. Phyllis counted seven rings, most of which were set with precious stones—diamonds, rubies, sapphires, green garnets and emeralds. All of the rings looked like they were antiques, such were their fancy settings.

The woman reached up and moved something around her collar, and as she did this she noticed Phyllis looking at her. Phyllis gave a quick smile and then turned back to Barry.

'How long until the action starts?' Phyllis asked her friend.

He looked at his watch. 'I think it's about time.'

At the front of the room, a tall woman with a beehive sort of hairdo and sparkly glasses mounted the rostrum where the auctioneer's lectern was positioned. She had in her hand a small wooden hammer—her auction gavel.

'Good evening, ladies and gentlemen,' she announced into the microphone on the lectern. 'Welcome to The House of Wendlebury's. Tonight it is our great privilege and pleasure to be auctioning yet another valuable First Folio by the greatest writer the world has seen, the Bard of Stratford, William Shakespeare.'

At this, a round of polite and refined applause ribboned about the room.

'But first, we have a most important group of Dutch and Italian oil paintings from the seventeenth century to go under the hammer . . .'

Phyllis looked at Barry, and he gave her a wink.

The next forty minutes passed in a blur of fast talking from the auctioneer, as painting after painting went under the hammer. Staff members (including floppy-haired Siiimon) were sitting at a table next to the auctioneer's lectern, their ears glued to their cell phones as they took absentee bids from people who were unable to be at Wendlebury's. Other customers who were present in the room bid by discreetly raising their hand or a special little yellow Wendlebury's paddle they had been given when they had registered for the auction. Phyllis craned her neck as she tried to see who was bidding.

When a painting had reached its final bid, the auctioneer brought her gavel briskly down, banging it sharply against the lectern, before going on to the next painting.

Phyllis was captivated by the whirl and the pace of the action, and was surprised when all of the paintings had been sold—everything had seemed to happen so quickly.

Then the time had come. Barry leant over and said quietly, 'Now for the big one.'

Next to the lectern, a huge screen was lowered from the ceiling. In front of this, rising up through the floor, came a tall gold-painted wooden plinth with a heavy glass cube on top. Underneath this glass cube was a big, thick book.

Barry whispered, 'There, Miss Wong. What you see beneath that glass is worth millions.'

Phyllis tingled, not at the thought of the money, but at the idea that something so old was so precious and desirable.

'Ladies and gentlemen,' said the auctioneer in a royal-sounding voice, 'I present to you a rare and coveted First Folio by William Shakespeare!'

Polite applause once again ribboned throughout the room. The muscly men in front of Phyllis squirmed excitedly in their seats as they fluttered their hands together. Some of them whispered, 'Ooooh . . .'

Onto the screen behind the First Folio, an image suddenly flashed: a portrait of Shakespeare himself—the exact same portrait that was on the title page inside the cover of the First Folio. Then words slowly appeared above and below the portrait:

Mr. WILLIAM

SHAKESPEARES

COMEDIES,
HISTORIES, &
TRAGEDIES.

Publifhed according to the True Originall Copies.

LONDON
Printed by Ifaac Iaggard, and Ed. Blount. 1623.

'Tonight's volume,' continued the auctioneer, her voice becoming even more regal, 'is a beautiful example of the First Folio, in even more pristine condition than the one we sold a little over six months ago. It is one of only two hundred and forty known complete copies remaining in the world. It is presented in its original leather binding of red with gold bands on the spine; a binding which we presume the first owner of the volume had commissioned after picking up the sewn pages from the printing firm of Jaggard and Blount in the year of publication, 1623. There is no buckling or splitting in the leather, and all of the pages are clean and printed on superior quality paper. This is the finest example of a First Folio that we have ever seen.'

A ripple of bold enthusiasm spread around the room at that, and one of the muscly men leant forward and perched on the edge of his chair, flexing his shoulders.

'I trust,' said the auctioneer, 'that there will be some spirited bidding for this scarce and beautiful tome, as we do not know when and where, indeed *if*, another of these almost legendary offerings will ever turn up.'

'Hmm,' hmmed Barry Inglis in a suspicious tone. 'I wonder . . .'

One of the muscly men looked quickly over his shoulder at Barry and hissed, 'Shh, *please*.'

Barry glanced at Phyllis and gave a *schoolboy who's just been told off* expression, and she almost giggled.

'And now,' said the auctioneer, 'I will start the bidding at two million dollars. Do we have an opening bid?'

Immediately, the muscly man on the edge of his seat raised his yellow Wendlebury's paddle above his shoulder.

Phyllis's breathing became quicker.

The auctioneer saw the paddle. 'Two million. Do we have two million, two hundred and fifty thousand?' She looked around the room and at the staff on their cell phones. There was a pause for a few moments and then one of the staff nodded.

'Bidding is at two million, two hundred and fifty thousand,' the auctioneer announced. 'Two and a half million?'

The muscly man raised his paddle; one of his muscly friends patted him on the arm encouragingly.

The auctioneer took the bid. 'I'm looking now for two and three quarter million? Two and three quarter . . .?'

Somewhere else in the room, another bidder raised her paddle. Phyllis heard the muscly man groan.

'Two and three quarter million,' announced the auctioneer. 'Do we have three? Three million dollars anywhere?'

The staff on the cell phones were chatting quietly and quickly to the customers on the other ends of the lines. Phyllis watched the muscly man fidgeting and looking at his friends; she noticed that the back of his neck had small beads of perspiration studding it.

On the other side of the aisle, the curly-haired woman dressed mostly in black was also leaning forward in her chair, one hand resting on her ruffled collar.

Siiimon looked up from his cell phone and nodded at the auctioneer.

'Three million dollars!' the auctioneer proclaimed. 'Three million to the phone bidder. Any advance on three million?'

There was a hushed silence. Then the muscly

man hoisted his yellow paddle defiantly above his head. 'Three and a half million!' he almost squealed.

The auctioneer's eyes widened behind her sparkly glasses. 'Three point five million,' she said, nodding at the man.

Phyllis saw to her side the curly-haired woman leaning even further forward.

'The bidding stands at three point five million dollars,' declaimed the auctioneer. 'Are there any further bids? Do I hear three point seven five?'

From down at the front of the room, a bearded man raised his paddle.

'Three million, seven hundred and fifty thousand,' announced the auctioneer, and the muscly man groaned again, his shoulders sagging.

'Four million!' called a woman glued to one of the cell phones. 'My bidder from Switzerland.'

'Four million dollars,' repeated the auctioneer. A collective gasp swelled in the auditorium.

'Four and a half million!' cried the muscly man, waving his paddle around as though he were trying to swat at a cloud of mosquitoes.

'Four and a half million!' The auctioneer sounded very pleased.

Phyllis's heart was racing. She saw that Barry Inglis was sitting very still, not giving anything away, but she detected that his eyes were bright and darting about the room.

'Four and a half million,' the auctioneer said again, looking all around for any further bids.

'Five million,' came the response from the woman with the Swiss cell phone bidder.

'Five million dollars,' the auctioneer almost shouted.

The muscly man groaned again. He looked at his friends, nodded at them, then waved his paddle frantically and shouted, 'Five and a half!'

'Five and a—' began the auctioneer.

'Six!' came the bid from the Swiss buyer on the phone.

'Six million dollars,' the auctioneer declared. 'Do I hear six and a half million?'

Phyllis counted the seconds—one, two, three, four. They seemed to go forever, and she felt the Time hanging about her . . .

'Yesssssss!' Mr Muscles was on his feet, thrusting his paddle as if it were a tennis racket and he was trying to lob an invisible ball over and over. 'Six and a half! Six and a half million!'

The curly-haired woman was clutching her collar more tightly as she watched the escalation of the bidding.

The auctioneer repeated the amount and looked across at the woman with the Swiss bidder on the end of the phone. More seconds passed, heavy seconds, thick seconds, as everyone waited for a response.

Then the woman with the phone said something to the Swiss bidder. She took the phone from her ear and shook her head at the auctioneer.

'No further bids?' asked the auctioneer to the whole room.

Silence.

'Then,' she said, holding her head high, 'if there is no further interest, I declare the First Folio by William Shakespeare to be sold for the sum of six and a half million dollars. Going once . . .'

Phyllis looked all around the room.

'. . . going twice . . .'

The muscly man was almost collapsing with anticipation, his wide shoulders wibbling through his tight shirt.

There was a loud, echoing BANG as the auctioneer slammed her gavel onto the lectern.

'SOLD! For six and a half million dollars to the gentleman in the second-last row!'

'Oooooooooh,' gasped Mr Muscles. He fell back into his chair, and one of his friends mopped his brow with a neatly pressed handkerchief.

And that's when all hell broke loose.

Lurking in the ruffle

Daisy, by breed and nature, was a sensitive dog, and ever alert. Even when she was sleeping (which she tended to do a lot), she was always half-conscious of what was happening around her.

Added to that, her ancient instincts—to hunt and go after small rodents and other sorts of larger prey—were still very much alive within her. Tonight, deep inside Phyllis's magically gimmicked shoulder bag in The House of Wendlebury's auction room, the little terrier's ancient instincts began to re-surface.

It started with a whiff of something. Even though she was ensconced within the bag, enveloped by the warm darkness and surrounded by Phyllis's bits and pieces, a strange smell had wafted towards Daisy's nostrils. Daisy opened her eyes but did not move. She stayed perfectly still, allowing the smell to reach her snout as clearly as it could.

She knew that odour. She had smelt it every now and then at different places in the city, often when she and Phyllis were walking past dingy alleyways or places where trash had been piled up, ready for collection.

It was the smell of things that gathered in such places, and tonight, for some reason, she could smell it here at Wendlebury's.

There was a rodent in the room!

The hairs along Daisy's spine hackled, and she concentrated even harder.

She moved her head a little so that her ears were closer to the sides of the bag. She had to listen, to help her find the direction where the rat was hiding.

Muffled sounds came through the heavy canvas walls of the shoulder bag. Daisy concentrated, trying to separate the sounds that were washing in . . .

'. . . *Going once . . . going twice . . .*'

No, those weren't ratty noises; those were words, from the humans, excited words . . . Daisy concentrated some more.

BANG! went the gavel.

'*SOLD! For six and a half million dollars to the gentleman in the second-last row!*'

The little dog gave a tiny sniff as she listened to the now very big excited words. But still, they were not the sounds she was trying to hear . . .

Then her whiskers tingled. She heard what she was waiting for.

A scratching, soft and faint, so soft and faint that only a mini foxy like her could hear it. She knew exactly what it was. It was the sound of claws, moving gently through something that was softish. Through some sort of fabric, perhaps.

Daisy calmed her breathing and made her heartbeat slow, so that she couldn't hear anything else but the scratching sound.

It came again, scrizzling and scrabbling, and— *it was close*. It was coming from the other side of Phyllis!

And it had to be dealt with!

The next few moments were upside-down moments: with a huge spring, Daisy leapt up through the top of Phyllis's bag, out into the brightness of the room, across Phyllis's lap and into the aisle. There she crouched on the carpet and looked balefully up at the woman with the curly hair who was sitting next to the aisle.

Phyllis gasped.

Daisy was growling, deep and marble-gargling low. The woman looked down—and it was as if a rocket had gone off under the terrier's tail: suddenly Daisy was yapping, as fast as machine-gun fire, and then, in a blink, she exploded off the floor like a miniature hairy tornado, leaping up onto the woman's lap, trying to bury her front paws and snout in the woman's ruffled collar.

'*Arf! Arf! Arf! Arf! Arf! Arf! Arf! Arf! Arf!*'

'*Aaaaargh!*' screamed the woman, shooting her arms into the air and trying to get her head and neck away from Daisy. 'Get it off! Remove it! Help me!'

Everyone in the room turned and watched, amazed and horrified at what looked like an attack from out of nowhere. The muscly men jumped up and moved quickly away.

Phyllis leapt to her feet and grabbed Daisy from the woman's lap and shoulders. Daisy kept barking wildly at the collar around the woman's neck as she was pulled away.

'*ARF! ARF! ARF! ARF! ARF! ARF! ARF! ARF! ARF!*'

'I'm so sorry,' Phyllis apologised to the ashen-faced woman. The woman had raised her multi-ringed fingers to shield her face, and the gemstones in the rings glinted brightly at Phyllis, especially the diamonds and the green garnets.

Barry Inglis, now on his feet, snatched up Phyllis's bag and held it wide open. Phyllis quickly deposited Daisy into the bag and Barry ushered her away, up the aisle and past the guards and other employees of Wendlebury's, down the steps and out into the cold night air.

There, Phyllis staggered, her heart beating fiercely, the sudden rush of the chilly night hitting her hard.

Barry took her by the elbow to steady her. 'Are you all right?' he asked, his tone a little peeved.

She took a few deep breaths. 'I'm . . . I'm okay.'

'Come on.' He led her quickly away from The House of Wendlebury's.

Inside the shoulder bag, Daisy had settled a bit and Phyllis could feel the soft weight of her friend against her hip. But Phyllis's heart continued to beat fast and furiously.

'What got into her?' Barry asked as they turned the corner. 'I've never seen her behave like that before.'

'I . . . I don't know. She must've smelt something . . . or heard something . . .'

'It's lucky you got her away from that woman like you did. Otherwise things might've got nasty.'

'Yeah.'

He sighed. 'Oh, heavens. I won't be able to show my face at Wendlebury's any time soon. No siree. I only hope that that Siiimon didn't see what happened. He'd have me banned, for sure.'

'Sorry for all that, Chief Inspector.'

'Ah, well. These things happen. No real damage done, was there?'

'I hope you don't get into trouble,' said Phyllis.

'Now, trouble, Miss Wong, is what I'm paid to deal with. It is my dance partner in the ballroom of life, as it were. If there *is* any trouble—' He stopped

172

walking and looked at her. 'Are you sure you're all right? You're shaking and . . . good lord . . . you're as white as a sheet!'

'I think I need to sit down somewhere.'

'Yes, you do. C'mon, there's an excellent café on the next block. The best chocolate sundaes you've never yet tasted. My treat.'

Phyllis nodded. 'Sounds good.'

He led her along the street, keeping a watchful eye on her as she walked. From the way she looked, he thought she appeared to be in a sort of daze, or perhaps the onset of some kind of fever.

Something had shaken Phyllis Wong, but she wasn't exactly sure what it was.

Uncertain

Late that night, after Minette had returned from her gig at the Baubles of Baalbek Nightclub and Chief Inspector Barry Inglis had deposited Phyllis back with her, Phyllis lay in bed in Minette's guest bedroom with Daisy curled up by her side on top of the blankets. Phyllis was as wide awake as the moment she had been born.

Something was wrong. Phyllis could feel it. Something about what had happened at the auction wasn't right.

She'd seen something, in the blur of seconds when Daisy had leapt from her bag and attacked the curly-haired woman. Something that jolted the young conjuror. But, in those frenzied seconds of Daisy barking wildly at the woman and people jumping up to get out of the way and Barry hurrying to help get Daisy back into Phyllis's bag, whatever it was that Phyllis had seen had blurred in her mind.

She shut her eyes and tried to concentrate. She tried to visualise the scene again: how the woman recoiled; how Daisy attacked furiously at the woman's ruffled collar; how the woman had screamed to get Daisy away from her and had covered her face with her hands.

. . . how she had covered her face with her hands . . .

Phyllis opened her eyes suddenly as the image of the woman's rings speared into her memory. She recalled seeing the flashes of brightness from the gemstones—the brilliant white diamonds and the big, glowing green garnets. They were far brighter than the rubies and emeralds and other precious stones. Especially . . .

. . . the green! Suddenly Phyllis saw the scene again, as fresh as if it were happening all over right in front of her. Only this time she realised she'd seen something different to what she thought she'd seen at the auction. It hadn't been the green garnets in the woman's rings that had glowed at Phyllis. It had been the woman's eyes.

The woman's eyes had been glowing green!

A chill went through Phyllis, from her fringe to her toenails. She took a deep breath as the realisation dawned on her.

She knew how the First Folios were appearing, all of a sudden, here in the twenty-first century. The woman sitting by her in the aisle at The House of Wendlebury's was a fellow Transiter!

Phyllis's heart was beating quickly, and a surge of wonderment oscillated up and down her spine.

It was strange knowing this. She was feeling a mixture of emotions about it all. Firstly, she was excited that she had met—or, to be accurate, not *quite* met—another like herself. There was something a bit comforting in that, knowing that another Transiter was around. This didn't completely surprise Phyllis, of course; W.W. had told her that there were other Transiters . . . what had he called them? Yes, that was it: *fellow wayfarers.* Others who had stumbled upon the Pockets. And the woman in the dark clothes with the long curly hair was clearly one of them.

Secondly, even though Phyllis felt excited about the woman, she was also uneasy about her. Something felt not quite right about what the woman was doing. If she were Transiting back to 1623 and getting the First Folios—twelve of them, if all the Folios that Barry Inglis had found out about had indeed been brought back by her—well, was that *wrong*?

It was wrong if the woman was stealing them, but *was* she stealing them? Maybe she was buying them, and then selling them again, in the here and now . . .

Phyllis bit her lip. She was feeling butterflies of uncertainty in her tummy. She just didn't know . . .

Something W.W. had said to her flashed into her mind: *Some use the Pockets for procurement, Phyllis . . . some* misuse *the Pockets of Time . . .*

She felt that the woman with the dark curly hair was up to something fishy. Something sneaky. How bad or wrong that thing was, Phyllis wasn't sure. But she felt she needed to find out more . . .

Phyllis lay awake for a long time, wondering. And during this time, it was as if the two feelings she had—the excitement and the uneasiness—were having a little tug-of-war inside her.

She felt alone (apart from having Daisy by her side). She couldn't tell Barry Inglis what she knew, or what she suspected; her great-grandfather had told her to try, as far as possible, to safekeep the secret of Transiting. Besides, Phyllis knew that the Chief Inspector was a down-to-earth, no-surprises-around-the-corner sort of man. Chances are, even if she were to tell him about her secret, he'd never believe her.

Phyllis turned over, and Daisy roused, opening one eye and checking that her friend was all right. When she was sure Phyllis wasn't going to get out of bed, the terrier stood, turned around three times and lay down again, curling herself snugly against Phyllis's back.

Dad'll be home tomorrow, Phyllis thought as her feelings pulled and tugged at her. *I'll talk to him. Maybe he can help . . .*

Harvey Wong arrived home the next morning, and Phyllis was mighty pleased to see him. She was always glad when he was safely back from a trip.

At lunch, Phyllis asked him, 'Dad? You know in business? Is it wrong if someone's buying something up and then selling it for a huge profit?'

Harvey smiled. 'Ah. You are considering becoming a businesswoman, then?'

Phyllis shook her head. 'Only if magic is business,' she said before taking a bite of her sandwich.

'It's show business,' said Harvey Wong.

'Yeah, but in big business—like your sort of business—is it wrong to make huge profits quickly?'

Harvey chewed his sandwich and thought. 'That depends,' he replied. 'It depends on how the property was acquired.'

'Huh?' Phyllis slipped a tiny bit of crust down to Daisy who was waiting patiently on the black-and-white tiled floor of their kitchen.

'Don't feed the four-paws at the table,' said Harvey.

'Sorry. How does it depend?'

'Well, say for example that someone bought something and swindled the people from whom he was buying it. Say that he offered them a ridiculously low amount and they accepted the offer.

Then say he onsold the property for a whopping profit, and that the people he'd swindled were hurt by his dealings. I'd consider that wrong.'

'Could he be arrested for that?'

'In some circumstances, I suppose he could. If it could be proved that he hoodwinked the sellers, perhaps. That he tricked them into selling. But sadly in most cases the law couldn't touch him. It's wrong, yes, but not illegal. But wrong it is. I think it's morally bad.'

Phyllis listened carefully.

'To hurt people in business is not good, my girl. It should not be done. But, sadly, all too often it *is* done. Greed is a goddess for many people; their greatest desire is to make money and more money, and they don't care whom they hurt or exploit on the way.

'Sometimes people do it on the share market, also. They call it "insider trading" when someone trades huge amounts of stocks and shares for enormous profits because they have information about those stocks and bonds that is not public. That is illegal, and people go to jail for insider trading.'

'So it's like stealing?' asked Phyllis.

'Yes,' said Harvey. 'It is.'

Phyllis stopped eating. She knew what she had to do. She had to find out if the curly-haired woman was *stealing* the Folios from somewhere in Time. She had to discover how the woman was getting them.

It was time to use the Pockets.

Plans upheaved

At the Millennium Hotel, a small, expensive hotel on the Upper River Side of the city, the curly-haired woman hurried into the lobby, pushing the entrance doors so hard that they almost knocked down a man who was about to leave the building.

She rushed through the foyer, and the receptionist, busy organising the next morning's breakfast orders, looked up. 'Ms Colley,' he said, 'is everything all right?'

She glared at him but didn't stop, clutching the collar of her fur-lined coat tightly around her neck as she headed for the elevator. 'Do NOT speak to me!' she hissed. 'NEVER speak to me unless I speak to you first!'

The receptionist gave a small gasp—not because of her rudeness, which he was used to, but because of her eyes—and he dropped the breakfast order cards onto the desk.

The woman jabbed her finger on the elevator button. Almost immediately the doors slid open and she entered, jabbing another button inside to close the doors swiftly. The elevator rose silently to the fifth floor.

She strode out and unlocked the door to her suite of rooms, quickly went in and slammed the door behind her. She undid the buttons of her coat and carefully reached into the mink fur of the coat's collar. Her fingers felt warmth, and she withdrew her small friend from the fur and set her down on one of the plush sofas in the centre of the sitting room.

'Everything,' said Vesta Colley to the small, red-eyed white rat, 'is calm again, my dear Glory.'

Glory—for that is what she had christened the rat when she had found her in a dingy street in London nearly four hundred years ago—looked up at her. The rodent twitched her white whiskers and made a tiny sound. '*Squeeeetch.*'

Vesta Colley took off her coat and threw it onto a chair. She reached up and tousled her hair, letting the curls billow out fully, as though she were trying to free herself from the memory of what had happened at The House of Wendlebury's. She shook her head and undid her lace collar. 'That confounded dog. It had no place there. It could have taken you out, my dear Glory. It could have seen the end of your days . . .'

Glory started grooming her tiny paws, her

tongue making a *snik-snitchering* sound as it darted up and down across the fur.

'But at least we sold the book. Again.' Vesta Colley sat on the sofa next to Glory, and started unlacing one of her long black boots. 'Another First Folio,' she said, a curl of satisfaction creeping into her low voice. 'Another fine First Folio for the modern world of fools . . .'

She took off the boot and started unlacing the other one. She was halfway through when she stopped, her face clouding. 'But something's going on,' she said, more to herself than to Glory. 'That man was there again, that sandy-haired man in the blue suit. Always the same blue suit, he wears. A fellow of fine appearance, Glory. A handsome man. Bright blue eyes, constantly looking around. He was there with that wretched girl who brought the dog. Why does he come, every time we sell the books? Why does he come, yet never he bids? Always the watcher, never the buyer . . .'

Her eyes glowed brighter, greener, as she went back to unlacing the boot. She was a slender, strong-featured woman, tall and with an intelligent face. Her eyes, when they were not afflicted with the Transiter's Green, were a hazel colour and keenly observant. One of her eyes was set a little lower than the other, and it had a slightly droopy eyelid, and from that eye she didn't have perfect vision. But this didn't make her look sleepy or stupid; quite the opposite—it suggested that she knew secrets. That there were a lot of things she was aware of that others were not. That she had a cache of valuable knowledge inside her head.

Which was entirely true.

Vesta Colley knew much. But it wasn't the hunger for knowledge that propelled her through her life and her Transits, or the desire to learn or to discover new things. It was a hunger of a different sort. It was the hunger of greed.

She removed the boot and placed it neatly side by side with its mate. 'Methinks,' she uttered, 'that the man in the blue suit is onto us. Methinks he might be suspicious of our little enterprise. Maybe he is trying to uncover our plan . . .'

She stood and went to a table in the corner that was arranged with bottles of expensive drinks. She took the cork from one of the bottles—a fifty-year-old bottle of whisky—and poured some of the deep amber-coloured liquid into a crystal glass. This she held up to the light, swirling the whisky around inside it.

Slowly the green in her eyes started to fade, and their natural hazel colour began to strengthen.

'It is perhaps time for us to stop bringing any more First Folios into this world, Glory my love.

Otherwise it might not be only the wretched *dog* that will be smelling a rat . . .'

Glory scuttled up onto the back of the sofa and ran along it to be closer to her mistress.

'No,' said Vesta Colley, still looking at her drink. 'Methinks that shall be the end of the First Folios. It was starting to get too easy, anyway. No, my dear little skitterer, we shall bring forth something much greater than those. Something far more rare and valuable. Something that will net us more money than even *I* have imagined possible. Then I shall retire, for I am growing weary of the Transits.'

She stopped swirling the drink and held the glass still, looking up at it and feeling a tingle of new amazement as this fresh, bold plan began to emerge in her mind.

'And I know just the very thing to bring forth,' she murmured. 'Something that the world has hoped for, but has never expected. Something, as that auctioneer said, that is almost legendary!'

Slowly her lips curled into a sneer—a thin, hard sneer infused with a deep hatred and a rising surge of cruelty. 'Furthermore, I believe it is time to enact my final burst of destruction. To bring down the very place whence these things came . . . to put an end to the mindless frivolity that the people waste so much of their lives on. To make my ultimate, anonymous ripple on the wretched tide of History!'

Her eyes gleamed as a smile of unimagined possibilities spread across her face. She lifted the glass higher and toasted: 'To legends, and those bold enough to seek them out!'

Then, in a single gulp, she drained the glass.

A scrap to go on

Phyllis decided that she would Transit back to Shakespeare's time and try to visit the printers of the First Folios. From there, she hoped, she would be able to trace the trail of the valuable volumes.

First, though, she needed to find something from London in the early 1600s. A sort of *guiding signal*, W.W. had called it. A 'passport'.

But where could she find something that had come from London, almost four hundred years ago? There was an obvious place where she could start her search: Mrs Lowerblast's Antiques & Collectables Emporium, downstairs. Mrs Lowerblast had so much old stuff down there, crammed into every nook and cranny, that there was an excellent chance she'd have something Phyllis needed.

Phyllis smiled, but almost immediately her smile evaporated: she remembered that Mrs Lowerblast was away for a month—she'd gone to Italy on one of her annual antiques-buying expeditions, and her shop was closed for the duration. *So much for that idea*, Phyllis sighed.

But then another idea came to her. She had something no one else had: the magic basement. She figured that maybe—if she was lucky—there might be something down there from all that time ago that W.W. had collected in his Transits. After all, he'd had the old scarab he'd used to take her back to Egypt, hadn't he? And that had been stored in the basement.

She spent almost an entire Saturday looking down there. While Daisy snoozed on one of the sofas, Phyllis went through every shelf, every drawer in every cupboard, every box and basket and skip and trunk and chest. She found new (old) magic props she hadn't known were there, tucked away in some of the gloomy corners, or hidden and forgotten at the backs of drawers. She could easily identify the magic props—with her experience, she could spot a piece of stage apparatus a mile off—but she couldn't seem to find anything that even remotely looked like it might have come from seventeenth-century England.

She went through all the racks of costumes, all the cloaks and Oriental-style gowns and W.W.'s tuxedos and capes and his assistants' outfits—everything ranging from slave girls' spangly harem attire to realistic gorilla get-ups, some of which were looking a little moth-eaten and the worse for wear. She pottered about amongst the hats and headwear: top hats, turbans, feathered headdresses, pith helmets, cone-shaped clowns' hats, fezzes, fake crowns and tiaras glittering with paste jewels. But here also there was nothing that hinted of the right Time and place.

Phyllis went and sat next to Daisy and pondered. *The problem*, she thought, *is that even if any of this stuff does come from a long time ago, I'm not sure when it comes from and I'm not sure where. And there's nothing that looks right.* She reasoned that if she were to accidentally choose the wrong thing, she might end up anywhere.

She was sitting there, frowning about it all, when her cell phone rang. She flipped it out of her coat pocket and saw Clem's face on the identification screen—he was wearing a rubber pointy nose and crepe hair eyebrows which were bushier than a bird's nest.

'Clement, my old friend,' she greeted him.

'Hey, Phyll, what're you doing?'

'Just . . . looking for something.'

'Looking for what?'

'Oh, nothing much.'

'Okay.' Phyllis thought she detected a note of flatness in his voice. 'Hey, do you want some help?' he asked.

'No thanks, Clem, I'll be fine.'

'Okay,' he said again, his voice a bit more flat. 'Want to hang out, then? I've got all my warts off now, and I don't feel like xylophone practice.'

'You *never* feel like xylophone practice.'

'Nope, that is the state of my life.' He sighed. 'I wish Mum had never heard of a xylophone. D'you know, she's got this idea into her head that I should become a concert xylophonist! Man, if she wants that, I'd have to practise so much they may as well lock me in my room and throw away the key!'

'Ha. Somehow I can't see you ever becoming a concert xylophonist.'

'So how about we go and see a movie? There's that new one about the vampires and the zombies and the mix-up at the hospital when they're born, *Creche of the Living Deadoids*—'

'I'd love to, Clem, but not today. I'm just a bit busy.'

'Okay. Well, tomorrow?'

She stroked Daisy's ears. 'How about I give you a call?'

'When?'

'When I've found what I'm looking for.'

There was a long pause. Then Clement said, 'Yeah, you do that. Gotta go. Have fun.' And he rang off.

Phyllis put the phone away, and she felt a knot

190

of squeamishness—she got the feeling that Clem was upset, and she hated being the cause of that. 'Oh, Daisy girl,' she said.

Daisy looked up and blinked her large brown eyes. She gave Phyllis's hand a gentle snouting, and Phyllis giggled at the feel of the little moist nose tickling her palm.

'I wish I knew what I was looking for,' she said to Daisy. 'I wish I knew where I could find something from Shakespeare's time. I wish I knew where to *start* looking for it . . .'

She stopped, as an idea came upon her. She smiled. 'Hey, Daisy, *I* mightn't know where to start looking, but I know someone who can surely point me in the right direction.'

❊

Phyllis Wong had a special sort of status down at Police Headquarters. It came about because she had helped Chief Inspector Barry Inglis with a case—a most perplexing case, the most perplexing in his career so far—very recently. It meant that Phyllis could turn up at the station and see him, if he were not tied up with a case, whenever she needed.

So now, the first thing on Monday morning, Phyllis walked downtown, past all the shops and stores with their windows bursting with Christmas decorations and Hanukkah menorahs, straight up the steps of Police Headquarters and to the front desk. There she was welcomed by a familiar face.

'Season's greetings,' said Constable Olofsson, a young, down-to-earth member of the constabulary. 'What can we do for you today, Phyllis Wong?'

'Three guesses,' winked Phyllis.

'You want to join the force?'

'No.'

'You want to borrow some handcuffs to practise an escape routine with? I've already told you I can't lend you any of those; they'd have my badge quicker than you could whistle—'

'Nope, try again.'

'Now let me think . . .' Constable Olofsson looked skywards (or she would have looked skywards if the flaking ceiling of the police station hadn't been in the way) and pulled a thoughtful face. 'Ah! You want to see that Chief Inspector friend of yours?'

'You got it, Constable.'

'Yes,' said Constable Olofsson, matter-of-factly. 'I am very on the ball. I can anticipate any situation, no matter how unpredictable it may be. It's all part of my extensive training in the fine art of detection.' She winked at Phyllis. 'I'll see if he's free.'

'Thanks.'

The Constable picked up the phone. 'Chief Inspector? Olofsson. I have a young magician here. Says she wants to see you.' Phyllis waited as

Constable Olofsson listened. Then the Constable took her ear from the phone and asked Phyllis, 'He says do you have your dog with you?'

'No,' answered Phyllis. 'She's at home.'

'No,' Constable Olofsson told Barry Inglis. 'Right. Will do. Yes. Thanks, Chief.' She put the phone down. 'He'll see you now,' she said. 'But he's only got a few minutes.'

'Swell,' said Phyllis, quickly displaying her empty hand, front and back, to Constable Olofsson. With a quick flick of her wrist, Phyllis produced a playing card—an ace of clubs, with THANK YOU handwritten across the front. She dropped it down on the desk. 'Thanks, Constable,' she called over her shoulder as she headed for the stairs.

'You're welcome,' Constable Olofsson called back, picking up the card and shaking her head before returning to her computer screen and her game of *Dungeons of the Deadly*.

Phyllis bounded up the three flights of stairs to Barry's office and rapped on the door.

'Come,' he called.

'Hi, Chief Inspector!' She entered his messy domain and promptly went and sat in one of the chairs in front of his desk. He was sitting in the big leather chair on the other side.

'Good morning, Miss Wong. And what brings you down to my neck of the woods?'

'I need to know something.'

'Do you?' Barry moved some papers on his desk, and Phyllis saw, in the pile, some photocopied images of Shakespeare's First Folio and some other images that looked similar. 'What is it you'd like to be enlightened about?'

'It's sort of weird,' she said.

'I'm head of the Fine Arts and Antiques Squad. Weird is commonplace to me, like putting on my shoes. Go ahead, ask.'

'Well, where would someone go if someone wanted to find something that came from London, early seventeenth century?'

Barry Inglis stopped arranging the papers and looked at her, his left eyebrow arching.

'Like from Shakespeare's time?' he asked.

Phyllis smiled. 'Yep.'

'Why do you want to know?' he asked.

'I . . . I've sort of got interested since we went to the auction. I don't know . . . something about the era fascinates me . . .'

'I see. What sort of object did you have in mind?'

'Oh, anything. Anything that really dates back to that Time and place.'

The Chief Inspector regarded her carefully. 'Anything?'

'As long as it's genuine.'

'Hmm.' He gave her a *go on, tell me more* sort of look—a look he often used to draw out information from suspects during questioning.

Phyllis put her hands under her legs and pressed down on them. 'I . . . I'd just like to touch something from way back then,' she tried to explain. 'To help me feel . . . well, closer to the Time, I guess.'

He nodded. He had always, ever since he had first met her when she was a small child, been aware that she thought differently to many other people. Even though sometimes she seemed to say highly unusual things, or do out-of-the-ordinary things, he had come to appreciate the fact that she was different, and he respected the way her mind enquired about things. (Secretly, he believed that one day she would make a first-class detective, but he kept this opinion firmly to himself.)

'I see,' he said. 'Well, it may not be so simple. Objects that old—objects that we *know* are that old—aren't that easy to come by nowadays. Oh, sure, artworks turn up every now and then, and sometimes furniture, and recently these First Folios—' he pulled a small grimace at the mention of them—'but they usually turn up in the bigger and better auction houses.'

'Like Wendlebury's?'

'Like Wendlebury's. Those are the kinds of places that collectors buy seventeenth-century antiques and artworks. Of course, one could be lucky, and find something in a junk shop or second-hand store or antiques store, but not often. And if you did find something in that sort of place, you'd have to know what it was, or hope that the seller knew what it was.'

'I see.' Phyllis thought. Perhaps that's what she needed to do: haunt the shops over on the street that had all the antiques places and curios and second-hand stores all in the same block. She frowned—that would take forever, and she wanted to get on to this quickly. Besides, there was no guarantee that any of those shops would have anything from the seventeenth century for sale, and even if they did, would Phyllis be able to afford it? And what if all she could find was some big old table or wardrobe or something? How would she Transit with something like *that*?

Barry saw her frowning. 'Actually—' he began, and paused.

From this point on in her life, Phyllis Wong would always love the word *actually*. She looked up.

'Actually,' Barry said again, 'I think I can help. You said you just wanted to touch something from the time, yes?'

'Uh-huh.'

From another pile of papers at the far side of his desk he withdrew a large blue plastic folder. This he placed on the desk between him and Phyllis.

'You're in luck. I have to return this to Wendlebury's this afternoon . . . should've done it days ago, but I've been snowed under.'

'What is it?' asked Phyllis, staring at the folder.

'Open it and find out.'

Phyllis leant forward and did so. Inside the folder was a large sheet of thick, slightly creamy-coloured paper. Phyllis noticed that it had a weave to it, as though it had been made from some sort of linen or similar material. There was no writing on it, only a few small, pale ink blots, and two of its corners had become torn and separated from the main part of the page. The corners were sitting there with the rest of the page, like pieces of a jigsaw puzzle that were about to be put together.

'What is it?' she asked.

'It's a fragment of paper from that First Folio you saw auctioned the other night. It was found tucked into the inside back cover when the seller brought the Folio to Wendlebury's. The experts at Wendlebury's called me in to get a test done on it to make sure it was genuine and not a fake. It's the same sort of paper—the exact same sort of paper—that the rest of the Folio was printed on.'

'And is it genuine?' Phyllis could feel her heart pumping a bit faster.

'To all intents and purposes, it is. We dated it back to the early 1600s.'

'Wow.' She looked up through her fringe at Barry.

'Go ahead, touch it,' he said. 'Here.' He took a pair of white cotton gloves out of a top drawer of his desk and handed them to her. 'Pop these on first, though. We can't have the oils from our skin spoiling something so old.'

'Thanks.' Phyllis slipped her hands into the gloves—they were too big and she felt like she had frogs' fingers. Gently she touched the paper.

As she did so, something special happened: a tiny zing of something like electricity went through the glove, into her hand, along her arm and down her spine. She scarcely breathed as she rested her gloved hand on the page.

Then Barry Inglis's phone rang loudly, breaking the Time-stopping silence, and Phyllis jumped. Barry reached for the phone quickly.

'Inglis here. Really? Good lord! When . . .?' He swivelled his chair around to face the window as he listened carefully.

Phyllis looked back down to the old page, and she saw that one of the separated corners of the page—the corner closest to the edge of the desk— was not there. When she had jumped, her hand must have accidentally knocked it off the folder, off the desk and onto the floor. She gave a small gasp as she realised what had happened.

Barry was still busy with his conversation; it seemed he hadn't noticed the fallen corner. Quietly, Phyllis bent down and looked on the floor. There was the corner, just by her feet. Delicately, she picked it up and, keeping her eye on the Chief Inspector, went to place it back in the blue folder.

But a thought ricocheted into her brain. She didn't put the corner back there. Instead, she slipped it into her bag, which was on the floor by her feet. Silently, smoothly, as only a magician can, she straightened, and gently she closed the blue folder. She slipped off the gloves and folded them neatly, placing them on top of the folder.

It fell onto the floor, she thought. *Now I'll borrow it, and bring it back when I've done what I need to do. I'll explain that it must've fallen . . . into my bag. It's not like I'm stealing it or anything. It can't do any harm. I need to know about all these First Folios . . .*

'I'll get some of my people down there straight-away, and I'll be along directly,' said Barry Inglis into the phone. 'Don't let anyone enter the scene. Thanks, Chatterton.'

He put the phone down and turned back to face Phyllis. 'Miss Wong, I'm afraid I have to go. Detective Pinkie Chatterton has uncovered something that needs my attention. Ah, I see you're finished.'

'No, Chief Inspector, I'm only just beginning.'

He gave her a quizzical look. 'Huh?'

She grabbed her bag and stood. 'Thanks for your time, you've been a fabbo help. See you round!' And, with a big smile, she was out the door in seconds.

'Hmm,' hmmed Barry Inglis, looking at the gloves on the blue folder before starting another search for his car keys which were buried somewhere in the mountains and valleys of paperwork covering his desk.

Using her Pockets

Phyllis decided on black for her first expedition alone.

From her History lessons at school she knew a little about the clothes they wore back in Shakespeare's time. One of her teachers had shown Phyllis and her classmates a slideshow of the types of clothing people wore back then: the men's tight-fitting button jackets they called *doublets*, the bodices and the skirts worn by the women and the framework that went under their skirts (Phyllis had liked the name of the framework— it was known as a *farthingale*, and was made of whalebone or wire), and the tube-shaped bundle that women wore to give them the appearance of having bigger hips (the boys in her class had enjoyed a good sniggerfest when they'd learnt that this was called a *bumroll*).

Phyllis decided that she couldn't hope to dress in the authentic fashion of the time, but wearing black would be the next best thing if she didn't want to stand out in the crowds. The last thing she needed was to draw too much attention to herself. So she dressed in a dark shirt, black sweater and jeans, and a pair of dark runners. She chose her long black coat that came down past her knees, and tied her hair back in a ponytail. She didn't want to be choking on mouthfuls of it when the wind picked up in the Pocket.

Daisy lay on the bed, watching her as she got dressed. 'You're a good girl,' Phyllis said to her. 'I'm going to be gone for a little while—'

At the sound of the word *gone*, Daisy sat up and extended a paw, her little face crinkling in the way it always crinkled when she heard words that unsettled her.

'But,' said Phyllis, taking Daisy's paw and shaking it gently, 'you'll hardly even notice. Time will fly and I'll be back before you can sneeze.'

Daisy gave a little gargling-of-marbles sound.

Phyllis held her paw. 'Maybe I'll take you with me another time. But not now. Not this time. I have to get used to this, and I don't want anything happening to you that shouldn't . . .'

Phyllis stopped and, still clasping Daisy's paw, she took a deep breath. 'Okay, Miss Daisy, it's time.'

She took one of Daisy's favourite treats from a tin on her dresser and gave it to her. Daisy wagged her tail and settled down with the biscuit. She was enjoying it so much—as she always did—that she didn't notice Phyllis picking up her shoulder bag and quietly leaving the bedroom.

The elevator was waiting, and Phyllis went straight in. She inserted her key in the basement lock on the control panel and turned it. The doors closed and the old contraption began descending.

As she went judderingly down, Phyllis wished that the journey through the Pockets could be like this. Even though the old elevator didn't give the smoothest ride, it was way smoother than some of the turbulence she'd go through if she Transited through an Anamygduleon or another Andruseon.

Then, with a final lurch, she was in the basement. The doors slid open and Phyllis walked out onto the landing at the top of the stairs. She flicked on the lights and reached back into the elevator to shut its doors so that it could go back up, in case other people wanted to use it to travel to their floors.

After it had gone, Phyllis peered down the staircase and into the basement.

From above, she couldn't see any sign of the TimePocket. There was nothing strange about the light or the space on the stairs—no shimmering, or molecules of matter that shouldn't be there. Phyllis bit her lip and frowned. Maybe the Pocket wasn't there any more? W.W. had said things were constantly shifting . . .

She realised then that she had never seen the Pocket here from above; she had entered it with W.W. by coming *up* the stairs. She smiled, slung her bag over her neck, across her shoulder, and held its strap securely. Then she went down the stairs two at a time.

She stopped at the bottom and took a moment to check herself. She registered what she was feeling: excited and scared. There was an enormous, exhilarating current of excitement flowing through her veins—she was about to do something huge, something so huge that her brain was still coming to terms with it all, and she was about to do it *by herself.* That was an almost dizzying thought. And, rushing around inside her, as though it were chasing the excitement in there, was a soft feeling of fear. Yes, she admitted to herself, she was scared. Uncertain things do that to you, she thought. But she was reassured to feel that the excitement was outweighing the fear, and this gave her extra courage.

She found that she was breathing fast, so she took a few deep lungfuls of air and steadied herself. That's when she remembered that she didn't have something she needed to take with her: her Transiting journal. She'd been writing details of the Pockets in it, and also the details of the publisher of Shakespeare's First Folios. She'd totally forgotten to put the journal in her bag, and she felt the zing of the just-rescued-from-the-clutches-of-dread feeling that you get when you've just avoided forgetting something important.

Where did I leave it? she wondered. She'd last had it a few days ago when she'd been pottering about in the basement, trying to find something that might have come from Shakespeare's Time, before she'd paid her visit to Barry Inglis in his office. Phyllis interlocked her hands, and the reassuring feeling of her thumb and little finger curling around each other helped her to focus on where she had been looking.

Ah! Over by the shelves, near the costume racks by the far wall. She hurried to the place and began searching through all the costumes, half of which she hadn't hung back up again and which were strewn across the floor. She got down on her knees and began going through the piles of clothes and hats and other bits and pieces.

There lay the old leather-bound journal, underneath a couple of silver waistcoats and an oversized royal stage crown. She pulled it out, re-tied the leather cord around the book, and dropped the journal into her shoulder bag.

Just as she was standing, she heard a loud, jolting, juddering sound.

She jumped and stood, and then she heard the doors of the elevator squeaking open. She couldn't see the elevator from where she was, behind the shelves and the costume racks, but she knew that sound only too well.

She must have left her key in the control panel. She felt like saying *d'uh* to herself, but instead she shook her head and made her way back to the stairs. She hurried up them—deliberately skirting around where she felt the Pocket was—and reached into the elevator. Sure enough, her key was still there.

'Get your brain on, Phyllis,' she muttered to herself. She turned the key, took it out, and sent the elevator back up to the lobby. It rose slowly, shudderingly, and disappeared above her. Now, without the basement key in the control panel, no one would be able to come down here.

Dropping the key into her bag, she hurried down the stairs again and stood at the bottom. She looked up, concentrating, squinting at a point about two-thirds of the way up the staircase.

Slowly, as though they were materialising from a shadowy cosmos far out in Space, the faint green edges of the Pocket began to appear.

Phyllis smiled, and every pore of her skin tingled.

Molecules of pale light started moving around, dancing their Time-changing swirls. The lights grew brighter, and pulsated and throbbed, and Phyllis felt they were beckoning her to come to them.

She reached into her coat pocket and carefully

withdrew the corner scrap of First Folio paper. She had put it in a plastic packet, the sort she used for card tricks where she only needed to have two or three cards with her. She knew she needed to protect the piece of paper from the turbulence in the Pocket and from her perspiration and from anything else that might damage it on the journey.

Clutching this, and arranging her bag more securely over her shoulder, she took her first step up the staircase . . .

. . . and stopped suddenly.

There had been a noise, a faint sound like something moving, near one of the stacks of old theatre trunks and chests piled close to the bottom of the stairs, on the other side of the handrail.

Phyllis edged closer to the handrail and peered over into the shadows beyond the trunks and chests. She held her breath and listened as she watched carefully for any sign of movement.

After a few moments of silence, she said, quietly, 'Hello?'

More silence.

She peered more intensely, but she couldn't see anything out of the ordinary—gloom was shrouding the floor on the other side of the trunks, but the dimness didn't seem to be concealing anything.

She thought it might have been a mouse or rat or something—she'd seen some down here in the past but she was never bothered by them, and she decided to get back to what she should be doing. Turning to the upper reaches of the staircase, she focussed once again on the shimmering molecules of beckoning light.

Her Pocket was waiting.

Her spine began to tingle, her palms grew sweaty, her feet felt as light as feathers as she started climbing the stairs.

Closer and closer she came to the green-bordered Pocket. Brighter and brighter the lights grew, twinkling beads of brightness she had seen before. The dense darkness lay beyond, a blanket of blackness . . .

She felt the thickness of everything ahead as she stepped closer . . .

Blurriness now . . .

She could hear the wind—the buffeting wind, the roaring wind . . .

Something behind her, too, faint, approaching . . .

Two more steps . . .

She was on the threshold now. She shut her eyes against the pitch black and the huge wind ahead, and she began to hear the soft, vibrating hum of all that was to come and all that had been and all the uncertainties and mysteries and marvels that lay in wait . . .

. . . and with a single step, she was gone!

The enormous turbulence threw her all about, and somehow, from somewhere deep in her mind, a poem came to her:

And then it was, I left the stair
and rode the wind, through Time-
    wrapped air,
propelled along the black highways,
sent back to glowing yesterdays . . .

With a great stumble, the wind-blown Phyllis lurched forward onto a narrow set of stone stairs above a street.

She opened her eyes slowly. Her body was vibrating all over, as though she were very cold and she couldn't stop herself from shivering. But she wasn't shivering; she was coming down from the relentless, jumbling forces that she had passed through, and her body must be trying to settle back into a state of being normal again. The vibrating must be a part of this process, as was the feeling in her tummy that she wanted to be sick. She remembered this from the time she had Transited with W.W., and she told herself that it would pass soon enough.

She was still clutching the corner of the First Folio in the plastic packet. Carefully she slid it into her coat pocket and started to breathe more calmly.

She looked around. Slowly, the sounds and the smells of the street began to creep up to her, and the place seemed to grow lighter.

This looked like the Time, she thought. People were hurrying through the street, dressed in fashions of the early seventeenth century, according to what her teacher had shown them. Men were striding along in doublets and hose, some of them wearing knee-length capes and ornate ruffled collars. Others were clad in simpler vests and breeches and black shoes. The women Phyllis saw had long skirts and bodices and some wore bonnets. Everyone around her was moving quickly. *This must be a busy part of town*, Phyllis thought.

The street itself was narrow, and the houses on it, with their dark wooden beams against white-washed walls, were crammed together side by side, their upper floors jutting out into the street. Phyllis looked up. It was like she was standing in a sort of semi-open cave, she thought, with just a little glimpse of the greyish sky above.

Suddenly she wrinkled her nose, and clamped her hand quickly over it. An awful stench had flowed out of one of the nearby houses, and Phyllis turned and looked back up the street to see a woman leaning out of one of the small leadlight windows of a house not far away, pouring some brown sloppy stuff out of a big pot. The slush splattered down onto the cobble-stoned street, some of it gurgling down a small drain near the gutter but most of it splashing all over the stones and onto some of the passers-by. Some of these unfortunate people shouted incredibly rude words up at the woman and kept hurrying on their way. The woman shouted some incredibly rude words back and disappeared inside, slamming the window shut.

Phyllis shuddered and, clutching her bag firmly across her shoulder, she started down the stairs and up the street, away from the putrid place.

Most of the people jostling around her were too busy going here and there to pay her any attention. She had to keep moving, so that she wasn't banged into or (with some of the ruder people) pushed firmly out of the way. This was very unlike where she lived.

The whole place was filled with noise: clattering footsteps against the cobblestones, shouted conversations, barrels of beer being rolled clunkingly along, the occasional rat-a-tat barking of a dog or the foghorn-like honking of caged geese being trundled along on wooden carts.

I'd better make sure this is London, Phyllis thought. She spied a woman with a not-too-cranky sort of face coming towards her, and stepped into her path.

'Excuse me, madam,' she said over the noise from the street. 'Am I in London?'

The woman stopped, but only for a couple of seconds. She looked at Phyllis warily, eyeing her hair and clothes and face. Then she replied as though Phyllis were a lump of something extremely stupid. 'London? Of course you are, you daft thing. Where d'ye think it is? The moon?'

And with that she gave Phyllis a small shove out of the way and continued on.

'Well, nice to meet you, too,' Phyllis muttered when the woman was out of earshot. But she wasn't rattled by the abrupt encounter; she just felt glad that she was in the right place.

She walked on and came to a cross-street, with four separate ways going off in four different directions. Here she stopped, unsure of which way to turn. She went and stood against the wall of a shop that had fish, eggs and dark-coloured meat spread out on a table behind the small front window, away from the main bustle of the street. She took out her journal and opened it.

She quickly flipped to the page where she'd noted down the printer's address, which she'd found on the internet:

Isaac Jaggard, Printer and Binder at the sign of the Half-Eagle and Key in Barbican, London.

'The sign of the Half-Eagle and Key, in Barbican,' she read quietly. She guessed that Barbican was a part of London, like a precinct or something. She had to find out where it was.

That meant asking more questions.

She shut the journal and held onto it tightly. Then she stepped out away from the shop and looked for a friendly sort of person.

An old man came along, his head bent low and a couple of large leather-bound books under his arm. When Phyllis saw the books, she immediately stepped out in front of him.

'Excuse me, sir?' she asked.

He slowed his pace for a moment, looked at her strangely and asked, 'What do you require?' before continuing along the street.

Phyllis walked alongside him. 'Do you know where I can find Isaac Jaggard's Printers, at the sign of the Half-Eagle and Key? In Barbican?'

At that, he stopped and looked at her again. 'You want to buy a book?' he enquired.

'Erm . . . I'm interested in their books,' she answered.

'Well, young friend, if it's books you be after, the best place to find them is yonder, in St Paul's churchyard. That be where the book purveyors sell their tomes. They all set their tables up there— the printers and the stationers and the booksellers and the scriveners and the bookbinders. You'll find more books there than you could ever read in one lifetime, even with all the years ahead of such a young person as ye'self.'

'St Paul's?'

'Aye. I've just come from there meself. Had these new printed sheets bound.' He proudly held out the books, and Phyllis saw how shiny and new the leather covers looked. 'You'll find St Paul's on this side of the Thames River, up the street, that way.' He pointed behind Phyllis.

Phyllis nodded. 'Thank you. But do you know where Jaggard's shop is?'

'Oh, aye. I certainly know it. He's a most worthy printer, is Isaac Jaggard. You'll not be a far distance from it from where you are standing.' He half-turned and pointed back up the street, in the other direction. 'Go up there until you get to the Gay Goose Inn, then you should be turning left into Gropeturnip Lane. Go down Gropeturnip until you come to Aldersgate Street—that be a big street, wider than this'un. Walk on up Aldersgate and you'll find Barbican to yer right. Turn into Barbican and go up a little way and you'll soon see the Half-Eagle and Key Inn. Isaac Jaggard's establishment is immediately next door to it.'

Phyllis had whipped out her journal and a pencil and she was scribbling down the instructions. 'So Barbican is a street?' she asked.

'Aye, that it is,' answered the old man. Just then

he felt the first spots of rain on his balding head. 'Blast the heavens,' he muttered. 'I'd best be getting my tomes home before they get spatterstained from this water. Good morning to you, young—' he looked at her strangely again—'young'un. I hope ye find what you are after.'

And, with a curt but not unfriendly nod, he hurried on.

'Thank you,' she called after him, and he gave her a farewell wave over his shoulder.

Phyllis closed her journal against the raindrops and held it sheltered under her arm. She smiled, took a big breath, and hurried along towards the Gay Goose Inn and Gropeturnip Lane.

Discovery at Jaggard's

The young conjuror managed to brave the crowds and the smells and the bustling higgledy-piggledy lanes and streets, and, thanks to the old man's instructions, she soon found the printing shop of Isaac Jaggard without too much fuss.

She opened the glass-paned door, and a small bell above it tinkled lightly. She stepped down into the premises and found herself in a dimly lit room, long and narrow. Immediately in front of her was a tall wooden counter with stacks of paper—wide sheets of thick paper that looked like they would be soft to the touch—arranged neatly to one side.

Beyond this Phyllis saw a big, black printing press. A man was standing at either end of the press. One of them—the younger-looking man—was feeding sheets of the wide, thick paper one by one into a roller and turning a wheel, which drew each sheet of paper through the press. The other man, who had a neatly trimmed grey beard and a gold earring, was gently pulling one of the printed sheets of paper out the other end of the press, handling it delicately as though it were the wings of a butterfly. Phyllis guessed that he was being careful so that the still-wet ink on the paper wouldn't smudge or be spoiled.

When the printed sheet of paper was clear of the press, he carefully placed it in a large wooden drying cupboard which had dozens of narrow shelves in it. Phyllis watched as he slid the page into one of these shelves. Then he looked across the counter and saw Phyllis.

'Good morning,' he said, a quizzical look on his face. He had never had anyone like her come into the shop before, dressed the way she was, and he was trying to place from where she'd come.

'Good morning.' Phyllis smiled and came closer to the counter.

The younger man stopped feeding paper into the press and he, too, looked strangely at Phyllis.

'How may I be of your assistance?' asked the older man.

'I wonder if Mr Jaggard is here?' Phyllis asked.

The man wiped his hands on the big white apron he was wearing. 'I am Isaac Jaggard,' he said. 'And who might you be, then?'

'I'm Phyllis. Phyllis Wong. May I ask you a few questions?'

Isaac Jaggard regarded her for a few seconds. It was unusual to have young people in the shop asking questions. 'We're very busy,' he said.

'I won't take up too much of your time,' said Phyllis.

'What would you be enquiring about, Phyllis Wong?' he asked her.

'About your printing of Mr Shakespeare's plays.'

Then he smiled at her. He signalled to the younger man to leave the press, and the younger man went off into the rear of the shop and started arranging some big hides of leather. 'Mr Shakespeare?' Jaggard said, coming forward to the other side of the counter. 'You like Mr Shakespeare's works, do you?'

Phyllis nodded. 'Oh, yes. He's swell.'

'Swell?' asked Isaac Jaggard. 'What mean you, swell?'

'Um . . . wonderful,' said Phyllis quickly.

'Ah.' Isaac Jaggard winked at her, and his eyes crinkled at the edges. 'Aye, we think likewise. Full of wonder, indeed. That is why we are publishing all his collected works. Such a shame he could not be alive to see the book.'

Phyllis looked confused.

'Aye, it be seven years or thereabouts since he departed this good world. A great loss to the theatres, and to those of us who love to see players strutting the stage. There was no one like Mr Shakespeare, and I dare wager it, there will be no one to come in the future like him. He were a brilliant man, Phyllis Wong. Brilliant like the brightest star in the heavens.'

'Many people still think so,' said Phyllis.

'Aye, and that's a good thing. And it's largely thanks to his player colleagues ,Mr Heminges and Mr Condell that we are able to publish his—how did you say it—his *swell* words. We wish to keep his memory alive, and the swell words he penned.'

'You're doing a marvellous job,' Phyllis told him.

Isaac Jaggard gave her a bigger smile. 'Thank you, Phyllis Wong. It always is good to be appreciated. Especially by the younger ones.' He took out a piece of white cloth from his pocket and wiped some ink from his hands. 'Now, you said you wanted to ask about our printing of the plays?' he asked her.

'Oh yes.' Phyllis slung her bag off her shoulder and put it on the floor. 'The First Folios you've been publishing—'

'First Folios?' repeated Isaac Jaggard. 'Hmm. That is a good description of them. I suppose it *is* the first time that this size of book has been published with all Shakespeare's plays inside . . . and these are the most accurate versions of the works. His friends Heminges and Condell acted in his company at the Globe Theatre, and they kept their scripts, and that's what we've used to publish the plays.'

'Wow.' Phyllis felt a small surge of excitement—she was breathing the very air of History right now. 'You use Shakespeare's actual scripts?'

Isaac Jaggard laughed. 'Oh, no. Just the *copies* of the scripts that were given to the actors. No, Phyllis Wong, we'll never get our hands on the foul papers. If only we could . . .'

'The *what*?'

'The foul papers. The original drafts, penned by Mr Shakespeare in his own handwriting. No, Mr Shakespeare guarded those foul papers, those handwritten scripts, with his life—he never let them out of his sight, even when they were being copied by a member of his company. You see, they made *copies* of his originals and gave 'em out to all the actors, and they were the scripts used for performing. It was these script versions that we've used to put together what you call the First Folios.'

'I see. And how does someone buy one of your First Folios?' Phyllis asked.

'Well, they usually go and see the bookseller. Edward Blount is his name. We've printed the First Folios in association with him. He comes and collects them from us—they're not bound in covers or anything when he collects them; they're just the pages sewn together, and when a customer buys their copy of the First Folio from Mr Blount, the customer usually goes away and has the pages bound in leather or calfskin or vellum or however they want them bound. Ed Blount has a stall in the churchyard of St Paul's.'

'Where all the booksellers are,' said Phyllis, recalling what the old stranger had told her earlier.

'Aye, that be correct.' Isaac Jaggard stopped and scratched his beard, as he remembered something. 'But, now that you ask, not everyone buys that way. We have one customer who comes to us direct. She's bought not one First Folio, but . . . oooh . . . let me think . . .' He scratched his beard some more, then called out to the younger man: 'Indigo? How many copies of the big Shakespeare have we sold to Mistress Colley?'

Mistress Colley, Phyllis noted in her mind.

'Ooh, must be close to a dozen, as I'd recall, Mr Jaggard,' called the younger man from the back of the shop.

'Aye, you be not far off the mark, Indigo,' Jaggard called to him. 'Yes, Phyllis Wong, this woman, Mistress Colley, she comes in here every now and then—sometimes several times in the space of a few weeks, other times we don't get a visit from her for a year or longer—and buys a First Folio. Sometimes she buys more'n one on the same occasion. She is a most . . . *individual* sort of woman, wouldn't you say, Indigo?'

Indigo looked up and gave a wry smile. 'You could put it like that, Mr Jaggard.'

'Aye. She's very forthright, no nonsense about her. Almost demanding. And she dresses like a man, too. Every time we've seen her she be wearing britches and long boots and a gentleman's cloak.'

'And she be keeping company with a rat,' added Indigo, shaking his head.

Isaac Jaggard nodded. 'We think she does indeed. Indigo saw a thing scurrying around her shoulders on one of her visits.'

Phyllis shuddered.

'But she's a good customer. The big Shake-speares don't sell cheap, and she always has the money.'

'How much does a First Folio cost?' asked Phyllis.

'Well, if we sell direct—and we only sell direct to her—they cost one pound each. That be more than most people around here could afford in half a year of wages, Phyllis Wong. Ed Blount charges the same across at St Paul's, but he doesn't include binding the sheets in the cost. People have to pay for their own binding if they buy from him.'

'And do you bind the copies you sell to this Mistress Colley?'

'Aye. She's always most particular about how she wants the Shakespeares bound. She always requests—no, she always *demands*—that each First Folio be bound in a deep, dark-red calf leather. And then the bound book has to be wrapped carefully in a soft vellum covering—that's the skin of a young goat, is vellum. And the vellum covering always has to be dyed green, a dark green. She's most fussy about all of that, isn't she, Indigo?'

'Fussiest customer we ever did see,' Indigo responded as he stacked the leather. 'She and her rodent.'

'And she's the only customer who comes in here and buys the First Folios directly from you?' asked Phyllis.

'She is,' replied Isaac Jaggard. 'I once asked her why she didn't just pop over to see Ed Blount and buy her copies from him. She said she wanted to get them from us because it would save on any wear and tear. She said she wanted her books in the most perfect condition possible, and she had a better chance of getting them like that if she bought them directly from us, with no extra handling involved.'

Phyllis nodded. 'Mr Jaggard, why does she buy so many copies, do you think?'

'Ah. I enquired that of her myself, not so long ago. She wouldn't answer me. Just paid for the book that day, said goodbye and off she went, her cloak billowing about her like there was a gale blowing. Oh, I remember that day only too well . . . her eyes were strange, they were. Like they were glowing—greenish, as the eyes of a cat on a dark night. Well, her good eye was, at least. Just like a cat's . . .'

No, not the eyes of a cat, Phyllis thought. *The eyes of a Transiter.*

'Very strange it were,' said Jaggard. 'Never have I seen eyes like that before or since.'

'She be a very strange woman completely,' said Indigo with a grimace. 'And nasty. Oh, yes, nasty, indeed. I remember the first time she bought one of the Folios. She were just leavin' the shop here and she'd stepped out onto the street, and lo and behold someone emptied a pot o' slops from a window above, all a-splatter on the ground right next to Mistress Colley's boots. Mistress Colley wasted not a moment—she dashed up the stairs o' the house and the next thing I see, when I ran outside the shop, was a man bein' dangled by his ankles from the third-storey window. Mistress Colley was holdin' him there and shoutin' the worst cusses I ever did hear from a woman's lips. The poor fellow was terrified, beggin' her to stop and to let him back inside. Then, just as a crowd was gatherin', a peddler came past with his cart and when he was in front of the house, Mistress Colley let go of the poor man's ankles and he dropped like a metal sinker, BANG into the cart. Luckily it were full of cabbages, but even so, cabbages can be most injurious.'

'That be true,' said Isaac Jaggard. 'The unfortunate man broke his shoulder and both arms in the fall. 'Twere a miracle he didn't get killed by them cabbages.'

Phyllis felt a sense of creeping dread growing inside her, as she was finding out more about this woman, Colley. She shook her head, and returned to the question of the First Folios. 'Does she always pay you cash when she gets a new Folio?' she asked Jaggard.

'Every time. She never buys on credit. And every time I always give her the proper receipt.'

Phyllis frowned. She'd found the information she needed—that Colley was *buying* the First Folios, and not stealing them. But still, Phyllis felt unsatisfied . . . it didn't seem right, what this woman was doing . . .

'Would you like to buy a copy yeself?' asked Isaac Jaggard.

'I'd love to,' Phyllis said. 'But . . . I haven't the money.'

'No, it is a huge amount, aye. Never you mind. But, Phyllis Wong, I'd like you to have something. To remember your visit to Isaac Jaggard's.'

He went back to a tall rack of shelving behind the printing press. From one of the shelves there he took out a small piece of black metal type, nearly an inch long and a quarter of an inch wide. He came back and handed it to Phyllis.

'A little keepsake, if you like. A little piece of what we use to set the Shakespeares.'

'Wow! Thank you.' She turned the block of type over in the palm of her hand. On the top of it, mirror-reversed, was a raised letter: **P.**

Isaac Jaggard smiled as he watched her examining it.

'Mr Jaggard, how old is this?'

'Hmm. Well it's not new. I bought all the type from an old printer a few years ago. And I doubt it were quite new even then. Oh, let me think . . .' He scratched his beard again . . . 'Maybe it's ten years old. Maybe older. I could not be sure.' He stopped scratching his beard and regarded her. 'You're a curious young girl, if thou don't mind me saying such.'

She beamed at him. 'I don't mind you saying that at all,' she told him. 'I'd rather be curious than ordinary.'

'Aye, well you'll go far with that attitude, Phyllis Wong. You'll go far indeed.' Suddenly he looked over her shoulder, through the front window of the shop. 'Egads! I live and breathe!'

Phyllis turned and she too looked out the front window. She saw passers-by, but nothing out of the usual. She turned back to Isaac Jaggard. 'What's the matter?'

'Ha. He's gone now.'

'Who's gone?'

'A most strange fellow. A dwarf. A dwarf with a long red beard. Looking into the shop for a moment. Now, one don't see many like that around. Sometimes the King has one in his court, a dwarf I mean, but they are few and far between in London . . .'

'It seems to me that London's full of strange things,' Phyllis commented.

'That it is,' said Jaggard. 'That it truly is. And now, I have work to be returning to. Many pages to print before suppertime tonight, Phyllis Wong.'

'Goodbye, Mr Jaggard. And thank you.'

'Thou art most welcome,' he said, giving her a wink.

She held her opened palm up to him and showed him her block of type. Then, as smoothly as silk being slid away, she passed her other hand over the type.

Isaac Jaggard's eyes became huge as he saw that her palm was now completely empty. She turned her other hand over to show him that it, too, was empty. His eyes became huger.

'Disappeared!' he gasped. 'Heigh-ho! How can you do such a thing?'

'Magic,' replied Phyllis, smiling.

'Ordinary you are definitely not, Phyllis Wong,' said the printer, shaking his head.

She picked up her bag and, with a cheery wave, she left him.

✳

When Phyllis left Isaac Jaggard's shop, she realised that she'd become a bit disoriented; she had no idea from which direction she'd come to get there. Even with the instructions from the old man which she'd written in her journal, she'd managed to become lost.

She spent nearly two hours wandering the streets and alleys, pausing whenever she came to any stairs and peering intensely up them, hoping to find a TimePocket. She hoped that if she stayed still when she was doing this, controlling her breathing until it slowed down and clearing her mind of as much as she could clear, then she might be able to see the glimmer or the faint presence of an Anamygduleon or an Andruseon or Anvugheon or Anaumbryon.

Although there would have been lots of stair-cases inside buildings to check, she felt it was safer to remain where there were more people coming and going. And that meant staying outside. Most of the staircases she came across were littered with rotting vegetables or broken bottles or cats having kittens (that had only been on one of the staircases, and it had given Phyllis a little shock); others were crowded with people rushing up them or down them as they set about their business.

But then, rounding a corner near a noisy tavern, she found what she'd been looking for. In front of her, leading up to a street that was higher than the one in which she was standing, was a ramshackle staircase that gave her a strange feeling.

She stopped, slowed her breathing and let her mind empty. She half-closed her eyes and looked to the upper reaches of the crooked stone stairs. And she saw it almost immediately.

This Pocket was different to the ones she'd already Transited through. It was shaped like a large almond and instead of a pale green light around its edges, the edges of this one shone with a bright orange glow before fading away and shining again. And what lay inside it—a dark blue-black, like the colour of W.W.'s midnight-blue tuxedo— seemed denser, thicker . . .

But it was a Pocket! *Let's go*, she told herself. She pulled her bag firmly across her shoulder, patted her coat pockets to make sure she had all her things (including her piece of metal type and the corner of the First Folio page) and then, from the pocket of her jeans, she took out one of the small, red, spangly balls she used for her cups-and-balls routines. This she clutched tightly in her left hand. This was her passport home.

Holding her head high, she ran up the stairs towards the Pocket, her heart beating faster.

And, unseen by anyone from that Time, she was gone!

The journey home was wild and bumpy; this time she seemed to be pulled almost ferociously into the Pocket, and the darkness smothered her straightaway. The wind was fierce; she shut her eyes as hard as she could, but the air currents still found a way to prise open her eyes at the corners, and she couldn't help the teardrops escaping—not tears of pain, but tears from the air pressure. Her cheeks ballooned out and her coat and bag buffeted and blew behind her. She felt like she was Transiting at an angle, leaning forward into the darkness, being propelled like a paper plane along the rapidity of the cosmos.

As the darkness came into lightness, she tried not to think about her stomach—it felt like someone had reached down her throat and grabbed the insides of her tummy and was trying to pull it up through her mouth. *Think of something else,* she told herself. *Think of Daisy and her cold wet snout and the way she licks her paws when she grooms herself and the way her little tail wags . . .*

She heard the soft, high-pitched humming of

the air around her, and then the wind started to fade and the light began growing brighter. There were the molecules of brightness ahead, those small, twinkling baubles that she'd seen at the entrance to the TimePocket when she'd left the magic basement.

With a mighty lurch forward, Phyllis stumbled out of the Pocket so fast that she tripped and, unable to get her balance, tumbled down the stairs, her legs going over her head and her arms buckling under her.

'*Oooooof!*' she gasped as the breath was knocked out of her and she kept on rolling down, down, down . . .

She came to a hard stop on the floor. And moaned loudly.

She waited a few moments to see if she was hurt. Luckily she couldn't feel any sharp pain—just the discomfort of having been knocked about on the hard stairs. She knew she'd have some bruises coming up very soon.

She lay there, waiting for her head and her stomach to settle. Her eyes were throbbing and she felt as if she were an accordion—and that some invisible musician had just played some wild sort of tune on her, pulling and squeezing her through the centuries.

In this semi-dazed state, she didn't notice the elevator's doors above her. They opened and closed and then the elevator rose up towards the lobby. Phyllis was too zonked to hear it depart.

Eventually she rolled over and rubbed an elbow. Slowly she got to her feet, steadying herself against the stair's banister. *That was some trip*, she thought. *I've really got to work on my re-entry if I'm not going to end up a permanent bundle of bruises.*

Then she heard the juddering full-stop of the elevator as it landed again in the basement. She looked up the stairs, past the Anamygduleon she'd just Transited through, and saw the elevator doors vibrating.

'Huh?' she wondered aloud. 'How come that's come down again? I'm sure I took my key out of it before I left. No one can operate that without the key . . .'

She went up the stairs, opened the elevator doors and went inside. There was a key, sitting in the basement lock in the control panel. Phyllis frowned. She took the key out, then quickly checked her pockets and her bag to see if this was *her* key or her dad's—maybe her dad was home; he was the only other person with a key to the basement of the Wallace Wong Building.

She couldn't find her key anywhere. She looked at the key in her hand. *This is screwy*, she thought. *This is my key. But I took it out before I left, and put it in my* . . . She put her hand to her mouth as she realised something. The Time must be different! She must have returned here to a time *before* she had left! She must have come back a few minutes before she had Transited to London . . . That would account for the elevator behaving strangely earlier, too . . .

Phyllis's heart was beating fast. Her first solo journey and the discombobulations and the pressure of the Transitaciousness (as W.W. had put it) were making her dizzy. She needed a good dose of normal right now.

She inserted her key into the control panel, turned it and pressed the button for the third floor, to her apartment. She needed to play with her Daisy.

Heads-up headline

Two days later, after Phyllis had settled back into the modern world and spent some happy time with Daisy, and after she had written down the details of her journey to Isaac Jaggard's so she wouldn't forget all the things that he had said to her, she still couldn't help but feel unsatisfied.

She felt that things weren't really right. She knew that the woman whom Isaac Jaggard had called Mistress Colley was not *stealing* the First Folios; she was buying them, and then selling them for a huge profit. That wasn't illegal, her dad had said, to buy and sell like that, but to Phyllis it didn't seem *fair*.

She thought it seemed *underhanded*.

Because that Colley woman wasn't breaking any law, Phyllis couldn't see what could be done to stop her. Phyllis was becoming exasperated about the situation. How would it look, after all, if she went and told Chief Inspector Barry Inglis about what she'd discovered? He'd listen to her, all right—he always listened to her and treated her like she was a worthwhile person, and she always liked that—but even *he* would think she was crackers. He'd probably ring up her dad and suggest she spend a bit of time with some doctor with a nice soft couch and a soothing manner.

Maybe, Phyllis considered, *that's what the world's like. Maybe the world is a place where people can get away with things that aren't really right while at the same time not breaking the law.* Phyllis didn't like that idea at all. It seemed selfish and ugly and unfair.

Perhaps it's a question of how people see things, she thought. *All sorts of situations can be seen in different ways. Look what happened with Leizel Cunbrus.* Phyllis felt that she herself hadn't done anything wrong, but people thought she had. Leizel had seen to that, with the way she'd carried on, even though she hadn't really got burnt at all.

It's like people seeing things from different angles, and coming to different conclusions. A bit like what W.W. was trying to explain; about people witnessing events from different distances, and how those events appeared to be happening at differing times.

Maybe the world isn't such a black-and-white place, Phyllis decided. *Maybe right and wrong aren't that easy to work out.*

Maybe she needed some chocolate . . .

She was having breakfast with her dad the next day when she was jolted by a headline.

Harvey Wong was sitting opposite her and Daisy at the kitchen table, half-hidden behind his morning newspaper. Phyllis was layering her toast with chocolate-hazelnut spread when she looked up and saw the headline facing her.

She dropped her knife and it clattered off her plate and onto the table.

'Careful, love,' said her dad without looking around from behind his paper.

'*Rfff*,' said Daisy, waiting on the floor next to Phyllis's chair for any stray crumbs or bits of crust that Phyllis might feed her.

Phyllis said nothing. Her mouth was open as she read the front-page headline for the second time—it was almost as if the words just weren't sinking in to her head:

LOST SHAKESPEARE FOUND

ORIGINAL HANDWRITTEN SCRIPT OF SHAKESPEARE'S MISSING PLAY *CARDENIO* TO BE AUCTIONED

The Greatest Literary Discovery of the Last 400 Years—Written in Shakespeare's Own Hand—Experts Predict Astronomical Result

Immediately, Phyllis was filled with a huge, rolling ball of suspicion. This wasn't a coincidence—this was surely the work of the Colley woman.

'Dad? May I have the front page please?'

'Sure.' Without distracting himself from the paper—he was checking the stock reports, and this always took his full attention—he slid the front sheet of his newspaper out and handed it across the table.

'Thanks,' said Phyllis. She folded it over so she could read the article beneath the headline:

Exclusive report by E. Phillips Herrick

A play written by William Shakespeare, thought to have been lost since it was first performed in 1613, has reportedly been discovered and will be offered for sale next month at The House of Wendlebury's fine arts auctioneers.

The play, *Cardenio*, has long been presumed lost after it was staged by the theatre company The King's Men in London 400 years ago. Despite many efforts to find a copy of this legendary work, no trace of it—no fragments or scenes—have ever been located.

The discovery of any missing play

penned by Shakespeare, widely regarded as the greatest writer ever to have lived, is a ground-breaking event. But this is doubly ground-breaking: the manuscript copy of *Cardenio* being offered for sale is reportedly handwritten by Shakespeare himself. To find a lost Shakespeare play that has been written by the playwright's own hand is extraordinary.

It is the only time that anything of this nature has been discovered. Before this, there have only been six words written by Shakespeare's own hand thought to be still in existence. They are his name, written as his signature, on three separate wills.

Fine arts experts are confidently predicting that the handwritten manuscript will fetch a world-record price, because of its rarity and state of preservation. It is reputed to be in near mint condition.

It is expected that interest will be fierce, and buyers will be bidding from around the globe. Estimates are, according to a spokesperson from The House of Wendlebury's, impossible to make.

Whatever price the manuscript fetches, one thing is for certain: the auction world will be ablaze with excitement next month.

When Phyllis had finished reading the article, her hands were sweaty. This changed things. The handwritten manuscript of *Cardenio* couldn't have been bought and paid for at Isaac Jaggard's shop. *Cardenio* had been stolen!

Carefully she folded the paper along the borders of the article, using her thumbnail to make the folds scissor-sharp. Then she neatly tore the article out and folded it over.

'Dad?'

'That's me.'

'What time is it?'

Harvey's newspaper rustled as he checked his watch. 'A little before eight.'

Good, thought Phyllis. *He'll still be here.*

'I've gotta go,' she said.

Harvey looked over the paper at her. 'Where?' he asked.

'Downstairs.'

He gave her a *where exactly downstairs* look with his eyebrows.

'To the café,' she answered.

'Okay. Make sure you're back before I head off to the office, all right?'

'Sure.' She pocketed the newspaper article, tore off a crust from her toast, popped it down into Daisy's grateful mouth, and hurried out of the kitchen.

As soon as Phyllis went into The Délicieux Café, she was almost pounced upon by Pascaline Ravissant's husband, Pierre.

'Ah *bonjour*, my favourite conjuror! Eet 'as been too lerng zince I 'ave been seeing you!'

'*Bonjour*, Pierre,' Phyllis greeted him as she scanned the café.

'Whert would you like zis merning?' he asked, addressing her over his shoulder as he always did with his customers.

'Um . . .'

'I know! Ze *pain au chocolat, oui*? Zat erlways teeckles yer tastebuds, you leetle chocaholeec.' He smiled and wiggled his moustache at her.

Phyllis saw who she was looking for. 'Oh! Yes please, that'd be peachy, Pierre. Thank you.'

'Peachy ees whert I do,' he said. 'Cerming right erp.'

He winked at her and sped off to the counter. She hurried over to the corner table, where Barry Inglis was half-slumped across his newspaper. He had the look of a man who had just been told that he had to work for the next fortnight without any break at all.

'Hey, Chief Inspector! You all right?'

He looked up, his eyes clouded. 'Miss Wong. How good to see you. Please, have a seat.'

She pulled out the chair opposite him and plonked herself onto it. 'I've seen the headline,' she said quickly, pulling it out of her pocket and showing it to him.

'As have I, Miss Wong. As have I.' He displayed the front page of his newspaper to her. 'Good lord, this is getting fishier and fishier.'

'You can say that again.'

He sighed, and had a slow sip of his double espresso. 'As you know, for some time I've had my doubts about all these Shakespeare Folios turning up one after the other,' he told her. 'They've been popping up too frequently to be . . .' he thought for a moment, '. . . to be real. But, real they seem. Heavens above, the experts have tested them and every time they find that they're all genuine books from 1623. They haven't been faked. And now, this!'

'A lost play,' said Phyllis.

'In the Bard's own hand,' Barry added, in a hopeless sort of voice. 'You can't imagine how much extra work this means for the Squad. We got the heads-up about this *Cardenio* business yesterday from Wendlebury's—they came to us before they went to the press—and to say I've had a sleepless night, Miss Wong, would be the understatement of the century.'

Pierre appeared by Phyllis's elbow and placed her chocolate croissant on the table, along with a big glass of water. 'Zere, you breelliernt girl. Enjoy!'

'Another double espresso, *s'il vous plaît*, Pierre,' said Barry. 'Oh, merciful heavens, make that a quadruple! I'm gonna need all the help I can get today.'

'Bert erf curse, Chief Inspecteur!' And, with another wiggle of his moustache, Pierre was off again.

'No,' Barry continued, 'I've been on the net all night, finding out anything I can about *Cardenio* and its history. Humph. That's the one good thing about the internet, I suppose—at least I can work from home, and in my pyjamas.'

Phyllis smirked and tried not to giggle— somehow she couldn't imagine Chief Inspector Barry Inglis in anything but his dark blue suit or his tennis whites, which he wore whenever he played on Sunday mornings. She wondered whether he had a teddy bear for company.

'So did you discover any ground-breaking facts?' she asked.

He shook his head. 'Not much, apart from what we've both read in this morning's paper. *Cardenio*'s been the Holy Grail, if you like, of the theatrical and the literary worlds for centuries. People have been hoping and searching for it. And now . . . here it is! Or soon will be.'

'I bet it'll go for a fortune,' said Phyllis.

'Without a doubt, Miss Wong. We're sure

that every government of every country that has a serious interest in English literature and the written word will be making a bid. Why, to have the original handwritten copy of a Shakespeare play in its national library would do any nation proud. And then there are the private collectors to think about as well. There are some mighty rich people out there, some people who have so much moolah that they could *buy* a small country if they wanted to. I well imagine that some of those individuals will be in on the bidding action, come next month.'

He ran a hand through his sandy hair, pushing it back off his forehead.

'How much do you think it might fetch?' asked Phyllis, taking a bite of her croissant.

'Ah. We have no real idea. It's almost impossible to guesstimate, because nothing like it has ever appeared on the market before. But just between you and me—' he leant towards her—'we're thinking it could go for as much as five hundred million dollars!'

Phyllis did a spit-take, sending a small shower of moistened crumbs into Barry's face.

Politely, without making any fuss, he took out his white handkerchief and wiped them away. 'I don't blame you for that reaction one little bit, Miss Wong. I almost did the same thing when I realised it myself.'

Phyllis started feeling a small knot of anger somewhere deep inside her. 'Chief Inspector?'

'Yes? Ah, *merci*, Pierre.'

'*De rien*, Chief Inspecteur,' said Pierre, depositing the quadruple espresso in front of Barry and hurrying away.

'Well,' said Phyllis, 'you know how this *Cardenio* is Shakespeare's actual foul papers?'

Barry gave her a sudden look. 'You never fail to impress me, Miss Wong. How do you know about foul papers? I only just learnt the term last night, while I was researching . . .'

'Oh, I found out about it just recently too,' she told him.

'Hmm,' hmmed Barry Inglis.

'I also found out that Shakespeare himself never let his foul papers out of his sight. He protected them and guarded them and no one was ever allowed to have them but him.'

'Yes? Your point being?'

'So what if the foul papers of *Cardenio have been stolen*?'

'Stolen?'

'Stolen. That'd be a crime, wouldn't it?'

He frowned. 'Of course it would be. But we'd have to prove that they'd been stolen. We'd have to establish that a theft had taken place. And if a theft *has* taken place, then it must've happened a long time ago. According to all the reports I've read, *Cardenio* was lost just after it was performed in 1613. So if the foul papers were stolen around that time, it'd be very difficult—no, I dare say *impossible*—to go back and reconstruct the crime and find the perpetrator.'

'Impossible?'

'Of course. Not even your magic could work it out, Miss Wong.'

She gave him her inscrutable smile and said nothing.

Barry sipped his espresso and pulled a face as though he had just sat in a bucket of custard. 'Good lord, that's strong!' He put the cup down. 'And furthermore, Miss Wong, if we *did* establish that the foul papers were stolen, it would also be next to impossible to go back through history and trace the path of the manuscript. Who owned it, who sold it to whom, that sort of thing.'

'I see,' Phyllis said.

'Unless the foul papers had been kept in a secret private collection somewhere, and this was a *recent* theft, well—' Just then, Barry's phone rang. He pulled it out of his pocket. 'Inglis speaking. Morning, Chatterton.'

Phyllis listened as Barry listened.

'Really?' he said. 'Next week? And we can examine it then? . . . Uh-huh. Okay . . . Is that a fact? I can't say that that surprises me, I sort of thought it'd be the case . . . Strange, though, don't you think? . . . Of course you would . . . Okay, thanks for the update, Pinkie.' And he rang off.

'That was one of my men, on the case,' Barry told Phyllis. He sipped his coffee and pulled his bucket-of-custard face again. 'Not that we've really *got* a case; more like a bag full of suspicions.'

'What did he say?' Phyllis asked.

Barry regarded her closely. 'This isn't to go any further, right?'

'Right.'

Barry lowered his voice. 'He told me that The House of Wendlebury's don't actually have the foul papers yet. They won't have them until late next week. So their experts—and my Squad—can't inspect or do any testing on the manuscript until then.'

'Why haven't they got it?' asked Phyllis, her eyes narrowing.

'The seller has to travel with it. Seems she won't send it on before she arrives—she wants to be with it at all times. And who could blame her? If it were mine, I wouldn't let it out of my sight for a split second. That's all it takes for something to go missing, Miss Wong, believe you me. A split second can make all the difference and change everything . . .'

'Where's she travelling from?'

'Now that, I do not know,' replied Barry Inglis.

'Ah-ha,' murmured Phyllis, as she realised. *She hasn't got it yet. She's only* promised *it to the auctioneers, but she still has to steal it!* 'Did you say next week they'll have the foul papers?'

'I did. That's when Wendlebury's will see *Cardenio.*'

Phyllis stood. 'Thanks for talking to me. I have to go now. Bye!'

'Go carefully,' Barry Inglis said.

She smiled and waved at him, and waved at Pierre too as she left the café. She *would* go carefully. She had to be careful, and she had to go now. She knew exactly what she had to do.

She had to visit Mr Shakespeare himself!

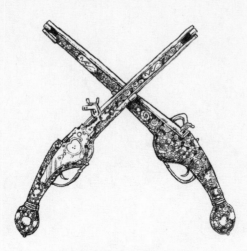

PART THREE

Now you see it . . .

Frustrations

Mistress Vesta Colley looked at her reflection in the mirror on her dressing table in her lavish suite at the Millennium Hotel. She was tired, and it showed, especially in her one droopy eye. She frowned as she dabbed at her dark lipstick with the corner of a fine linen handkerchief.

She was not happy.

It shouldn't be taking this long, she thought as she threw down the handkerchief and picked up her gold-plated hairbrush. *It has never taken this long in the past.*

With annoyed strokes, she began brushing her curls, letting the fine bristles of the brush pull through them as though they were trying to unknot the problem facing her. Behind her, on top of one of the antique tables, her red-eyed rodent companion, Glory, was creeping back and forth, watching her in the mirror.

'I can't understand it, my dear Glory,' muttered Vesta Colley as she drew the brush through her

251

hair. 'It's never taken me this amount of time to find a set of stairs upon which to Transit.'

'*Squeeeetch-squeeeetch-squeeeetch*,' squeaked Glory. She stopped creeping and sat there, still as a stone.

'It is peculiar,' Vesta Colley said to her reflection. 'I have been searching for days. But to no avail. Every staircase I come to—every staircase upon which I sense that there will be a Pocket, that there *should* be a Pocket—is empty. I am sure that there are people in this city who see me and who think that I am a madwoman, the way I have been constantly rushing up and down stairs. And, when I do find some stairs with a Pocket on them, the Pocket isn't strong enough. Three times now, Glory, *three times*, I have Transited through these minor Pockets, only to find myself back in Time just a week or a few days before I have left this place, not back to the Time I need. The Pockets are weak, my ratty friend. I need a *strong* Pocket, a powerful transporter . . .'

'*Squeeeetch-squeeeetch-squeeeetch*,' squeaked the rat.

Vesta Colley finished with her hair and banged the brush down. 'And, whereas in the past I have been able to return to a set of stairs where I know there has been a Pocket that I have Transited through successfully—why, now when I revisit those stairs, the Pocket is no longer there! What is going on? This has never been the case of things before! Not in all my five hundred and seventy-three years of Transiting have I known Pockets to disappear. They have shifted about, yes, but to disappear? No, things have changed, Glory. Things are different now . . .'

She picked up a small pair of eighteen-carat gold scissors and began trimming her fingernails. She snipped her thumbnail quickly, snappily, impatiently.

'What has changed, Glory, that I am having these difficulties? It seems as if,' she continued snipping the nail on her next finger, 'it seems as if there is not room enough now. Maybe the highway back is becoming more crowded . . . maybe there are other Transiters taking my routes, using my Pockets, venturing into the vortexes that are mine, and *mine alone*!'

With a sudden snip, she accidentally cut into the flesh under her fingernail. A small line of deep red appeared there, and she winced. 'Fie!' she exclaimed, watching as the blood welled up. Vesta Colley hated disfigurement of any kind, especially when it came to herself—she always desired to be as perfect in appearance as she could, despite her lazy, droopy eye.

'*Squeeeetch-squeeeetch-squeeeetch!*' Glory smelled the blood and scampered across the table, down onto the floor, up the back of the chair, down Vesta Colley's arm and onto the dressing table. There she started licking the rich redness from her mistress's finger.

Colley closed her eyes. 'Dear Glory,' she murmured. 'I must keep trying. I *will* get my prize. And then, with all the wealth it will give me, all the great richness, I shall stop my Transiting . . . it is wearing me down, Glory; my eyes can only take so much. Yes, I shall retire on the spoils of my final accomplishment and become powerful—powerful in ways I have never been able.'

She stared deeply into the mirror, and spoke in a faraway voice: 'I will buy entire cities, Glory, all the buildings and roads and parks and harbours in them. I shall own these things, and I shall own the *people* who live and work there. I shall be more powerful than a Queen or a President. I shall control *all that is mine.*'

She looked down at the rat cleaning her wound. 'Ah, my dear Glory . . . that is good . . . that is *good.*'

Beginners please

Phyllis held the small piece of metal type from Isaac Jaggard's tightly in her fist. The wind was buffeting her, blowing her almost inside-out, and the light was fading until the blackness of the years, hanging like a heavy curtain around her, smothered the way ahead.

Her stomach rose and fell; she battled to breathe against the fierce rush of air that barraged her nostrils. From somewhere right behind her, she could sense something, something close to her, almost touching her. It was as if the wind was so strong, the force of the gale so rough, that it was grabbing at her one moment and thrusting her onwards the next . . .

She leant forward into the tremendous force, putting her head down against her chest. She held her shoulder bag firmly against her hip, and felt Daisy wriggling around frantically inside it. The little dog had been clingy before Phyllis had left, and hadn't let Phyllis out of her sight, following her around her room and then down into the basement, and even when Phyllis had offered her a small biscuit-treat, Daisy hadn't been interested in it. All she had wanted was to be with Phyllis, and so Phyllis was left with no choice but to take her small four-pawed pal along with her.

Back to a faraway London.

Phyllis patted the outside of the bag, trying to soothe Daisy inside it. The young conjuror leant further into the relentless wind, pressing her chin against her chest, scrunching her eyes shut as tightly as she could.

I hope this bit of type will take me where I need to go, she thought. *I hope it's right* . . .

Then she began to hear the vibrating, soft, high-pitched humming. The darkness on the other side of her eyelids started to melt away, and a light was emerging. The wind was dropping, and Phyllis leant back, and back further, until she was standing upright again.

The last vestiges of the breeze faded away; Phyllis's body trembled uncontrollably for a few moments; her legs were hollow and shaky. She felt her eyes throbbing as she opened them.

She'd arrived.

She did two things straightaway: she opened the top of her bag and reached inside to give Daisy a loving pat and ear-cuddle. And, as she told

Daisy that everything was okay, Phyllis looked around at their whereabouts.

She was at the bottom of some wooden stairs. She peered up and saw what looked like a small, square trapdoor. It was open, and sunlight was streaming down onto the stairs.

Daisy popped her head out of the shoulder bag and she too peered up. '*Rrrrr?*' she growled uncertainly.

'Let's go see where we are, Daisy girl,' whispered Phyllis.

She started up the stairs, when all at once there was a loud BANG!

Phyllis's head snapped up to see a large wooden keg slamming and rolling down the stairs towards her and Daisy. It was coming so fast—like a torpedo—that Phyllis momentarily froze. But then her instincts kicked in and, quickly, just as the keg was about to flatten them, she pressed herself and Daisy and her shoulder bag hard against the stone wall at her side and sucked her stomach in.

With only a few millimetres to spare, the big, heavy keg crashed past them, clunking and bumping down the rest of the staircase, and came to an abrupt stop on the gloomy floor below.

'*Arf! Arf! Arf! Arf! Arf! Arf!*' barked Daisy at the top of her lungs.

Phyllis looked down at the bottom of the stairs and saw other wooden kegs stacked on the floor there. 'We must be in a storage room of some tavern or inn or something,' she said to Daisy. 'I think we'd better vamoose, quick smart!'

She clutched her bag to her side and dashed up the stairs, squeezing through the trapdoor and up, out onto the street and well clear of the trapdoor.

Taking cover in front of the narrow leadlight windows of a candlemaker's shop, she smiled as she beheld everything around her. The people milling about the small street were dressed in similar fashions to those she'd encountered when she had Transited to visit Isaac Jaggard—the women's skirts and bodices, the men's doublets and breeches and their coats and hats all suggested to Phyllis that she was in the right Time frame.

But what *exactly* was the Time?

Her legs were not shaking as much now, and she could feel her stomach settling. Daisy poked her head and snout out of the bag again and Phyllis gently rubbed the top of her head, next to her permanently folded-over ear. 'Where are we, Miss Daisy?' she asked quietly. '*When* are we?'

At that moment, they heard a bell ringing loudly. The sound was coming from around the corner, and was heading in their direction. Daisy's ears swivelled towards the ringing, and she craned her neck.

Dong-ding-dong-ding-dong-ding-dong!

Then a man's voice could be heard, between the bell's peals. 'Hear ye, hear ye, good citizens of London town!'

Phyllis felt her heart quicken—they were in the right place!

The man came around the corner. He was a portly chap, dressed in a knee-length red robe, trimmed with white fur, and he wore a large, soft felt hat with a broad feather in it. He was shaking the bell vigorously—a fat, shining brass bell with a heavy oak handle—and its clangings echoed up and down the streets.

'Hear ye, hear ye, good citizens of London town,' he repeated loudly between the clanging.

'He's the Town Crier,' Phyllis whispered to Daisy. 'He's what they have instead of a newspaper . . .'

'Ah!' shouted a man hurrying to get past the Crier. 'What is't thou mammers about today, you droning, swag-bellied Bellman?'

The Crier gave the man a withering look and ignored his insults. 'Here be the news for today,' he cried, 'December the 20th in the Year of Our Lord, Sixteen Hundred and Twelve!'

Phyllis's heart quickened some more—they were in the right Time!

'Ah, take thy news and blow it out thy pantaloons, you fat-kidneyed harpy!' a woman shouted at the Crier.

The Crier rang his bell sharply at her, as if to say, *go away and fall into the nearest sewer, where you belong.*

'Ye beslubbering foot-licker!' a man yelled down at him from the upper-floor window of a house across the street. 'Make thyself gone!'

'Enshut thy trap-hole!' proclaimed the Crier, ringing his bell fiercely up at him as though it were a whip.

'Away with you, you mountain of wobbly flesh!' shouted the man, and many in the street laughed heartily.

The Crier took a deep breath and opened his mouth to start announcing the daily news when someone threw a rotting cabbage at him, knocking his hat into the gutter.

Phyllis got the impression that the Town Crier was not all that popular in this neighbourhood. 'C'mon,' she said to Daisy, 'let's away.'

'Rrff,' said Daisy.

Phyllis edged her way towards the far end of the street. As she went, she took her journal from her coat pocket and quickly thumbed through it to the map she'd copied down from an internet site she'd found a few hours earlier. It showed the streets of London, circa 1610. (Phyllis was glad of the internet when it came to things like this—you could find out just about anything if you knew what to look for.)

Most importantly, the map she'd copied into her journal showed the street in which the Globe Theatre was to be found—Park Street in Southwark. The Globe was where Shakespeare and his company of actors rehearsed and performed their plays.

A cold wind was blowing as Phyllis paused at the end of the street to get her bearings. Up on the side of the corner house was a narrow sign: *Threadneedle Street*. She found where she was on her map and saw that she had a bit of a way to walk: down Bishopgate Street to London Bridge, then across the bridge and right onto the Bankside. The Globe Theatre was a short walk along the River of Thames.

'Let's go, Daisy, my girl,' she said.

Daisy blinked her big brown eyes and snuggled deeper into the bag, out of the cold.

Phyllis pulled her collar tighter around her neck. She looked up at the clouds. They looked like they were carrying snow and that it wouldn't be too far away. She shivered; then she turned right out of Threadneedle Street and started for the theatre.

Not far behind her, someone else shivered too and wished that the snow would stay away as, furtively and closely, that person followed in Phyllis Wong's footsteps.

❋

It was cold crossing London Bridge, and windy. As Phyllis continued along the bank of the Thames, the chill breeze swept across the water and up at her, like an invisible, flapping curtain of iciness.

She hurried along. There were fewer people here on this side of the river, and the streets were not so close together. Some of the people she passed stared at her; others ignored her. No one bothered her; most folk were hurrying to get indoors away from the cold, or too busy to take any notice of this young, black-clothed girl walking purposefully, head down and eyes bright (with only the faintest glimmers of Transit green in them).

As she went, she smelled the stomach-churning stench that was wafting up from all the nearby tanneries. She tried not to breathe too deeply; after her Transiting, the last thing she wanted was more tummy upsets from such an awful smell.

Daisy curled herself into a tight ball inside Phyllis's bag. The little dog was feeling only slightly unsettled—being close by Phyllis's side was what she wanted, and right by Phyllis's side was exactly where Daisy was right now.

At last, Phyllis saw it: a large, circular, white building with a thatched roof. She recognised it from pictures she'd seen on the net. It was the Globe Theatre.

She felt light-headed as she approached the famous building. She came to a wall surrounding it, with a set of tall oak doors set into the brickwork. One of the doors was partly open.

Phyllis took a deep breath and ducked through the doorway, into a deserted courtyard that lay between the wall and the outside of the theatre. She stopped in the courtyard and looked up at the building. It was three storeys tall, with a couple of towers built into its sides. Here and there, around its whitewashed walls, small windows were dotted about.

Phyllis rubbed Daisy through her bag. 'We've got to get inside the theatre,' she said quietly.

Daisy poked out her head and licked Phyllis's wrist.

'There's how,' Phyllis murmured, spying a doorway over to the left, in one of the towers. 'Down you go, Daisy, best you stay out of sight for a while . . .'

The little dog snuggled back into the soft darkness of Phyllis's bag, and Phyllis went up to the door. Gently she pushed it. It was heavy, but it opened smoothly.

She ventured through the doorway, into the gloominess ahead. There were no candles or lamps burning here in the tower; the only light coming in was from the pale sunlight that, when it wasn't being covered by the clouds outside, was shining feebly through the narrow windows.

Phyllis let her eyes get used to the gloom. Then she saw, rising up in front of her, a narrow set of wooden stairs. Towards the top, they disappeared around a corner. She imagined that the auditorium and the stage might be to her left, on the other side of the wall next to her.

She was about to go up the stairs to see if her hunch was right, when, suddenly, a door at the foot of the stairs—a door she hadn't seen in the gloom—swung open and a ruddy-faced man came out. He saw Phyllis immediately, but didn't look surprised. Instead he gave her an impatient look.

'You're late,' he said in a gruff voice.

Phyllis blinked.

'But you're lucky,' he went on. 'The gentlemen still be here. Wait there, and be ready to go on.'

'Um . . . Yes, sir,' said Phyllis.

In a flash, the red-faced man went out through the door. Phyllis heard him calling out, 'There be one more, just arrived. Are ye still interested?'

'Send him in,' came another voice, from further away.

Phyllis wondered what was going on. In the whirlwind seconds of what was to happen next, she quickly found out.

The ruddy-faced man appeared again. 'Look you sharply,' he barked at Phyllis. 'They're ready for you now. Through here and do not tarry.' He held the door open and almost shoved Phyllis through.

And immediately her eyes went as big as plates.

She was standing on the stage, a big, wide stage with a column on each side. The columns looked like marble, crowned with gold-painted capitals, and they rose up to a ceiling which covered the back half of the stage. Phyllis looked up and she smiled as she saw the sun and the moon and a constellation of stars, all of which had been painted brightly and boldly onto the ceiling. It felt like an enchanted place, and Phyllis liked it straightaway.

She looked out, ahead of her, to see a vast empty yard. This, she knew, was where the groundlings—the people who bought the cheapest tickets to the plays—stood to watch, clustered around close to the front of the stage and filling the yard. On all sides of the groundlings' pit, rising up the full three storeys, were tiers of enclosed rooms in which the box seats were set. The back walls of some of the boxes had been painted with scenes of fields and ancient Greek temples and other lavish images. Tickets to these rooms were more expensive, as they permitted a better view of the stage and all the action.

Her gaze rose higher, and she saw, at the very top of the theatre, the sky, with the clouds rolling gently across it. There was no roof at all above the groundlings' area. No wonder the tickets for that section were cheap—when it rained, the ground-lings would get drenched!

I'm here, she thought, her spine tingling and zingling and her eyes filling with the wonder of the place. *I'm on the stage of the Globe Theatre . . .*

A voice from above made her start. 'And what are you?' it asked, loudly and clearly. It was certainly the voice of an actor.

Phyllis looked up, and all around. She saw, in one of the boxes on the first tier directly in front of the stage, two figures. She could only see their outlines; the day was not bright and the light was gloomy, especially in the boxes which *did* have ceilings. And there seemed to be a fine fog, a spindly sort of mist, that was floating about the building.

Phyllis gulped. She was used to being on stages when she performed, but this stage was different—bigger and more open and more . . . *raw*.

'I say,' repeated the shadowy man, 'what are you?'

In her best, most confident stage voice, she answered: 'I am a performer, sir.'

'A performer?'

'Yes, sir.'

She saw the outline of the man who had spoken move closer to the other man, and she could see the other man's head nodding. Then the first man spoke again: 'A performer? And thou art a *girl*?'

'I am,' answered Phyllis Wong.

'Strange that a girl should call herself a *performer.*'

'Where I come from,' Phyllis called up into the smoky-looking mist, 'girls can be performers.'

There was silence. A shaft of sunlight broke through the clouds, onto the stage, and Phyllis put a hand above her eyes to shield them from the glare as she kept looking up.

Then the voice spoke again: 'It is obvious, indeed, that thou comest from a very different clime to the stage upon which you find yourself.'

You can say that again, Phyllis thought. She smiled up at the shadowy men.

'We are curious. What *sort* of performer art thou? Are you an actor? An acrobat, or a singer or a balladeer? A dancer, perhaps?'

'I am a conjuror,' Phyllis answered proudly.

'A conjuror?' repeated the man.

'A prestidigitator,' she said.

She saw, through the glare and the mist, the second man writing something down with what looked like a long feather quill.

'A magician,' she added.

'Oddsbodkins! We have not had anyone with your speciality during the auditions.'

'Auditions?' said Phyllis.

'Aye. That is not why you are here? Wherefore else wouldst thou come today?'

'Oh. Of course. That's why I'm here; to audition for your company.'

'Well, then, present us some of your magic . . . erm . . . what is thy name, young woman?'

'Phyllis. Phyllis Wong.'

She saw the second man's quill moving again.

'Well, Phyllis Wong,' the first man called down, 'amaze us with your ways. We await with bated breath!'

Phyllis smiled. She took her hand away from her brow and gently placed her bag by her feet. 'Gentlemen, behold my conjurations!'

And the second man above her scribbled eagerly.

Don't call us . . .

Phyllis rolled up the sleeves of her black coat, all the way to her elbows. It was chilly on the stage of the Globe, and she felt her arms go all goose-pimply.

'Behold, gentlemen,' she declaimed boldly. 'Nothing up my sleeves . . .'

From above, the second shadowy figure scrawled away with his feather quill.

Phyllis reached down and picked up her shoulder bag. She opened it and out popped Daisy's head. The little dog blinked, wondering at her surroundings, and Phyllis patted her soothingly on her neck. 'Allow me to present to you,' Phyllis called to the men above, 'my faithful assistant, Daisy.'

'*Rerf!*' barked Daisy, looking all around.

The first man chuckled. 'A most noble assistant, Phyllis Wong,' he called down.

'I thank you,' said Phyllis. 'Watch her carefully, for she, like me, is a performer of magic!'

Phyllis saw both of the silhouetted figures

leaning forward, resting their arms on the low wall at the front of their box.

Gently, she pushed Daisy back down into the bag, and then she closed the top. She held the bag aloft, over her head, and she spoke in the mysterious sort of voice she always used whenever she said magic words: 'Abracadabra . . .'

The second gentleman leant back and scribbled that down.

'Now you see her,' announced Phyllis. She brought the bag down and held it in front of her. Then she opened it wide, as wide as it could be opened, and held it out so that the two men were able to see down into the inside of it. 'Now you don't!'

The men craned their necks and inspected, as best they could from that distance, the interior of Phyllis's shoulder bag. It was empty! All they could see was the black velvet lining, and nothing else.

Phyllis put her hand under the bag and pushed the empty black interior upwards, turning the bag inside-out.

'The dog has vanished!' gasped the second man.

'Vanished into thin air!' said Phyllis, holding the bag higher to afford them a better view.

'Vanished into thin air,' repeated the second man. 'I like that. Aye, a fine way to put it.' And he quickly wrote the phrase down, his feather quill dancing away in the gloom.

'Astounding!' exclaimed the first man.

Phyllis turned the bag the right way inwards. 'And now,' she continued, 'for a change . . . let me *produce* some change.'

She placed the bag carefully at her feet again and reached inside (she gave her furry companion a *good work, Daisy, you're a star* sort of pat as she did this). She fiddled about for a moment, then took out a long yellow fan. Phyllis straightened up and, with a snap of her wrist, the fan opened. Finely penned Chinese calligraphy was painted in red along the fan's folds.

Phyllis wafted herself with the fan, and then waved it in wide circles about herself. The graceful curves it made through the air were like the wings of a beautiful, bright bird floating through the sky.

She showed the fan on both sides as she let it sail around her. Then, with another snap of her wrist, the fan was closed again.

Phyllis saw a metal pot at the front of the stage, a few feet in front of her. She advanced towards the pot, deciding to use it in this trick. She raised the closed fan before her and waved it. In a blink, a big, shiny gold coin appeared at the top of the fan!

She reached up with her other hand and took the coin. This she held between her thumb and first finger, giving her spectators a good view of it. After a few seconds, she tossed the coin across the stage and into the metal pot. It made a loud CLINK sound as it dropped inside.

(It also made a sort of *squelchy* sound, which Phyllis hadn't expected. She thought that the pot was probably a spittoon, and it probably had contents that she didn't want to think about too closely.)

The men upstairs looked at each other, then turned their attention back to the stage.

Phyllis raised the fan again, and once more a large, gleaming gold coin appeared at the end of it. She took the coin away, held it up for all to see, then again she tossed it into the spittoon. There was another CLINK and a soft *squelch*.

She repeated the action another five times, every time making a beautiful gold coin appear and every time taking it, displaying it and then throwing it into the spittoon. The action grew faster as each coin appeared and was deposited into the spittoon. CLINK *squelch* CLINK *squelch* CLINK *squelch* CLINK *squelch* CLINK *squelch*! (Phyllis was glad that this trick didn't require her to retrieve those coins from that insalubrious receptacle.)

Finally, she opened the fan and displayed both sides. The fan was empty—there were no pockets or compartments or secret places on it. It was just an ordinary, elegant fan.

Both men upstairs clapped warmly.

'Most wonderful!' said the first.

'Excellent, indeed, madam!' called the second.

'Thank you, sirs,' Phyllis said, taking a small bow.

'Now, let us hear thy song.'

'Um . . .' Phyllis stared up at the two shadowy men. 'My song?'

'Yes, thy song. Of course all actors—all *performers*—must present a song as part of their audition. We need to hear if thou art able to carry a tune, and do it sweetly.'

'Oh.' Phyllis thought quickly. *A song* . . . Then she remembered a tune that she had heard her great-grandfather performing in one of his first Hollywood movies, a short comedy titled *Neddy Noblock Comes to Town*. She'd learnt the words to the song by heart when she was younger and she thought she could remember most of them now. There was something special about the song; it always reminded her of W.W. and, now that she and he were sharing the secrets of Transiting, it would take on a new importance for her as she sang it here.

But, she thought, *it might need a little something to liven it up.*

'Well?' one of the men called down. 'Are we going to be blessed with thy singing or shall we wait here all day?'

Phyllis smiled up at their silhouettes. She crouched down, plunged her hand back into her shoulder bag (Daisy gave her fingers a quick lick), delved around in there for a bit and pulled her hand out again.

Then she took a deep breath, counted to three in her head and, with all the loudness she could muster, she began to sing:

'First you bring me laughs, then I have
    sorrow,
you're just here today and gone
    tomorrow,
why am I left here on my own?
Tell me, why must I always be alone?

'I want to travel with you,
do what you do,
see what you see—and I'll be happy.'

The two men looked at each other and—unbeknown to Phyllis—they both winced. For, to tell the truth, Phyllis Wong was far better at performing magic than she was at singing songs.

Then, as she sang on, Phyllis raised her right arm towards the men in the balcony, and a long arc of brilliant yellow flames *whoooooooshed* out towards them. It shot across the stage before petering away to nothing.

'Ye Gods!' exclaimed the first man.

'Zounds!' cried the other.

Phyllis sang on:

'I want to skip when you skip,
flip when you flip,
dip when you dip—and I'll be happy.'

Phyllis raised her other arm now, and sent a long shower of fire off to the left. *Whoooooooooosh!* It blazed for mere seconds before disappearing.

'If you go north to south,
or east to west,
I'll follow you, I will,
and everything will be best.

'I want to travel with you,
do what you do,
see what you see—and I'll be happy.'

Another brilliant blaze shot out from her right hand with another soft *whooooooooosh!*

Then something unexpected happened: as Phyllis kept singing, and as she shot out the flames from her hands, *music started to play*—jaunty, chiming music that accompanied her words and kept the tune perfectly. Phyllis looked around, but she couldn't see where it was coming from. The men above looked around, too; they were likewise surprised.

The unexpected, chiming music swelled her up with a new gusto, and she sang on:

> '*I want to travel with you, could be a*
> > *treat to*
> *do what you do, it'd be sweet to*
> *see what you see—and make it snappy!*
>
> '*I want to skip when you skip, if I could only*
> *flip when you flip, we won't be lonely,*
> *dip when you dip—and I'll be happy.*
>
> '*If you go north to south, let me too,*
> *or east to west, you ought to know,*
> *I'll follow you, I will,*
> *and things will be best.*
>
> '*I want to travel with you,*'
>
> (Flames shot to the left—*whooooosh!*)
>
> '*do what you do,*'
>
> (Flames shot to the right—*whooooosh!*)
>
> '*see what you see—and I'll be happy.*'

276

Suddenly the music stopped abruptly, and the ruddy-faced man who had shown Phyllis onto the stage burst forth from the wings. He was brandishing a long sword in one hand, and with the other he was holding, by the scruff of the neck, a short red-bearded person with a balding head and spectacles.

'What witchcraft is this?' the ruddy-faced man demanded angrily, pointing the sword at Phyllis. 'What sorcery? Fire from the fingertips?'

Phyllis snatched up her bag and backed away, but he came closer.

'And *red-bearded dwarfs*?' The man's cheeks were turning even more scarlet. He looked up at the two men in the box. 'See, sirs, what I find backstage, banging away on empty and half-filled beer bottles with a couple of spoons? The sorceress brings a dwarf with her! 'Tis evil, that's what it be! 'Twill bring a plague upon our house!'

Phyllis was trembling.

The two men in the box stood. Then the second man, still holding his quill and writing paper, vaulted swiftly over the front of the box and landed in a crouching position on a big pile of dark purple curtains that had been put in the groundlings' pit, ready to be hung later.

Gracefully he stood and faced Phyllis, his single gold earring glinting, as were his dark, deep eyes.

Phyllis gasped. For the first time, she was able to see the man's face—a face she had seen in paintings and engravings many times recently. 'Mr . . . Mr Shakespeare,' she stammered.

William Shakespeare slid his quill and paper into the side pocket of his dark brown coat. He straightened his broad white collar and said to the man with the sword, 'Nay, Ralph, she is not a sorceress.'

'But the fire, Mr Shakespeare,' said the ruddy-faced man, his blade still pointed at Phyllis, his hold on the dwarf still firm. 'She brings the flames; she brings the dwarf! She be diabolical!'

'Nay, Ralph, what you saw was merely the latest thing in stagecraft. A new invention for the theatre. I have heard that in the distant Orient the actors possess such marvellous effects. I have been told that things of fire are harnessed there and used for great spectacular occasions . . .'

'I . . . I'm not a witch,' Phyllis said, looking nervously at the point of the man's sword. 'I'm a stage magician.'

'That she is,' said William Shakespeare.

Slowly, the man lowered his sword, but his eyes still harboured a blazing distrust of Phyllis, and a terror of the dwarf he was holding.

By this time the other gentleman had arrived in the groundlings' pit. 'That be right, Mr Heminges?' asked Ralph.

'Aye, Ralph,' said John Heminges.

Ralph grunted, and shook his head—he was still not fully convinced.

Now that Phyllis was no longer getting the death-stare, she got a good look for the first time at the red-bearded dwarf who was squirming in Ralph's grasp. 'What the dickens?' she blurted.

'What the dickens?' repeated Mr Shakespeare. 'That is good . . .' He whipped out his quill and paper and scribbled it down.

Phyllis's mouth was open as she watched the dwarf struggling. 'Let me go!' he was grumbling. 'Stop bumping me!'

'*Bumping?*' Shakespeare said, stroking his short beard. 'I like this, too.' Quickly he wrote down the word.

'Let him go, Ralph,' said John Heminges.

With a forceful shove, Ralph released his grip.

'What art thou doing here, dwarf?' asked Mr Heminges.

'I . . . I just . . .' began the short fellow.

'I know why he be here,' said Ralph, his sword moving through the air like the tail of a cat, ready to pounce. 'He's here to steal. He's here to sniff about for your plays, Mr Shakespeare!'

At this, Shakespeare's manner seemed to change. A dark look crept across his face, and he glared at the dwarf. 'Is that right, thou false, cunning villain?'

'Steal?' squeaked the dwarf. 'No, no, no, I'm with her!'

Phyllis gasped. 'How?'

Shakespeare turned his glare to Phyllis. 'Well, Phyllis Wong? Is this the truth?'

Phyllis just shook her head in disbelief. She didn't know what to say.

'Tell me,' Shakespeare said to her, taking a slender pearl-handled dagger from the garter on his tights, 'why exactly be thou here? Thou didst not arrive at the Globe to audition for our company, didst thou?'

Phyllis was sweating. She clutched Daisy in her bag close to her side. 'I . . . I came to . . . to warn you about *Cardenio*,' she said desperately.

Mr Shakespeare's eyes widened with fury. '*Cardenio*?'

Phyllis nodded.

Shakespeare glanced at John Heminges. Then he said to Phyllis, in a low and wary voice, 'How know'st thou of *Cardenio*? Nobody is privy to this work. I have barely finished writing it. How art thou aware of it?' He came towards her urgently, the dagger before him.

'Mr Shakespeare, you must safeguard it,' Phyllis urged. 'Someone is going to steal it! You must—'

'We must ensure that you and your short companion do not tell anyone of this!' Shakespeare interrupted her. 'We are having too many of our plays being copied and pirated by rogues who come in here, stealing my words, writing them down as the actors deliver them on the stage! Now you tell me that my new play is to go this same route? Before it has even been *performed*? We must stop you from your felonious purpose!'

While everyone was watching Phyllis and Shakespeare, the dwarf, unseen, reached into a pack he was wearing strapped to his back. He pulled out a small black console and pressed a button on its side.

'Aye,' said John Heminges. 'It was lunacy of us to even watch this girl. Children should not be in the theatre, and girls are not allowed on the stage— why, we would be arrested and the theatre shut down if it were discovered!'

'Aye,' Shakespeare said. 'Our curiosity got the better of us today. Ralph, take them to the property room beneath the stage. Lock them away until we decide what shall be done with them!'

'It be my pleasure, Mr Shakespeare.' Ralph went to grab them. 'Come with me, ye dwarf and sorceress!'

'Come get an eyeful of THIS!' shouted the dwarf. He thrust the console at Ralph, Shakespeare and Heminges. All at once, a crazy pattern of bright, flashing, strobing lights blazed on the screen and a cacophony of zapping, crashing sounds erupted. It was as if a hundred thunderstrikes were colliding in fierce, chaotic confusion.

The three men were dumbstruck, their eyes transfixed to the screen as they blinked at the stunning brightness of the display, trying to comprehend what they were seeing.

'Come with me!' urged the dwarf, grabbing Phyllis by the wrist.

She did not resist. The dwarf threw the console at the men—with his quick reflexes, Shakespeare caught it—and then the dwarf raced offstage, hauling Phyllis with him. She clutched her shoulder bag tightly as they fled.

Shakespeare, Heminges and ruddy-faced Ralph stood mesmerised by the alien technology in their presence. By the time they realised what had happened—quite a few spellbinding minutes later—Phyllis, Daisy and the strange red-bearded dwarf had crossed London Bridge and were getting their breath back, hidden behind some big oak barrels in a quiet laneway near Billingsgate.

Short explanation

'How on Earth did you get here?' Phyllis asked Clement.

'Easy,' he replied, taking off his semi-bald wig with the red hair around the sides, and scratching his neck under his bushy red beard. 'I just followed you.' He straightened his glasses and gave her a proud grin.

'What?'

'I followed you.' He patted Daisy, who was sitting alertly on Phyllis's lap.

'But how? How could you follow me?'

'Easy.' He pulled a *see, you're not the only clever one* sort of face.

'Clem!' she said in her *tell me or I'll throttle you* sort of voice.

'Well, the first time, I followed you back to that printer's. I watched you from outside the window.'

She thought back. 'Oh, yeah,' she said, remembering Isaac Jaggard spying the red-bearded dwarf looking into his shop. 'But Clem, how did you follow me?'

'Ha. It was simple. You left your key in the elevator.'

Phyllis shut her eyes, nodding.

'I was miffed,' Clement told her, 'that you didn't want to hang out. At first, I was. I thought that if you didn't want anything to do with me, then I didn't want anything to do with you. But then after a while I got bored with that. And I got bored out of my eyeballs with all the extra xylophone practice Mum made me do when she saw me hanging around the apartment. So I figured I'd find out what you were up to.'

'Uh-huh?' Phyllis said.

'So, yeah, I came over to the Wallace Wong Building that day and hid behind one of those big pot plants in the lobby and then I saw you going down to the basement . . . those little windows in the doors in the elevator are good for seeing who's in there as they go up or down. I knew where you were, at least, but also that I couldn't get down there because it's always key-controlled. The elevator, I mean. But I came out and pressed the button anyway, just in case. Then, when your key was still in there, I was in luck! The elevator came up, I got in and went down to your secret basement—man, Phyll, I had no idea you had all that stuff down there! Far out! And you were nowhere to be seen, but I could hear you tossing stuff around somewhere, so I hid near the stairs.'

'You promise me you'll not tell anyone about the basement? That's my secret place.'

'Cross my aorta nineteen different ways,' he said, making a star-shape across his chest with his index finger. 'Hey, Phyll! You're a time traveller!'

Phyllis looked at him. 'We don't use that expression, Clem. I'm a *Transiter*. And you're with me,' she said slowly.

Clem gave her a *we're in this together, Phyllis Wong* sort of wink.

She looked exasperated. 'But aren't you freaked out by the Transiting? I mean, it's not something you do every day, like going to the store or crossing the street . . .'

'Why would I be freaked out?' he asked back. 'Man, I've done freakier stuff playing *Gloaming: Asteroid Zombie Scrolls of the Drynachan Moors* or *Dancing with the Zombies*. Hey, apart from all that wind and stuff, this is like a walk in the park!'

'Yeah,' said Phyllis. 'A real picnic.'

'I just had to hold on tight to your coat, that's all,' Clement said. 'Or else I'd be blown away!'

She remembered she'd been aware that her coat had been buffeted and pulled from behind. 'So *you* were what I could feel behind me the last few times I've Transited. You.'

'Uh-huh.'

Then she asked him, 'So how about when you Transited with me on *this* trip? I didn't leave the key in the elevator before we came here. How'd you get down to the basement then?'

'Ah. Well, Phyllis Wong, I made a little discovery of my own.'

'Yes?' she said, frowning.

'Well, where I was hiding, behind that big pot plant—I betcha didn't know that there's a door there.'

Phyllis's brows came together as she listened.

'Yep,' said Clement. 'You don't really see it when you walk through the lobby; it's the same dark wood as the rest of the panelling all around the walls, and that lobby's always really dim, and the door's behind the plants, like I said. So a few days later I opened it and found out there were stairs behind it. And guess where the stairs lead?'

'To the basement,' Phyllis said.

'Correct. They come out through a door underneath the other big stairs down there, below the elevator. The door's hidden behind that huge pile of old crates and baskets and stuff.'

Phyllis felt miffed. She had no idea there was another entrance to her basement. 'So,' she said, 'you've been spying on me?'

'Well . . . not *spying* . . .'

'Yes, *spying*!'

At the sound of Phyllis's raised voice, Daisy gave her hand a quick, placating lick.

Clement took off his glasses and wiped them on his coat. 'I . . . I just wanted to know . . .'

'Wanted to know what, Clement?'

He sighed. 'I just wanted to know that you were okay. That's all.' He put his glasses back on and fiddled with the rubber on the half-bald wig in his lap.

Phyllis regarded him for several long minutes. Then a faint smile appeared on her lips. 'You promise me another thing.'

'What?' he asked.

'You are never, I repeat *never*, to tell anyone about what I do. About my Transiting. No one, not even Dad, knows about this. If you tell a single soul, I don't know what I'm going to do with you. But whatever it is, it won't be friendly.'

He looked up through his false red bushy eyebrows at her. 'I promise, Phyllis Wong. I fully promise that I'll never tell anyone about this.' He smiled, and he felt a warmth deep inside himself.

Phyllis smiled back. Then she said, 'What on Earth made you decide to dress up like that? You look like a reject from *The Hobbit*!'

'I think it's very good, actually,' said Clement. 'Evangeline said it suits me.'

'*Evangeline?*'

'Miss Hipwinkle, to you.'

Phyllis shook her head slowly.

'She said that the half-bald wig and the bushy beard and moustache and eyebrows give me a rakish air. She said I looked debonair, and that no one would ever recognise me.'

'Boy, she saw you coming a mile off!'

Just then a sharp, pungent smell wafted from across the river, and Clement screwed up his nose. 'Ergh! There's that stink again! I smelt it when I was following you to the theatre. What is it? It reminds me of Leizel Cunbrus!'

Phyllis caught it, too, and she put her hand to her nostrils. 'It's *worse* than Leizel Cunbrus,' she said. 'It's from the tanneries on the other side of the Thames. They use a certain something to soften all the leather. I read about it on the net.'

'A certain something?' Clement was scrunching his face so much his moustache popped off, and his beard was sticking out at weird angles. 'What? It smells like—'

'Believe me, you don't want to know,' said Phyllis.

Clement opened up his backpack and took out his phone. 'Boy, Mum's gonna kill me. That was a not-yet-released webPad 7 I left with those bozos at the theatre. She'll go nuts when she finds out I've lost it.' He turned on his phone, and his eyes lit up. 'Hey, Phyll, look at this!'

'What?'

'Look what's happening on my phone. Man, it's crazy!'

He showed her the phone's screen. There before them was a changing image—an amorphous, blob-like amalgam of bright gold swirls that were transforming into red spirals, and then purple threads, and then into glowing white tendrils. All of the colours and shapes were slowly corkscrewing into each other, getting smaller and smaller and then bigger again, and continually shrinking and expanding.

The patterns reminded Phyllis of something she had once found in W.W.'s and her basement; something that had mesmerised her and had crept into her thoughts often.

'That's the only signal we can get here,' Clem said. 'Not bad for . . . what Time is it?'

'Sixteen twelve,' she answered in a faraway tone.

He turned the phone off and Phyllis shivered.

Clement picked up his moustache from off the ground. 'Hey, you can answer me a question now: what's all that stuff about Card . . . Cardamom . . . what was it?'

'*Cardenio*,' Phyllis said. 'It's the reason I've come back. *We've* come back, I should say. And it's the reason we have to *go* back.' She stood, picking up Daisy and putting her into the shoulder bag.

Clement scrambled to his feet. 'Huh?' He shoved his half-bald wig and moustache into his backpack. 'Go back? Gee, for someone smart, you sometimes have the dumbest ideas. We can't show our faces there again . . . I don't like the look of that Ralph guy one little bit!'

Phyllis's eyes narrowed. 'We've got to get back into that theatre. We just have to.'

'But they won't let you in! Or, they will, but just to lock us up!'

As Phyllis was thinking, she looked over Clem's shoulder at a poster that had been pasted to the wall of the laneway: an audition poster for the Globe. An idea began coming to her. *They mightn't let girls on their stages*, she thought, *but there are other ways . . .*

'I think I know how we can do it,' she said, starting to hurry away. 'C'mon, Clem, we have to get back.'

'Hey, wait up!' Clement called, sliding his phone into his coat pocket and not noticing it falling out onto the street as he tried to catch up to his determined best friend.

Inveigling the Inspector

'**Y**ou want me to *what*?'

Chief Inspector Barry Inglis was standing with Phyllis at the foot of the stairs in the basement of the Wallace Wong Building.

'When I say the word, just run up the stairs with me,' Phyllis repeated. She held Daisy in her arms, and Daisy, too, was listening intently, a slightly quizzical expression on her little face.

Barry shook his head. He looked at Phyllis, then all around the vast, crammed basement—he had never been down here before. In fact, he had never, up until this point, even *remembered* there was a basement to the building, and he'd been living in the Wallace Wong Building for nearly fourteen years.

'Just . . . run up the stairs with you,' he said slowly. 'Miss Wong, are you intending to prank me or something?' Warily, he looked around for any cameras.

'No, Chief Inspector. This is important.'

He frowned. 'How can running up the stairs be important? Look, Miss Wong, I came down here because you said there was something urgent you had to show me. And now you're asking me to run up the stairs with you. I fail to see—'

'Trust me. Please. It *is* important.'

He sighed. 'You know full well that I have the greatest respect for you. Why, without you, there'd still be a case open and unsolved on the Squad files. But, good lord, I really have more important things to do with my afternoon. I should be at headquarters. I've got enquiries to make regarding the Shakespeare play, then I've got to go to the laundromat and then shopping for groceries and then watching the baseball game on TV, not to mention the—'

'This is all to *do* with the Shakespeare play,' Phyllis said urgently.

He stopped speaking when she said that. He looked at her, then he looked up the stairs. He was trying to work out how a set of stairs could be connected to the almost legendary Shakespeare manuscript when he was startled by a loud voice on the other side of the stairs' handrail.

'Hi, Chief Inspector!'

'Oh, my stars!' Barry Inglis jumped at the sight of the strange, short person with a hooked nose, thick grey sideburns, a very hairy handlebar moustache and a dreadful-looking scar above his left eye. 'Who the—*what* the—?'

'Clem!' said Phyllis. 'I told you, no disguises this time!'

'Huh?' he said. 'Oh, c'mon, this is hardly anything.'

Barry said to Phyllis, 'Is that really Clement?'

'Mm-hm. He's taken a new interest. Spurred on by his friend Miss Hipwinkle.'

Now Barry looked *really* confused.

'Never mind,' said Phyllis.

'Hey, Chief Inspector,' said Clement heartily. 'I heard that all the toilets at the police station were stolen last night.'

Barry gave him a sideways look. 'Really?' he asked in a dubious tone.

'Yeah. It's a real mystery. The police have nothing to go on.'

Barry regarded him for several long moments, during which the silence was heavy. Then he turned to Phyllis. 'Miss Wong, you said that this—these stairs—have something to do with the lost Shakespeare. Would you care to elaborate?'

'I could explain it all, but you'd never believe me,' she said. 'Look, this way you'll find out exactly what I mean. Just humour me and—'

'Miss Wong, I really don't have time to be—'

293

'What have you got to lose, Chief Inspector? All I'm asking is for you to run up the stairs with me—'

'*Us*,' Clement butted in.

'Us,' said Phyllis, giving Clem a *stop butting in* look. 'He has to do it too,' she told Barry.

'Yeah, we're a team,' Clement said.

'Take off the whiskers,' Phyllis told him.

Grumbling quietly, Clement started pulling off his hairy trimmings and stuffing them into his backpack.

Barry Inglis sighed. *What is going on?* he wondered. *How has the world shifted so much that I am standing here with a couple of kids—one of them one of the most intelligent people I know, admittedly—being persuaded to run up the stairs?*

'Go on,' Phyllis urged. 'Run up the stairs with us!'

Barry sighed again. 'Oh, all right, Miss Wong. Anything for a bit of peace!'

Phyllis beamed at him. 'Thanks, Chief Inspector.' Then, for a moment, she had a small qualm about revealing the secrets of Transiting and the TimePockets to him, almost like a pang of guilt. But she remembered what W.W. had written to her in his letter: that if she *did* decide to share the knowledge, then her good judgement must be paramount. She knew, deep down, that this was the best thing to do, and that Chief Inspector Barry

Inglis was the best person to share the knowledge with. And that now it was necessary to do so.

'Yeah, thanks, Baz,' said Clement.

Barry gave him another silent look.

'I mean, Chief Inspector,' Clem said.

Phyllis said to Barry, 'I promise, I'll explain what this is all about when we get there. But for now, this is very important: you have to hold onto my coat really tightly. And don't, under any circumstances, let go, not for a single second. Got it?'

The Chief Inspector's face was a hurdy-gurdy of confusion. 'Get *where*? Where are we going? What do you—?'

Phyllis raised a finger to her lips as she squinted at a point towards the top of the staircase. 'Shhh!' She gave Daisy a quick snuggle, then slid her into the change bag slung across her shoulder. With her other hand she took out the piece of metal type from her coat pocket and held it tightly in her fist. Then she moved forward so she was on the step above Barry.

Clement came around the side of the banister and stood next to Barry, giving him a quick wink.

Barry did not wink back.

'Okay,' Phyllis said. 'It's there. Hold onto my coat now.'

Clem grabbed the left corner of the back of her coat. Barry shook his head, then, slowly, he took hold of the right corner.

'Now,' whispered Phyllis, 'at the count of three, we run like the blazes!'

'Like the blazes?' repeated Barry.

'You heard the conjuror,' Clement said.

Barry sighed. 'Like the blazes,' he mumbled.

'One,' said Phyllis, grasping the strap of her bag tightly against her shoulder.

'One,' repeated Clement.

'Two,' Phyllis counted, steadying herself and squinting hard at the shimmering green outline of the Andruseon Pocket above them.

'Two,' repeated Clement, his heart starting to race.

Barry shut his eyes, waiting for this to be over.

'THREE!' shouted Phyllis. And she was off, racing up the stairs two at a time, towards the Pocket.

Like a couple of human caravans being towed, Barry and Clement ran behind her, holding firmly onto the back of her coat.

Suddenly Phyllis was there. She didn't slow down a fraction; as she felt the buffeting wind, she took a deep breath and plunged headlong into the Andruseon, taking her friends rapidly along with her.

✳

In Mistress Colley's suite at the Millennium Hotel, a pair of wheellock pistols lay on the dressing table, gleaming in the lamplight. Vesta Colley beheld their handles, decorated (to her instructions) in delicate mother-of-pearl, brass and stag horn, their long barrels finely embellished with gold engravings of her initials. And she smiled.

Next to them, Glory was nibbling on a small wedge of blue-vein cheese which she held in her pink paws.

'Whatever it takes,' Vesta said quietly to the rat. 'I am tired of this Transiting, Glory. In one fell swoop, we will take the greatest prize and wreak our destruction, and retire to a new life of total power and ownership and domination. And no one will thwart me, ever again.'

'*Squeeeetch*,' squeaked Glory, between bites.

Vesta Colley picked up one of the pistols and a silk cloth. Gently, almost lovingly, she began polishing the handle.

She Transited with these guns whenever she needed to go back to the seventeenth century. Although she would have preferred a modern pistol, which could fire off many rounds at the touch of a hair-trigger, she had to take these particular pistols. She didn't know why, but there was something about Transiting that meant that only weaponry that originally came from the era to which she Transited would work in that era. It was something she had discovered through bitter experience. To her knowledge, no other Transiter knew about this strange rule of the Pockets.

(She had found this out when she was trying to purloin a casket of rare rubies from an Indian maharajah in 1864. She had gone there equipped with a pistol she had acquired in 2009. When she had found herself cornered by the maharajah's guards in a building she had fled to, she had tried to shoot her way out, only to find to her eternal horror that the gun had exploded in her hand, causing her nasty burns and injuries to her fingers and wrists and to her eye. But she had also been fortunate on that occasion, because she was attempting her shoot-out at the base of a grand, sweeping marble staircase. She had stumbled upwards, the pain screaming through her, to find an Anvugheon, and she'd been able to escape instantaneously, plunging headlong into the dark hurricane-like void beyond. Her injuries, apart from those to her eye, had gradually healed after her Transiting back to the twenty-first century.*)

These two wheellock pistols would see her right. She'd had them made in 1607. She liked them, even if they could only fire a single shot before having to be re-loaded. They were French, lighter than

---

* The stairs, in the Taj Mahal, now closed to the general public, are still known to some as the Disappearing Staircase.

the German wheellocks, and more elegant. She admired their elegance and their hint of prettiness. And she was happy with the way she could carry them by sliding them down into her boots where they sat snugly, *comfortingly*, against her legs. They Transited safely, these wheellocks.

As she polished the mother-of-pearl inlaid pattern on the handle, a creeping anger started welling up inside her. 'We *must* find the right Pocket, Glory. I have to get *Cardenio* to the auction house no later than two days from now. They have scheduled their auction for next week, and they must have the play to authenticate it. The fools need to be sure . . . the safe-witted, cautionary, no-risks-for-us fools . . .'

'*Squeeeetch*,' squeaked the rat.

Vesta put down the pistol and took up the other. 'I need the Pocket,' she muttered to Glory as she buffed the gold on the barrel. 'I *must* find it. We must go and search again. Why am I being obstructed in my quest for it? Is our path to the past becoming crowded with rubbish? Congested by others who selfishly take up the routes that do not belong to them? Cluttered up by abecedarian blow-ins? I do not need such interferers on my journeys . . . I do not need such hindrances athwart me as I traverse Time . . .'

Vesta Colley's anger and frustration was nibbling away at her, much like Glory was nibbling away at the cheese. She buffed harder and harder against the' pistol until the barrel was almost hot through the silk cloth.

With a fierce gleam in her one good eye, she put down the cloth and looked at herself in the mirror. She slowly pushed one of her dark, luxurious curls away from her forehead as she stared at her reflection. Then, raising the pistol, she pointed it directly at her face in the mirror.

'Whatever it takes,' she whispered. 'Mistress Vesta Colley will stop at nothing.'

'*Squeeeeeeetch.*'

Secret and sudden arrival

It was raining gently as Phyllis, Daisy, Clement and Barry stumbled into the old city via some stairs near London Bridge.

They had all arrived without any major disruptions, apart from Barry being totally gobsmacked by what had just happened to him. His hair was sticking out at crazy angles and his ears were still ringing from the wind. His stomach was still trying to sort itself out after all the flipflops it had gone through during the Transiting. And he didn't know it, but his eyes were pulsating greenly as he emerged into the city.

Phyllis's stomach had been heaving even harder than it usually did when she Transited through a Pocket, and she had thought she was going to be awfully ill before they had arrived. Luckily, she had managed to hold on and now she, too, was starting to settle down.

Only Daisy and Clement had arrived without too much fuss—Daisy snuggling down in the warm darkness of Phyllis's change bag, and Clement seemingly used to the Transiting. All those hours spent playing his zombie games and being bombarded with quick, bright images and loud, blurting sounds seemed to have given him a sort of vaccination against the discombobulations of Transiting.

Now, as they all began to make their way to the Globe, Phyllis was answering Barry's questions.

'A *what*?' he asked her incredulously, his eyes throbbing.

'A Pocket. That's what we call them. They're the routes through Time.'

'Cool, huh?' said Clement.

Barry shook his head, trying to process what was happening. 'You're telling me, Miss Wong, that we have just gone back into the past?'

'Yep,' replied Phyllis. 'Look around, Inspector. This is Jacobean London.'

Barry Inglis stopped walking. He dug his hands deeply into his trousers pockets as he let his gaze wander about him. *Weird is not the word for this*, he thought. *It's far beyond weird. What the devil has happened? Either we've come into some huge, elaborate amusement park that's decked out to be London four hundred years ago, or what Miss Wong is telling me is correct. And I know her imagination is as wide as a planet, and I know she never lets the*

unknown hold her back, but . . . he bit his lip here . . .
well, even with all the magic she *can perform, even* she
*couldn't mock up an entire city and have it decorated
and filled up with people like this.*

Then he said out loud, 'And there's the wonder
of the thing . . .'

'The wonder of what?' asked Clement.

Barry blinked. 'Oh, never you mind, Clement.'

Clement shrugged. He slung off his backpack
and started rummaging around in it.

Barry thought he'd better check that he still had
everything he'd left with. Quickly he felt inside all
the pockets of his blue suit. Wallet: check. Police
ID card in its leather cover: check. Neatly pressed
handkerchief: check. Keys to his apartment: check.
Packet of breath-freshening mints: check. The nine
of diamonds playing card he always carried around
for good luck: check. His official police-issue pistol
in its leather holster, hanging from his shoulder
underneath his coat: check.

Phyllis had brought Daisy out of the bag and
the little terrier was having a widdle against a
lamp post. Barry went over to them. 'So,' he said
to Phyllis. 'Putting aside the fact that I am totally
dumbfounded by our present situation, and that
I have no idea how we got here, I do have one
question that I'm hoping you can answer.'

'Fire away,' she said.

'*Why* are we here? Why did you bring me here? Surely it's not just for fun, is it?'

'That's three questions, Chief Inspector.'

'Three questions to which I would be greatly pleased if you provided answers, Miss Wong.'

'Okay.' She reached down and clipped Daisy's lead to the back of the dog's little red-and-purple coat—she figured she'd let Daisy walk the rest of the way to the Globe, even if it was raining. 'No, it's not just for fun that I've brought you here. You're here because we have to stop a crime.'

He listened carefully.

'Remember that auction you took me to, where they sold the last First Folio? Remember the woman sitting across the aisle from us? The one with the long curls and all those gold rings?'

'The woman whom Daisy went for?' asked Barry Inglis.

'That's her.'

'I remember her. I've seen her at each of the Folio auctions, sitting quietly at the back of the room. I've been aware of her for some time.'

'Well, she's a Transiter too.'

'A Transiter?'

'Like me.'

'And me,' Clement butted in.

Phyllis said to him, 'Clem, you're my *assistant*. You're not a Transiter, not a real Transiter.'

He looked put out. 'Hey, I'm here, aren't I?'

'Yes,' said Phyllis, 'because *I'm* here. You came along with me. You've always come along with me.'

'It still makes me a Transiter,' Clement grumbled, returning his attention to rummaging in his backpack.

Phyllis said to Barry, 'That woman uses the Pockets to go back in Time, and that's how she's been getting the First Folios. Her name's Colley. They call her Mistress Colley.'

Barry's eyes narrowed. 'Go on, Miss Wong.'

'Oh, but she's not *stealing* them. Well, not in the legal sense of the word. See, I came back and visited the guys who printed the Folios and they told me that all the Folios she's got she's bought from them. She paid cash for them. Then she's Transited them back to our time and she's sold them for a huge profit!'

'She *on*sells them,' muttered Barry. 'Straight from here. That accounts for the near-perfect conditions of the books.'

'Yep. But that's not why we're here now. Chief Inspector, that announcement in the press that Wendlebury's is going to auction *Cardenio* . . .'

In a moment of dreadful realisation, Chief Inspector Barry Inglis of the Fine Arts and Antiques Squad raised his hand to his mouth, clamping it there tightly. A second later he took it away and exclaimed, 'She's going to thieve it!'

'The foul papers,' said Phyllis. 'I believe she's hoping to steal them directly from Mr Shakespeare himself.'

'Shakespeare,' repeated Barry in a voice Phyllis hadn't heard before—a voice that seemed to be coming from a long way away, the way a voice sounds when its speaker has come closer to something truly amazing. 'Miss Wong, tell me . . .' he spoke slowly, 'are we going to *meet* William Shakespeare?'

'We already have,' blurted Clement. 'That's why we had to come and get you.'

'He thinks *we're* trying to steal *Cardenio*,' Phyllis told Barry. 'He wants to lock us up so we can't.'

'I see,' Barry mused. 'Shakespeare himself, eh?' He tried not to show how excited he was (all he wanted to do at that very moment was to dance a tiny jig on the spot).

'We need to get back into the Globe Theatre,' Phyllis explained. 'Besides Shakespeare and his friends wanting to lock us up, they won't let kids into the theatre, *and they won't let girls*,' she said that with a shake of her head, 'on stage. I figure we need to get an adult in there, to try to stop Colley. That's why I brought you, Chief Inspector.'

'Do you think this Mistress Colley is here, now?' asked Barry.

'I don't know where she is. She could be anywhere. Any Time, any place.'

'Any place,' Barry repeated. His gaze moved warily around the street. 'Cities,' he said slowly, with a tinge of bitterness. 'They never really change all that much over time. Oh, sure, the buildings get higher and the traffic gets louder, but they're still cities. And where there are cities, there'll always be low-life. Perfect places for 'em. They can get lost amongst the crowds. They can bleed into the walls and disappear into the alleys and . . . dissolve away. Or so they think . . .'

'Stupid thing!' said Clement.

'What's stupid?' Phyllis asked.

'My phone,' he said. 'I wanted to show the Chief Inspector the crazy things it does when we come here, but I can't find it. I must've left it at home. I hope so—I hope I haven't lost it. I can't take another one of Mum's talks about the importance of looking after my valuable possessions and how lucky I am and how there are kids who can never—'

Barry cut him off. 'Miss Wong, exactly what year are we in?'

'Last time we came here it was 1612.' Phyllis pulled her journal out of her pocket and, sliding the loop of Daisy's lead up her wrist, she opened the journal and consulted it. 'It was December 20th, 1612.'

'So,' Barry wondered, 'is it the same Time now?'

'I don't know,' Phyllis answered. 'I'm still finding my way with the Pockets. I don't know yet how to pinpoint the exact Time and date of arrival. There are a lot of things to find out about all these Pockets,' she added.

'It's 1613,' Clement told them.

'Huh?' said Phyllis.

'It's 1613,' he repeated, in an *of course it's 1613* sort of tone.

'How d'you know that?' she asked.

'Because I'm clever,' he replied. 'I can tell things that are far beyond the normal reaches of the average person's brain.' He said that last bit in what he imagined was the voice of a mad scientist.

Phyllis gave him a hard stare, as if to say, *don't play silly boys with me, Clement!*

He sighed. 'Look.' He pointed across the street, past a laneway. A small chapel was being built, and it appeared to be nearing completion. A stonemason was carving a date into the lintel above the doors: *1613*.

'Whillikers!' said Phyllis. 'This is cutting it fine!'

Barry frowned and Clement looked puzzled.

'It was in 1613 that *Cardenio* was performed,' she said. 'Remember? The only Time we know it had a performance. Then it disappeared!'

'Of course!' exclaimed Barry Inglis. He looked up and down the street. 'C'mon, which way to the Globe?'

'Follow us.' Phyllis led Daisy down the street.

'Yeah, follow us, Chief Inspector.' Clement, who'd been rummaging around in his backpack again, gave Barry a wide grin and started off after Phyllis.

'*Bleeergh!*' Barry jumped, and Phyllis looked around at Clem. He was displaying more teeth than a single human being should be allowed to possess.

'I told you, no disguises,' Phyllis said to him.

'They're just *teeth*,' he protested. 'Not a full disguise. Evangeline says they're the best and most realistic teeth on the market. They're even better than my gran's dentures! Go on, Phyll, what harm can they do?'

'You look like an overly excited beaver,' muttered Barry, walking briskly alongside them.

Clement's grin went wider, and even *more* teeth somehow appeared at the corners of his mouth. He straightened his glasses and started humming to himself.

Phyllis rolled her eyes as she went with Daisy through the sprinkling rain. The young conjuror hoped, with every ounce of hope she had, that *Cardenio* had yet to be performed.

✳

'Through here,' Phyllis said over her shoulder.

She and Daisy led Barry and the bucky-toothed Clement through the gate in the white wall surrounding the Globe Theatre. She hurried across the courtyard, over to the theatre, and stopped by the wall there, sheltering under the thatched eaves above.

Clement joined her. 'I wish I'd brought my umbrella.'

'So this is the Globe,' said Barry Inglis softly. He stood in the courtyard, looking up at the building. A shiver went through him, but he tried to conceal it.

'Hopefully Mr Shakespeare is inside, working,' Phyllis said.

'Yeah, well if he is,' Clement said, 'he won't recognise me this time. No more red-bearded dwarf. Ha!'

Barry came to join them under the shelter of the eaves and Phyllis explained to him the way Clement had been disguised the last time they were here and how he had played music on the bottles during her audition.

'I see,' said Barry. 'You're right, Clem; at least today they'll have no idea of who you are.'

'I can go anywhere I want and no one'll ever know me,' Clement beamed, his fake teeth sticking out.

Daisy pawed at Phyllis's knee and Phyllis, realising she was really wet now, picked her up. She wiped the raindrops off Daisy's coat and, with a quick nose-against-snout nuzzle, she slid the dog down into her change bag and shut the top. Then she interlocked her left thumb and right pinkie, clasped her hands around each other, and thought.

'So, which way in?' asked Barry, looking around.

'You know,' she said, looking at Clem, 'what he just said makes sense.'

'Huh?' said Clement.

'About people having no idea who you are.' Phyllis looked at Barry. 'You can't go in like that, Chief Inspector.'

'I can't what?' he said, frowning.

'If Mistress Colley turns up,' Phyllis explained, 'she might recognise you. She's probably noticed you at the auctions—you've noticed *her*, you said so. How many Folio auctions have you been to?'

'Oh, good lord . . .' Barry thought. 'You're right. At least ten, it must be.'

'So that's ten times she's probably seen you.' Phyllis nodded. 'She'd remember your face, for sure.'

'How could she forget it?' asked Clement, wiggling his eyebrows.

Barry looked at him darkly.

'I only meant you're . . . you've got a . . .' Clement blushed.

'Never mind what you meant,' said Barry Inglis.

'We have to disguise you,' Phyllis said.

Barry said to her, 'You have a point. I have always liked your train of thought, Miss Wong.'

She gave a quick smile and said to Clem, 'Okay, Mr Invisible. What have you got in your bag of disguises to help out the Chief Inspector?'

Clement grinned so widely his teeth popped out onto the ground. He scooped them up and offered them to Barry. 'How about these for starters?'

The Chief Inspector pulled a sour-lemon face. 'What else have you got?' he asked.

'Oh, have you come to the right guy today,' said Clement. He squatted down and pulled out a long, flattish case from his backpack. He unclasped the case, lifted the lid, and three hinged trays rose up like a miniature staircase. The trays were filled with all manner of things hairy, rubbery, wobbly and generally bizarre-looking.

Phyllis said, 'Gee, you *are* taking this seriously.'

'Of course I am. Evangeline has instilled into me how important it is to do the best—'

'Cut to the chase,' said Barry. 'We're wasting time here.'

'Right, then.' Clement started speaking like a whirlwind as he pulled things out of his disguise box: 'This is the Robber Baron Deluxe—it's a real hair beard and moustache, all hand-knotted onto the gauze, as the best false beards and tashes always should be—I got it in grey, for that older look—and we can add a zigzag scar up on your forehead and some warts if you like and—oh, yeah, these are great, look at these really cool latex bits that stick on to your earlobes and give you old-man's ears, all long and droopy, and I've got this wig—I haven't tried it yet but Evangeline said it's the latest thing from Germany and I'm the first one to buy it and look, here it is, see how it's got a high forehead and then the hair just sprouts out of it from the top of your head and all around the sides and you can look like a college professor just by sticking that on and maybe a pair of specs as well, and—oh, man, I've got three different false noses and one's—'

'I think just the beard and moustache,' said Barry, picking them up and sniffing them.

'The Robber Baron Deluxe,' said Clem approvingly. 'Excellent choice, Baz . . . I mean, Chief Inspector. Hey, I'll just get the spirit gum and you'll look completely different in no time!'

'Yeah,' said Phyllis as Clement dexterously started sticking the beard and moustache to Barry's face. 'That'll work. It looks like the sort of beard men wear in this day and age.'

'I have never had to do this in my line of work,' said Barry as Clement brushed a smelly smear of the spirit gum under his nose. 'Dressing up, I mean. Some of the men have to, when they go undercover.

Pinkie Chatterton often puts on a wig or such stuff when he doesn't want to be recognised. He even dressed up in women's clothing on one occasion that I'm aware of . . . said it was to infiltrate a department store where there was a spate of designer handbag robberies. I did have my suspicions about the whole thing, I must admit . . .'

'Hold still,' said Clement.

'Hurry up, Clem,' urged Phyllis.

'There,' Clement said, pressing the moustache firmly onto Barry's face. He stepped back and admired his handiwork. 'Not bad. Your own mother wouldn't recognise you, Chief Inspector!'

'I am very glad she wouldn't,' said Barry Inglis.

Clement held up a small mirror, and Barry turned his head this way and that as he studied his bearded reflection. 'Hmm. Good work, Clement,' he said.

Clement smiled and nodded. He never had this sort of feeling of accomplishment when he played his games.

Phyllis smiled too; Clem *had* done a good job. More than good; Barry looked almost totally different now.

'Okay,' she said. 'Time to go in.'

'And face the music,' added Clement, packing up his paraphernalia and following her and Barry to the big oak doors.

The play's the thing!

When they entered the theatre, there was drama on the stage, but no play was being performed.

Phyllis stopped her friends in a shadowy corner at the back of the groundlings' pit. 'Look,' she whispered to Barry. 'That's Shakespeare, the guy pacing back and forth.'

'Well, I'll be handcuffed!' gasped the Chief Inspector, stroking his new beard. 'The Bard himself.'

'He's upset,' Clement observed.

Up on the stage, William Shakespeare was speaking angrily to a man who was half-lying, half-sitting in a crumpled heap on the boards. John Heminges was there also, looking worried, as were eight other people, all of them men. Some were dressed in fancy clothes, some were dressed in women's fancy clothes, and others were dressed more simply in dark clothing.

Phyllis whispered, 'It must be a rehearsal. Some of them are actors and the others are probably stagehands. And look, up there in the gallery at the back of the stage. They're the musicians.'

In the musicians' gallery, five men holding various instruments—a lute, a viol, a cornet, a trumpet and a crumhorn—were looking down on the scene, frowning.

Shakespeare's voice was raised, and it filled the theatre: 'How canst thou be so dimwitted?' he bellowed. 'Thou know'st it is strictly against the rules of this house to arrive here in this state!'

The man crumpled on the stage leant heavily on his elbow. 'I am most sor . . . sor . . .' he let out a loud hiccup . . . 'sorry, Mr Shakespeare . . . I can still be performing the part for you. *Hic!*'

'How canst thou expect to rehearse when thou cannot even stand?' thundered Shakespeare. 'We are premiering this play tomorrow afternoon! It will be the first ever performance of my *Cardenio*! Today be a most valuable and much-needed costume rehearsal! And here thou art, swine-drunk!'

Phyllis felt her blood run cold—tomorrow was the premiere!

The man's elbow slipped from under him and he went crashing down on his shoulder. Groggily, he propped himself up again. 'I only partook of one or two little glasses,' he said slurringly. '*Hic!*'

John Heminges spoke up: 'More like one or two little *barrels*! An excess of wine thou hast partaken, you sozzled knave! Thou art not good for any playing here, not in this theatre!'

At this, the man blinked heavily. He sat upright, swaying a little, and puffed out his chest. 'I show ye what I am good for,' he said, trying to pronounce his words clearly. 'Assist me to my feet, prithee. *Hic!*'

Shakespeare looked at Heminges (who shrugged) and he at Shakespeare (who rolled his eyes). Together they reached down and, grabbing the actor under his elbows, they hoisted him onto his feet.

The actor took a few slow steps upstage. Then he turned—everyone around him seemed to be doing a strange dance where they were drifting in and out of focus, like seaweed in the water—and put one hand on the hip of his knee-britches. His other hand he raised into the air as he started to declaim loudly:

'Cardenio, I bring thee word,
The Knight seeks thee out,
And therefore hither I come.
Quixote thinks thou a madman, so long a
    fool,
And he is intent (*hic!*) to discover your
    state.
Methinks your afflictions come wi' the
    passing

Of the Hours. For, like the tides that all
    befall us,
Time travels in diff'ring paces with
    diff'ring persons.
I'll tell you who Time ambles withal, who
    Time
dawdles withal, who Time rushes withal
and who he stands still withal. *Hic!*
O, Cardenio, vouchsafe unto me . . .'

The actor swayed, his eyes bulging. He got his balance again and went on:

'. . . vouchsafe unto me . . . *hic* . . .
    unto . . . *yeeeeeerrrrrrrgggggghhhhhh!*'

And, with a mighty eruption from his throat, the stage was awash with a lava-like spewing of thick vomit.

For a split second, the actor beheld his eruption. Then he put one hand on the front of his doublet and the other behind his back and bowed slowly. His bowing sped up and continued all the way to the stage, where his forehead met the floorboards with a loud CRASH!

'Ralph!' Shakespeare called. 'Clean it up!'

'Aye, Mr Shakespeare,' scowled the ruddy-faced Ralph, hurrying away to find a bucket and mop.

'He will not be sober for three days,' lamented John Heminges, looking at the unconscious man disdainfully.

'I thank the heavens for that,' Shakespeare said. 'The way he verily mangled my words! But, John, what are we to do? You cannot take on the parts played by this rascal; you are playing Cardenio himself. And I have more than a lion's share of performance, playing Don Quixote.'

Heminges looked at all the other players onstage. 'And all our men are doubling- and tripling-up on roles.' He frowned. 'I also know for a fact, Will, that the players at the Swan Theatre and at the Rose are all in production, with not a player to spare.'

Phyllis had been listening intently (she had also had to clamp her hand across Clement's mouth when the vomitacious activity had happened, as he was about to let forth a loud 'YUCKO,' which he frequently did whenever someone was sick in the playground at school). Now was her chance to set her plan into motion.

'We have a man here who could fill the part,' she called loudly.

'What?' hissed Barry Inglis.

Clement looked at Phyllis, then at Barry. Then he smirked.

Shakespeare, Heminges, all the other players and Ralph (busy mopping up the putrid mess)

319

turned in the direction of the voice. When Shakespeare saw Phyllis in the gloom at the back of the groundlings' yard, he leapt down from the stage and advanced towards her, Daisy, Barry and Clement.

'Ah, *the return of the conjuror*!' he declared, his voice low and threatening. Even though it had been some months (in Jacobean time) since he had seen her, he remembered her face vividly. 'What thieving ways have brought you back here this time, young woman?' He took his dagger from his garter and held its blade towards her.

'We're not here to steal,' Phyllis said quickly, urgently. 'Truly. We're here to *stop* a theft!'

'That's right,' Barry confirmed.

Shakespeare looked at him, eyeing him up and down. 'Who is this strange fellow?' he asked warily.

'I'm Chief Inspector Barry Inglis, of the Fine Arts and Antiques Squad of the Metropolitan Police Force.' Barry pulled out his little leather cover and flashed his ID card at William Shakespeare. 'Pardon the intrusion, Mr Shakespeare. We come on important business.'

Shakespeare ran his thumb up the handle of his dagger as he inspected Barry's badge.

''Tis not sleepy business,' continued Barry, 'but must be look'd to speedily and strongly.'

Phyllis stared at him—she'd never heard him speak like that before.

He put his hand momentarily to his mouth and whispered to her in an aside, 'I was in a production of *Cymbeline* when I was at police college,' he told her. 'Some things you remember.'

Phyllis pulled a *boy, are YOU full of surprises* sort of face.

'Thou speak'st my words,' Shakespeare said to him. 'Thou speak'st them well . . .'

'They are well written, Mr Shakespeare. No one writes words more finely than yourself.'

Shakespeare gestured with the dagger for Barry to put his badge away, and Barry pocketed it again. 'Thy apparel,' said the Bard. 'Never have I seen such a . . . is this, perchance, a *suit*?'

'It is,' Barry confirmed. 'It's the latest uniform, whither I come.'

'Strange,' mused Shakespeare. 'Yet, in my work, I have seen far stranger. Tell me, Barry Inglis, what it is thou art here to stop. This theft that young Phyllis Wong mentions. She told me, when she was here on a previous occasion, that it concerns my *Cardenio*?'

Barry turned to Phyllis. 'Tell him more, Miss Wong,' he said.

Breathlessly, Phyllis spilled the beans about Mistress Colley and how Phyllis knew that she was going to try to steal the foul papers of *Cardenio* and sell them for a huge sum—the biggest price ever seen for such an item. (Phyllis did not mention anything about the Transiting; even though she was addressing the man with possibly the greatest imagination ever, she did not want to make him any more suspicious of her and her friends. Nor did she mention anything about the First Folios; their publication would not happen for ten more years.)

Shakespeare and John Heminges, who had come to join him at the back of the groundlings' yard, listened to all of this in silence. Now and then Shakespeare rubbed the tip of his dagger through the point of his beard, as he studied Phyllis intently.

When she had finished her account he asked, 'And tell me, Phyllis Wong. Where doth this woman with the curls and the wicked intent come from?'

'From . . . from a long way away. She'll travel far to pull this off,' Phyllis answered.

'Pull this off?' Shakespeare slid his dagger into his garter and pulled out a sheaf of folded paper and his quill pen from his pocket. 'That is a fine expression,' he nodded, scribbling it down.

Clement nudged Phyllis with his elbow. 'Tell him about her rat you told me about,' he said, his eyes wide behind his glasses.

'Shh, Clem. Later.'

Shakespeare stopped writing and addressed Phyllis again: 'And how is it that thou, Phyllis Wong, are privy to such information?'

'I . . . I've just followed the pattern of the facts so far,' Phyllis said. 'I've traced what's been happening and what's come to light . . .'

'Come to light,' muttered Shakespeare, writing that down.

'She has a fine mind,' Barry said. 'It comes from her magic. She thinks in ways different to most people.'

'She's a one-off, all right!' added Clement.

Shakespeare raised his eyebrows, as if to say, *and who is this young person with the strangely protruding teeth?*

'That's just Clement,' Phyllis said quickly. 'My friend.'

John Heminges turned to Shakespeare and whispered into his ear. Shakespeare, looking thoughtful, nodded. He turned back to Barry. 'Hast thou ever acted on the stage, Mr Inglis?'

'I have,' said Barry. 'A long time ago during my training for the force.'

'And wouldst thou be prepared to take this rogue's parts in *Cardenio*? They are but four small walk-ons and three speeches, and much standing around, what we call hands-on-hips acting in the background.'

Barry looked at Phyllis. She gave him a nod. 'If you wish it, I shall tread the boards for you,' said the Chief Inspector.

Shakespeare quickly scribbled down the phrase.

'Most excellent,' John Heminges said. He clapped Barry on the back. 'We shall costume you and give you the script and start rehearsals again within the hour!' He turned to the actors on the stage. 'Refreshments for one hour,' he called, 'while we prepare our new player.'

Phyllis said, 'That's swell. Having him in the play means a good chance for the Chief Inspector to be in the thick of it . . .' Shakespeare wrote that down too, his feather quill quivering quickly, '. . . and from the stage he might be able to see Mistress Colley if and when she arrives.'

''Tis what we were thinking also,' said John Heminges.

'Of course,' Barry said, 'we can't just arrest her for turning up. We have to catch her red-handed.'

Shakespeare's quill was going ballistic now. 'What means this *red-handed*?' he asked as he scribbled.

'In the act,' Clement said. 'With her hand in the honey pot. Up to her eyeballs.'

'Ye Gods!' Shakespeare exclaimed. 'Such phrases! 'Tis like the heavens have opened!'

'You see our point, though,' said Barry. 'We have to catch her attempting to steal your foul papers. We have to catch her with them in her hands. Only then can she be charged with theft.'

Shakespeare stopped writing, and a look of dark anger clouded his face. 'No one touches those,' he said quietly. 'The foul papers are not to fall into anyone's hands but mine!'

'Nor shall they, Will,' said John Heminges. 'Not for good. Only for a few brief moments, so it can be proved she is stealing them. Our new acquaintances here will help see to that.'

'I will get more padlocks and chains for the box in which I keep them,' Shakespeare declared. 'The foul papers box I always keep with me, in the Globe or at my home. I will make her job impossible!'

'Settle thyself,' Heminges soothed him.

'I don't think padlocks and chains will stop her,' Phyllis said. 'I think she has more cunning up her sleeve than we realise. She hasn't let anything stop her so far—not Time or distance, or—'

She trailed off before she let too much slip. Shakespeare looked at her curiously. At that moment—because of what she had just said, and the passion with which she'd said it—he knew that Phyllis Wong was to be trusted.

'Miss Wong is right,' Barry said. 'We're dealing with a clever schemer, in this Mistress Colley. Now here's what I propose: during tomorrow's performance of *Cardenio*, while I'm up on stage with the other actors, I think it best that Phyllis and Clement—'

'And Daisy,' added Clement. 'Don't forget Daisy!'

Phyllis opened the top of her bag and Daisy popped her snout out and blinked at everyone.

'Ah, the vanishing pup,' said Shakespeare, the dark cloud beginning to lift from his face.

'And Daisy,' said Barry, flashing Clem a *let me get on with this please* look. 'Well, while the performance is going on, the three of them will be backstage somewhere safe, guarding your foul papers in their box. Will that be acceptable to you, Mr Shakespeare?'

'But if this Colley woman breaks through our watch?' asked Heminges. 'What happens if she slips in, and finds the young people with the box? What then?'

'Phyllis and Clement and Daisy won't be *with* the box,' Barry said.

'What dost thou say?' Shakespeare was becoming agitated again.

'They'll be hidden nearby. They'll be watching the box. It'll be sitting there, locked and waiting for her. When she opens it, and takes the foul papers, we'll pounce.'

'But how will we know when the dreadful deed happens?' asked Heminges.

'I know!' Shakespeare put three fingers into his mouth and whistled loudly. It was a shrill, piercing noise and Barry, Phyllis and Clement winced. Daisy barked excitedly—she liked noises like that. On the stage, Ralph looked up sharply from his mopping.

'Canst thou do that?' Shakespeare asked Phyllis and Clem.

Clem shoved three fingers into his mouth, cramming them in carefully around his gopher-like false teeth. Somehow the fake dentures amplified the noise, and he let out a whistle even louder and more shrill than Shakespeare's. He took out his fingers (covered with saliva) and asked, 'How's that?'

Heminges had a finger in his ear and was wiggling it around. 'Most . . . effective,' he said, his ears ringing.

'Ha!' Shakespeare laughed. 'Most excellent, young man! Repeat that as the alarm for us if the woman gets her hands on the foul papers. We shall come running—we shall stop the performance if needs be—and apprehend the felon!'

Barry Inglis almost smiled—he was not a man for grinning or such. 'I think it best,' he said, 'that we keep all of this a secret from the other actors and the stagehands. I've found, in my line of work, that when fewer people know about an operation, the more chance there is that it'll be successful.'

'Sound advice,' said Shakespeare. 'Agreed.'

'Good,' said Barry. Then it dawned on him that he had a role to prepare for, and a big knot of nervousness started to tighten, deep in his stomach. 'I'd better get my part from you, Mr Shakespeare. Study my lines and all.'

'I am Will, Barry. Call me that.'

Phyllis saw Barry's lips begin to curl upwards . . . for the first time, she thought she was going to be present for something almost as amazing as Transiting through the Pockets: her friend the Chief Inspector giving a full smile.

But she was not to witness such a rare event. Barry kept his mouth fixed firmly and said, 'Let's get this show on the road, Will.'

And Shakespeare scribbled down that saying too.

Whatever it takes

People were starting to notice the woman with the long, flowing curls who was rushing up and down stairs all over the city.

Vesta Colley had put on her favourite dark coat—a knee-length deep purple coat with capacious pockets and zippered compartments and a thick mink fur collar in which Glory could hide comfortably. The coat flared out from her hips—Vesta liked the way it did that; it reminded her of a dragon's wings before the creature took flight.

She had her wheellock pistols stashed securely in her high boots. Around her neck, falling below the black lacey collar of her shirt, she wore a heavy gold medallion that had been fashioned from the gold-plated cogs of an antique clock.

On her fingers she wore no less than six gold rings, five of them encrusted with glittering diamonds, brilliant rubies, deep sapphires and heavy emeralds. The sixth ring was a bold signet ring in brilliant gold, engraved with the initials *V.C.* inside a flourishing border.

Her hair was not tied back. Vesta Colley enjoyed the feeling of it whipping against her face when she Transited. It made her more alert and more determined. She didn't mind the stinging sensation as it flew wildly around her.

Whatever it takes . . .

But now, here in this twenty-first-century city, people had been noticing her. She had spent the whole morning, more than four hours, rushing about, catching taxis and jumping out whenever she spotted an outdoor stairway she hadn't yet come across. Whenever this happened, she would fling some money at the taxi driver and rush to the stairs, hardly stopping to peer up them to see if there was a Pocket located there. She would run straight up the stairs, hoping, wanting, yearning for there to be an Andruseon or an Anamygduleon on that stairway.

So far, there had been nought.

As she raced up the stairs she clutched, in her neatly manicured fingers, her 'passport' back to the Time she sought—a silver locket she had 'borrowed' from a wealthy woman back in 1613. The chain of the locket was wrapped around her fingers, and the edges of it were pressed hard into the palm of her hand.

Fortune, it seemed, had deserted her. Now she stood in one of the busiest streets in the city, in the precinct that was filled with the most expensive stores and salons. *Maybe*, she thought, *I should not be looking on* outdoor *stairways? Maybe the thing I seek will be found on stairs* inside *a building?*

Thus resolved, she hurried into the closest store on the next corner—a big department store that sold nothing that cost less than five hundred dollars.

She barged through the elegant revolving doors, pushing impatiently against them. An elderly woman in the revolving section immediately in front of her found herself speeding up unexpectedly as the doors swept around with a muffled *whoooosh*.

Vesta emerged onto the ground floor, which was festooned with huge boughs of tinsel and shiny Christmas decorations and many artificial Christmas trees and lavish baubles hanging from the ornate columns that stretched throughout the store. She heard a choir, somewhere at the far end of the floor, singing carols. The sound sickened her, and she hurried in the furthest direction from them she could go.

'*Squeeeeetch*,' squeaked Glory, clinging onto her mink collar. She disliked the music as much as her mistress did.

Vesta ran her hand through her collar, patting Glory soothingly. 'There, there,' she whispered. 'We shall be free of this soon . . .'

She shuddered and looked past the crowds doing their last-minute Christmas shopping. *So many people, so many things, so much foolishness,* she thought.

Then she spied what she was looking for. Down by the bank of elevators, tucked away to the side of them in a dimly lit place, was an old, wide staircase with a polished dark oak balustrade and grey-and-pink flecked marble steps. Vesta looked hard at it, and a slight shiver of anticipation ran across her shoulders, like an invisible Glory. This staircase seemed forgotten, there in the dimness. No one was using it; she could see that the shoppers were clustering around the elevator doors instead, then flowing into the mechanical contraptions and spilling out of them like a small ocean of eager flotsam.

Vesta sneered and shook her curls. She made her way through the shoppers, barging past their bags and parcels and their shoulders, and went to the base of the staircase.

Looking up the staircase, she saw that it rose for about forty steps before levelling out onto a landing. Then, around a corner of the landing, it ascended again. She craned her head back and looked straight up above where she was standing. She could see the underside of the staircase rising up and up and up. She counted the storeys. Eight.

Vesta Colley felt the shiver of anticipation scrabbling across her shoulders again, and she tingled.

There was a possibility here; she could sense it.

Taking a deep breath, and stroking Glory for luck, she bounded up the stairs in front of her, three at a time, her coat flaring out with her speed.

Maybe this would be the one . . .

✳

Rehearsals were over for the day and Phyllis, Daisy and Clem had made themselves comfortable backstage at the Globe.

They were sitting on the floor, having just finished a big supper of roasted chicken, boiled mutton, turnips and carrots, cheese, bread, apples and some sweet marzipan desserts made in the shape of birds—all generously provided by Mr Shakespeare and Mr Heminges.

'Man!' Clement groaned, leaning back against a props basket and holding his stomach. 'I'm as full as a fat lady's handbag!'

Daisy was busily licking the grease from Phyllis's fingers. The little dog, too, looked stouter than normal.

'We'd better leave the rest for the Chief Inspector,' said Phyllis.

Through the gaps in the curtained doorways leading onto the stage in front of her, she could see Barry strutting back and forth, practising his lines. He was reading them from a sheaf of parchment pages that Will had given him, handwritten by Shakespeare himself, with the strict instructions that they had to be returned to him as soon as tomorrow's performance of *Cardenio* had finished. (Barry had felt a strange feeling of amazement when he'd realised that he was holding some of the foul papers of William Shakespeare, and he didn't take the responsibility lightly.)

Phyllis thought he looked funny in his doublet and hose and beard and moustache, and she giggled as she watched him striding along on the boards.

'Hey, Phyll?'

'What?'

'It was nice of old Will and his friend to let us all stay in the theatre tonight, wasn't it?'

'They want us to keep watch,' Phyllis said, wiggling her fingers as Daisy's tickly tongue darted between them. 'Tonight as well as tomorrow.'

Clement leant over and unzipped his backpack. He took out his new webPad (his parents had given him yet another, from their latest stock) and switched it on to see if he could pick up any signals. 'They're really precious about keeping their play safe, aren't they?' he asked, waiting for any sort of image to show up on the screen.

'They have to be,' said Phyllis. 'It's their property and people are taking it and making money out of it.'

'That's what people do,' said Clement.

'Yeah, Clem, that's what people do. But, you know, I've been having a good think about it. It doesn't mean it's *right*.' Phyllis scooped Daisy up and put her on her lap. 'You heard what Mr S. said, how people were coming in to the audience and copying down the lines the actors were speaking during the performances. Then they'd go and put on their own play, using Mr S.'s script, without paying him for it. That's . . . that's almost the same as people going to the movies in our Time, when a picture's just come out, and filming it on their camera or phone and then giving it away or selling it. Or downloading music without paying for it, or a game or something.'

Clement stopped fiddling with his webPad. He blushed guiltily as he listened to her.

'Shakespeare has every right to be so guarded about his work. Like, why should he give it away? If someone came into your mum and dad's store and asked for a free washing machine, or a free webPad, would your parents give them one?'

'No way,' answered Clem quickly.

'So why should people expect to get other people's things for nothing?'

'You've got a point, I guess.'

'It's the same in magic, Clem. So many magicians have stopped creating new tricks because someone comes and copies what they've invented without paying them for it. Or someone puts a film of it up on the internet, showing how the trick's done. That's the same as taking someone's ideas and just trashing them.'

Clement said, 'Yeah. And to think it's been going on for centuries.'

'Some things don't change.' Phyllis frowned. She looked at his webPad. 'So, is anything showing up?'

He shook his head. 'Nup. Not a sausage. Not even those crazy patterns I got on my phone. This is just dead. Maybe I needed to charge it up more before we came.' He turned it off and slid it into his backpack.

Just then Barry barged backstage. 'That's enough practice for today,' he said, eyeing the leftover food with a hungry interest.

'Do you know your lines?' Phyllis asked.

'Near enough.' Barry took off his sword and sat on a pile of cushions next to Clement. 'I just hope I don't have any wardrobe disasters tomorrow afternoon. These pantaloons are not exactly the most comfortable trousers I've ever worn.'

Clement smirked.

Phyllis held out the plate with the rest of the chicken on it. 'Here, try some of this. It's good.'

'Thank you, Miss Wong.' He picked up a fork and took a piece of breast. 'By the way, Will and John Heminges said it's okay for you to sleep here backstage so you can keep an eye on things in case anything unexpected turns up. You should be comfortable . . . they said you can use some of these cushions that the wealthy audience members will be sitting on at tomorrow's premiere.'

'Swell,' said Phyllis. 'It should be cosy.'

The Chief Inspector chewed the chicken and helped himself to some bread. 'Will and John are also staying in the Globe, up in two of the boxes. They'll keep a lookout on things from up there.'

'Hey,' said Clement nervously, 'd'you think there are *ghosts* in here?'

'Why would there be ghosts?' asked Phyllis.

'Well . . . I mean, the place is so old . . . there're often ghosts in old places—they like to hang around places like this.'

'The Globe's not old, Clem.'

'Huh? Yes it is. It's over four hundred years old.'

'No,' Phyllis said. 'It's only fourteen years old.'

'She's right,' said Barry. 'Remember where we are, Clement. And *when* we are. This theatre was only built fourteen years ago.'

'Oh, right. Yeah.' He took off his glasses and polished them on the bottom of his shirt, which was untucked and sticking out from under his sweater. 'I forgot.'

'It's practically new,' Phyllis said, combing the fur on Daisy's back with her fingernails.

'About as new as I am,' Clement remarked, raising his eyebrows at the realisation. 'Well, almost.'

Phyllis smiled at him.

'Anyway,' Barry said between mouthfuls, 'I'll also be stationed in one of the boxes out there during the night. I think, between the three of us out there and the two of you in here—'

'And Daisy,' Phyllis added.

'*Rrrruuufff!*' Daisy barked.

'I sit corrected,' Barry said. 'How could I forget those dynamic ears and that snout? Between the three of us out there and the *three* of you in here, we should have a strong surveillance coverage of the Globe during the wee small hours.'

Phyllis stopped grooming Daisy. 'Chief Inspector?'

'Yes, Miss Wong?'

'If she comes . . . you won't be far away, will you?'

'I will be here,' he answered. 'You can always count on me.'

'And me, Phyll,' added Clement. 'I never let you down.'

Phyllis smiled, but she couldn't keep the feeling of uncertainty and the small fear of the unknown from clouding her thoughts about what was to come.

Time out of joint

The department store's gloomy stairs had been just what she needed, and Vesta Colley was now striding determinedly through the rain-washed streets of Jacobean London.

Her good eye blazed with triumph—a small triumph, for the greater triumph was yet to come—and her other eye, green and glowing, stared blankly ahead as she made her way through the dark city. Glory rode on her shoulder, twitching her whiskers against the snowflakes.

Not long now, Vesta thought. *Just slip in, grab the play, slip out again. And destroy all that created it.*

She stopped in the doorway of a milliner's shop and pulled out her small Date Determinator—a thumb-sized copper and brass implement that had three rows of engraved and geared brass numbers set into it, and three faceted emerald and yellow sapphire lights. This she had stolen from another Transiter, on a trip she had made in 1884. It had always been accurate and had never let her down.

She pressed a tiny button at the end of the Date Determinator, and the brass numbers started spinning around. Vesta held the Determinator steady as the numbers clicked away. Then, after half a minute, the gears slowed, and the three lights glowed—two of them bright green, and the other an intense, dazzling yellow. There was a loud CLICK, and the numbers came to a sudden stop.

Vesta inspected the rows of digits.

The first row showed 28.

The second row showed 06.

The third row showed 1613.

She was here. She was where she wanted to be. She was pleased.

She pocketed the Date Determinator and zipped it securely in. She leant back against the door frame of the closed shop and contemplated her plan. Tomorrow would be the performance. Tomorrow, Shakespeare would be at the Globe with his box containing the play. That was when she would be able to find it. Not until then. This evening, she would find a comfortable inn where she would spend the night. Then, tomorrow morning, before *Cardenio* was due to commence, she would go to her favourite goldsmith's in Gutherons Lane, and to some of the better jewellers in Cheapside. It would be good to collect a few more trinkets, she thought. A few farewell souvenirs from her trips to this place and Time.

After all, she did not intend to return here again. Her eyes had had just about enough.

There was also some powder she needed to buy. Some *special*, hard-to-come-by powder . . .

She patted Glory, who was nestled in her fur collar. She was just about to go in search of an inn, when something caught her eye.

Something on the ground, half-submerged in a shallow, muddy puddle.

Something dark, sleek and shiny.

Vesta's good eye narrowed. As she looked at this thing, her heart contracted, as though a steel clamp had closed around it. This thing in the puddle, this was not a thing that should be in this place and Time . . .

She bent down and picked it up and shook the water and mud off it. And the steel clamp around her heart tightened hard.

'What manner of intrusion is this?' she whispered, her eye filling with the unwelcome sight of Clement's cell phone. Her face became a pattern of horror as she clutched the phone. She shook it—violently, as though it were a living thing and she wanted to break the life out of it—but there was no power or life left in it.

'*Squeeeeeetch!*' Glory squeaked loudly, as she sensed her mistress's alarm.

'We are not alone, Glory,' Vesta muttered gravely. 'Someone else has come. Someone else is here in my shadow . . .'

'*Squeeeeetch!*'

'That is why we had such a difficult time finding the Pocket,' Vesta said softly. 'The more the Pockets are used, the less apparent they become . . .'

Her anger became stronger. 'Someone is here to try to stop me, my sweet Glory. To prevent me from pulling off the greatest plan of my life. No, they shall not. *They shall not succeed!* I will take *Cardenio!* With vengeance I shall take it!'

A new sense of purpose swelled within her—and it was savage. 'Now, because of *this*—' she flung the phone to the ground and smashed its screen with the hard, tall heel of her boot—'I will show the world my true power. I shall present my final act of brilliance in the most spectacular way!'

Her mind was all at once ablaze with her plan. 'After all,' she whispered to the rat, 'with that upstart Shakespeare out of the way once and for all, there will be no more plays issuing from his quill. *Cardenio* will be all the rarer for that, Glory, all the more special! And tomorrow afternoon will be the perfect opportunity to leave the mark of Vesta Colley on the smudged pages of History so that no one can rub it out!' She laughed—a low, deep peal of malevolence. 'And no one will ever know that it was even me!'

✳

It was well after midnight, but, backstage at the Globe, Phyllis couldn't sleep.

Daisy and Clement were out to it, Clement sprawling out on a bed of cushions he'd made in the corner and Daisy snuggling into the crook of his back. Clement's disguises box was open by his feet, and various things were half-in and half-out of it: beards, moustaches, false ears, fake noses and other strange and curious items.

By the light of a thick candle burning steadily on a box next to her, Phyllis watched Daisy's legs doing little dream-kicks as the terrier slept. *She's chasing the tigers again*, Phyllis thought. *Lucky girl.*

Phyllis tucked her knees under her chin. She thought about her dad, and realised she was missing him. She was looking forward to being home again, after all this business was done and dusted. All this business . . .

A line of concentration emerged on her forehead as she thought about the next day.

Anything could happen. That Colley woman could come here, sneaking in unseen somehow, and thieve the play. Or she could arrive and be seen by Clem and me and then Clem would sound the alarm, and then . . . Phyllis put her hands on her knees and joined them intertwiningly. *What would happen then? What exactly—?*

343

Suddenly there was a noise on the stage. Phyllis sprang to her feet and moved back into the shadows, away from the candlelight. She could hear footsteps.

They were coming backstage.

Her heart started racing. She felt her palms getting wet, and she wiped them on her jeans. Her breath was coming in short, shallow gasps.

The footsteps were approaching, quietly but steadily.

Phyllis stayed perfectly still. She could hear her heart hammering away against her ribcage, sounding like muffled drumbeats in her head . . .

Then the curtain separating front-of-stage from backstage was pulled swiftly aside, and a tall figure appeared.

'Miss Wong?' whispered the Chief Inspector, peering into the darkness. He was wearing his dark blue suit again. 'Are you there?'

'I'm here.' Phyllis came forward, her legs shaking as the relief surged through her.

'Good,' said Barry. 'Just thought I'd do my rounds. Make sure everything's okay.'

'Yeah, everything's fine.' She went and sat by the candle again.

'And I thought I'd get my costume ready for tomorrow. While no one's watching.' He gave her a wink and went quietly over to the costume rack by the back wall. From this he took down a big hanger that held his doublet and hose, his vest, his shirt with the ruffled collar, his short cloak, his pantaloons and his hat with a big plume in the hatband.

'Is that beard and mo itchy?' Phyllis asked as she watched him laying out the costume on a trunk.

'Surprisingly not,' he said. 'I'm very grateful that young Clement bought a fine quality set of facial hair. If this was synthetic, I'd be scratching myself silly.'

He took out of his suit pockets his essential belongings and began tucking them into the folds and pockets of his stage costume: his wallet, his Police ID card in its leather cover, his apartment keys and the nine of diamonds playing card. He had kept that ever since Phyllis had given it to him after she'd performed a flabbergasting card trick for him some time ago.

'You still carry that card around?' Phyllis asked.

'Always, Miss Wong, always. It reminds me that things are often not what they seem.'

'Often,' Phyllis agreed.

Finally he took his pistol out of the shoulder holster under his coat. He quickly checked that it was fully loaded, then he started looking for a place where he could hide it securely in the folds of the red velvet pantaloons he would be wearing over his hose the next afternoon during the premiere.

'Do you think you'll have to use that?' asked Phyllis, intrigued. She'd seen Barry Inglis with a pistol before, but she'd never been there when he had to fire it.

'I sincerely hope not,' he said. 'That's the worst part of my job, I don't mind saying.'

'I bet it is.'

'There,' said Barry, making sure the pistol was safely ensconced in the pantaloons, but not so snug that he wouldn't be able to whip it out quickly if he needed to. 'That should do the trick.'

'No, it's me who does the tricks.' Phyllis tried to make a joke, but her voice sounded flat.

Nevertheless, Barry Inglis winked at her (which was, for him, the equivalent of a smile). 'It certainly is. There is not a finer prestidigitator in all the world.' He took the pistol out again and returned it to the holster under his coat. 'I just wanted to make sure I could stow it there, for tomorrow. For tonight, it stays with me.'

He began putting all the bits of his costume back onto the hanger. 'I think, for now, you should try to get some sleep. You'll need all your alertness for the day to come.'

Phyllis nodded. She watched her friend take his costume and return it to the rack.

With a last look around the backstage area, Barry crept back to the curtains. 'I'll just be out in a box up there,' he whispered. 'You rest, and I'll see you all in the morning before the other actors arrive.'

'Okay.'

'Good night . . . or, rather, good morning, Miss Wong.'

'See you, Chief Inspector.'

He gave a small nod and faded away through the gap in the curtains.

Phyllis plumped up a few cushions and formed a sort of mattress. Then she lay down and rolled over onto her side. A few minutes later she had drifted off into a light, not-far-from-consciousness sleep.

Entrances and exits

'**H**eavens above!' gasped Barry Inglis. 'There must be thousands of people out there!'

He, Phyllis, Clement and Daisy (in Phyllis's shoulder change bag) were looking out from one side of the backstage area into the auditorium. The rain had stopped falling and, like a tide coming steadily in, the Globe was filling with people: well-dressed people trickling into the boxes all around the upper regions, and more boisterous, eager folk noisily flooding the groundlings' yard.

'Man,' said Clement. 'This place sure is popular!'

'It's what they used to do before movies and TV,' said Phyllis. 'The theatre was everything. That's why my great-grandfather became so famous in his day. He used to pull crowds like this with his magic.'

Daisy could sense the growing air of excitement and anticipation out there. She gave a short, sharp bark, and then another.

Phyllis patted her snout. 'Yes, Deebs. Settle down.'

Barry pulled down his doublet and straightened

his sword. 'It's like being at a baseball game,' he observed. 'This crowd ... *easily* must be two thousand ...'

'Closer to three,' corrected William Shakespeare, coming up to them with a large cedar box. 'I just checked with the ticket seller. We're just a whisker under the three thousandth patron. The house will be packed.'

'Sardine time,' Clement said, smirking.

Barry Inglis looked at the box that Will was carrying. '*Cardenio*?' he asked.

'The foul papers,' confirmed Will. 'The complete play. Every word writ by myself. The only parts missing are the short speeches of the character thou art playing, Chief Inspector.'

'Which I will return to you at the close of the performance,' Barry said. 'When I have played my part. Thanks for letting me hang onto them ... it's good to know I have them with me in case I get a sudden loss of memory.'

'As agreed,' Will said. He placed the box on a table by the back wall. 'It is double locked, and I have one key.'

'And I the other,' John Heminges said, coming backstage.

Phyllis went over to the table and ran her hands across the box. Her fingers tingled as she realised the importance of what was inside.

'It is precious, young conjuror,' Shakespeare said to her. 'As thou well know'st.'

'Beyond precious,' Phyllis murmured to herself, her hands still pressed onto the chest.

'We'll look after it,' Clement said confidently, pushing his glasses up his nose. 'Won't we, Phyll?'

'Arf!' barked Daisy.

'And, pray keep the vanishing pup still during the performance,' said Will. 'The groundlings do not like distractions.'

'She'll behave,' Phyllis said. She took her hands from the box and looked around. 'How about if Clem, Daisy and I hide over there?' she asked, indicating a large pile of baskets and property skips in the corner, to the left of the foul papers box. 'Behind all that stuff?'

'As good a place as any,' agreed Barry. 'We should be able to hear Clement's signal from there, if Colley arrives while we're onstage.'

Just then the other players came backstage, some of them dressed as soldiers, some as courtiers and some as women (some of the 'women' players wore closely curled wigs and large hooped skirts which swept widely around them on all sides, and Clement had to jump out of the way when one of them came close to him).

'Ten minutes to opening,' said John Heminges. 'Time to be still and to prepare our thoughts.'

Barry gave Phyllis a wink, and cocked his head in the direction of the hiding place.

She winked back, trying to force a smile above her nerves. 'Break a leg, Chief Inspector,' she said.

'I shall do my best not to follow your wishes literally,' he said. 'Thank you for the thought though, Miss Wong.'

Phyllis grabbed Clement and led him to the baskets and skips. Quietly they ducked behind them and settled.

'I wish we could see the play,' grumbled Clement. 'I feel like we're missing out on all the action back here.'

'We'll be able to hear it,' Phyllis said. 'They're just on the other side of that wall. And we'll be able to work out what's going on from the way the audience reacts as well.'

'I hope there's zombies in it,' Clement said, making sure he had a good hiding place to peek at the table and the chest.

'Don't count on it,' said Phyllis, rolling her eyes.

In the theatre, the noise from the audience was rolling around like low thunder coming from far away. A new feeling started to fill Phyllis's insides, joining her nervousness: the amazing feeling of quiet, mounting eagerness that she always got before a performance, whether she was due to perform herself or about to watch others.

She loved that eagerness and the way it fired her up.

She patted Daisy as she waited for the show to begin. Clement rearranged one of the smaller baskets on the pile in front of him so that he had an unhindered view between it and the basket next to it. Now, satisfied that he could see the foul papers box clearly, he sat back and waited too.

Then the trumpets sounded from the musicians' gallery directly above them. Both Phyllis and Clement started at the loudness of the blasts, and Daisy barked loudly.

'Arf! Arf! Arf! Arf!'

'Shh,' Phyllis quietened her.

The trumpets played a small fanfare, light and pleasant and loud, reflecting the excitement that was filling the Globe. Then the music stopped abruptly, and the noise from the audience subsided, fading away until there was barely a sound.

From the stage, Phyllis, Clem and Daisy heard an actor declaiming boldly:

'Ladies and gentlemen of our fair metropolis! Welcome, one and all, to our great wooden O, this most excellent theatre in the city of London. Welcome to the mighty Globe!'

A loud cheer erupted from the groundlings, and applause swelled from many of the upstairs boxes.

Phyllis tingled and held Daisy close. She peered

around the baskets and saw Barry Inglis waiting with all the other players. He was moving back and forth, almost as if he were doing a little jig on the spot. She had seen him perform the same sort of movement when he played tennis, while he was waiting for his opponent to serve the ball at him.

The actor onstage continued: 'For thy enjoyment on this afternoon of the twenty-ninth day of the month of June in the Year of Our Lord, sixteen hundred and thirteen, under the reign of our mighty King, we present, for the first time ever, Mr Shakespeare's latest epic tale—*The History of Cardenio*!'

More cheers and clapping came from the house. Phyllis saw John Heminges, dressed as Cardenio in the costume of a strange-looking hermit, give Will a hearty slap on the back.

William Shakespeare smiled at his friend, but Phyllis detected a certain grimness behind the smile.

'And now,' declared the actor onstage, 'without further ado, I pray that thou wilt gently judge our efforts. We strive to serve thee, and to present thee with the entertainment thou so rightly cravest. Behold, ladies and gentlemen: *The History of Cardenio*!'

To a huge surge of applause, the actor came backstage to join his fellow players. 'They seem a likeable house,' he said to Will and John Heminges.

'A fine thing,' Shakespeare nodded. 'That we need this afternoon.'

The trumpets above sounded an alarum, and Shakespeare turned to Heminges. 'Enjoy it, John. Play with thy customary gusto and they will love it.'

John Heminges put his index finger to his forehead, giving the Bard a small salute, as he always did when he was about to go on stage in a premiere performance. Then he pulled down his hermit's hat, pushed his tatty cloak back across his shoulders and went through the curtains onto the stage.

'And we're off,' Clement said loudly to Phyllis.

'Shhh!' One of the actors, who was costumed as a matronly woman, shushed him.

'Sorry, ma'am,' Clement whispered back.

The matronly woman pursed her lips at him and turned her attention back to the stage.

'Man,' Clement muttered to Phyllis, 'I'm glad ladies don't *really* look like that. Imagine if that was your mother . . . I'd rather cuddle a porcupine than—' He stopped, noticing that Phyllis was looking vexed. 'Hey, Phyll,' he whispered. 'I'm sorry. I didn't mean *your* mother . . . I wasn't thinking . . .'

Phyllis said, 'Huh?'

'I didn't mean anything about your mother,' he whispered, embarrassed.

She blinked at him. 'No, Clem, it's not that. It's something else.'

'You okay?'

'Just keep your eye on that box.'

Something the actor had said in his welcoming speech had given the young magician a jolt. Something about the date. It sounded familiar.

She moved Daisy off her lap and pulled her journal out of her coat pocket. Quickly she flipped through it to where she'd made her various notes about the Globe and Jacobean London.

The pages fell open to an entry with the date as its heading: June 29th, 1613.

Phyllis's eyes widened. Her blood ran cold. *This can't be today*, she thought desperately. *Not today, of all days!*

'Phyll?' whispered Clement. 'What's up?'

She shook her head. 'Just . . . never you mind, Clem. You just keep watching that box.'

'Sure,' he said, puzzled. He turned to peek again.

Phyllis's mind raced. *Maybe I can stop it*, she thought. *Maybe I can prevent the awfulness that's coming . . .*

As if in answer to her thought, the letter that W.W. had written her dropped out of the back of the journal. The words near the end of his letter seemed to leap out at her:

Never attempt to change the course of Time or the events of what humankind calls History.

To do so will upset the everlasting equilibrium of eternity.

As Phyllis read those words she felt sick. She knew that something truly awful was going to happen, something much bigger than the possible theft of *Cardenio*, this very afternoon. And there was nothing—nothing that would be right—that she could do to stop it.

❋

The Chief Inspector patted his pistol, tucked discreetly into the folds of his red velvet pantaloons. He was hidden behind the curtains by the doors leading onstage, looking out across the theatre. He was waiting to go on.

Nearly all the other players were waiting further from the stage, in the green room off to the right. When their cues came, they would hurry from there directly in to the performance. Only Barry and one other actor, who were due to make their entrances soon, were here, close to the stage.

The audience had been enjoying the play. There had been laughter, and shouting when the action had hotted up on stage, and pin-dropping silence during the sad and lonely bits and even some booing and hissing when some villains had tried to steal from Cardenio. Barry had kept one eye on the action and the other on the house. From where he was, he hadn't been able to spy the curly-haired figure of Vesta Colley anywhere.

Suddenly he felt a sharp nudge in his ribs. He jumped.

'You're on,' hissed the other actor next to him, who was wearing a lanky-haired wig for his part as an old soldier. 'Make haste, man, they have given thy cue already!'

'Good lord,' muttered Barry. He took a deep breath, hitched up his hose where they had sagged round his knees, straightened himself fully, and strode onto the stage. The old soldier followed him out.

Phyllis listened, her heart pumping with the dread of the afternoon and with nervousness for the Chief Inspector—her insides were a maelstrom of emotions. She heard him begin to deliver his lines on the other side of the wall:

'Cardenio, I bring thee word,
The Knight seeks thee out,
And therefore hither I come.
Quixote thinks thou a madman, so long a
    fool,
And he is intent to discover your state.
Methinks thy afflictions come wi' the
    passing
Of the Hours. For, like the tides that all
    befall us,

Time travels in diff'ring paces with
        diff'ring persons.
I'll tell you who Time ambles withal, who
        Time
Dawdles withal, who Time rushes withal
And who he stands still withal . . .'

He sounds a bit shaky, Phyllis thought. *But he's
keeping it together . . .*
John Heminge's voice came boldly in response:

'I have no desire for meeting thy master,
For it shall lead to the fury of two
        desperate men
Oppos'd by winters of discord and
        fighting,
Transported by calamity and—'

'Phyll!' Clement grabbed Phyllis's arm. 'Look!'
he whispered urgently.
She snapped her head around and peeked
between the baskets.
'That shadow,' Clement said softly.
Phyllis's eyes widened. She held Daisy firmly in
her lap and watched.
A dark shadow was seeping across the floorboards in front of the table with the box on it. It
spread steadily, growing bigger as it came closer to

the table. Then, smoothly and silently, the shadow seemed to bleed upwards, rising over the table legs and onto the table itself, covering the foul papers box like a blanket of darkness.

There was the sound of soft, determined footsteps, and then the shadow became defined: a set of legs, a torso, two arms and a willowy darkness at the top of it, enveloping the box and the table and the corner of the backstage area where Phyllis, Daisy and Clement were hiding.

'It's her,' whispered Phyllis. 'It's the lady from the auction! It's Mistress Colley!'

Vesta Colley had been carrying a small cloth bag, and this she dumped quietly on the floor beside the table.

'I'll whistle,' Clement whispered to Phyllis, putting his fingers to his mouth.

'No!' Phyllis pulled his hand away. 'Remember what the Chief Inspector said. We have to wait till she's got the foul papers in her hands. We give the signal when she's actually stolen them!'

Clement frowned but said nothing.

Vesta Colley stood before the box. She looked down upon it with a greedy gleam in her good eye, and a covetous smile spreading across her lips. 'Here it is, Glory,' she said to her companion in her fur collar. 'Here is Shakespeare's play. See the initials on the box? *W.S.* This is what we are after—that which is inside will change the course of our days!'

Glory gave a quiet squeak and nuzzled her snout against her mistress's neck.

Vesta Colley withdrew one of her wheellock pistols from her boot. She turned it in her hand so that she was holding it by the barrel, with the handle away from her. Quickly she looked around the backstage area, at the same time listening to the sounds coming from the stage. She waited a few moments; then, when Cardenio's speech became louder and more passionate, she held the pistol aloft and brought the thick wooden handle crashing down against the locks on the box. John Heminge's booming voice, on the other side of the wall, muffled the sound of the locks cracking off the box and clunking onto the floor.

'Now?' asked Clem.

Phyllis shook her head. 'Wait till she's got the play in her hands!' she whispered.

Vesta flung open the lid of the box and peered inside. Her smile grew bigger. A sheaf of papers, neatly tied with a dark red ribbon, greeted her. 'There it lay'st. The richest of the riches. The fools of the twenty-first century will bid themselves silly for this!'

She slid the pistol back into the top of her boot and reached into the box. Her multi-ringed, bejewelled fingers snatched out the manuscript of *Cardenio*. She laughed quietly.

'Now!' urged Phyllis. 'Whistle now, Clem!'

Clement put his fingers back to his mouth and blew hard.

Nothing happened.

Phyllis looked at him. 'Go on!' she hissed. 'Whistle!'

He tried again, blowing onto his fingers until his cheeks turned scarlet. Still, nothing. The only noise he produced was like a sparrow's burp.

He pulled out his fingers and whispered, 'It's the teeth! I haven't got the fake teeth in. That must be why I could whistle so loud before!'

'Blimey Charley!' gasped Phyllis.

Vesta Colley untied the ribbon around the foul papers and dropped it to the floor. She carefully rolled the manuscript and put it in one of the outside pockets of her overcoat.

'She's gonna leave!' Clement whispered.

A rush of outrage filled Phyllis's insides. 'Not if I can help it,' she declared. She handed Daisy to Clement and sprang to her feet. 'Where do you think you're going?' she yelled, jumping out from behind the baskets and skips.

Vesta Colley spun around. Phyllis stood before her, her fists clenched, her eyes shining with anger. 'I said, where do you think you're going?'

'Well,' the thief snarled. 'The little girl from the auction house. The little girl whose fleabag attacked me. The little girl who—' Vesta's eye gleamed hatefully, and her face contorted with rage—'*Transits*!'

She stopped as she noticed something about Phyllis. Something about her eyes, and the shape of her mouth and her chin. There was something . . . familiar . . . about this girl . . . something *strangely* familiar.

'Those papers don't belong to you!' Phyllis warned.

'They do now, little girl!'

'They're Shakespeare's!'

Vesta stared balefully at her.

'They're not yours to take,' Phyllis went on, her voice rising. 'You can't just come back here and steal them. You've overstepped the mark, this time, and you're through!'

'No,' the woman hissed, whipping out both pistols from her boots. '*You're* through!' She raised the guns' barrels and aimed them straight at Phyllis's head. 'Your Transiting days are over, little girl! Never again will you thwart the Transits of another. You're about to take your final journey!'

With the pistols firmly aimed at the young conjuror, Vesta Colley curled her fingers around the triggers.

And squeezed.

'*Arf! Arf! Arf! Arf! Arf! Arf!*'

Like a blur of furry lightning, Daisy shot around the sides of the baskets, her protective instincts kicking in at the sound of Vesta's threats, and her sense of smell alerted by Glory. The terrier rushed at the woman, leapt up and buried her sharp little teeth in the side of Vesta Colley's leg, above her boot.

The woman screamed and flailed her leg about, throwing Daisy off. Daisy flumped onto the floor, shook her head and was about to go for another bite, when Clement burst forth.

'Phyll! I found 'em!' The beaver-like teeth were sticking out of his mouth.

'*Yergh!*' gasped Vesta Colley, startled at the sudden sight of him.

Daisy remained still, watching, her straight ear upright and the other, folded-over, ear alert.

Clement shoved his fingers into his mouth and blew as hard as he could.

This time it worked! The whistle screamed into the air, piercing through the whole of the Globe Theatre, long and loud and lingering.

For a few seconds, the sounds on the stage stopped. Glory screeched into her mistress's collar. Vesta Colley looked shaken—her leg hurt and her ears were ringing from Clement's explosion. Her hands were trembling, but still she aimed the pistols straight at Phyllis's head.

Then the play resumed, but without two of its players: through the curtained doorway, Barry Inglis and William Shakespeare hurtled. They stopped when they saw that Phyllis was the target of Colley's pistols.

The Chief Inspector stood still, his hands by his sides.

Shakespeare stayed next to him, also unmoving.

'She's got *Cardenio*,' Phyllis told them, her voice quivering. 'It's in her pocket!'

Vesta Colley looked Barry up and down. For a moment, the beard and moustache and the outfit confused her, but then she discerned his features and the way he was standing. 'Ah-ha!' she said, slowly, threateningly. 'The man in the blue suit, *out* of his blue suit. So, a Transiter also?'

'You're under arrest,' advised Barry Inglis. 'You have the right to remain silent—'

'*You remain silent!*' she hissed sharply, like a snake uncoiling. Her arms stopped trembling and she held them rigid, defiantly bringing her hands together so that the barrels of both pistols were almost side by side. 'Otherwise, the little girl shall have her head blown to kingdom come!'

Phyllis's legs were shaking.

Daisy looked at Phyllis, then at the pistols in

Vesta Colley's hands. The dog knew it would not be good to rush at the woman again. There was danger in the woman's hands.

'Give me my papers,' Will said. 'They are not thine for the taking, madam.'

Vesta's good eye sleered across to him. 'They are yours for the *losing*, scribbler!' she spat.

Slowly, carefully, Barry pressed his right hand closer to the side of his pantaloons.

'Give them back,' Phyllis implored Vesta. 'Please! Don't do this!'

Barry's fingers disappeared smoothly into the folds of the red velvet against his hip.

'Shut the door of thy mouth!' Vesta Colley shouted at Phyllis.

'Leave her alone!' Clement shouted back at her.

Colley's face turned white with anger. 'One more sound from ANY of you and I shall let loose with my volleys!'

The group fell silent, waiting.

'Now,' Colley said, her voice knifeblade-sharp, 'I am going to walk away from this scene. I shall make my exit, untroubled and undisturbed. And if any of you try to follow me, to find me, to hinder me in the future and all of the futures to come, I shall finish you in ways you could never imagine!'

The Chief Inspector felt the cold hard steel of his pistol, and his hand curled around it.

'But first,' hissed Colley, 'before I leave, I shall take something more with me.' She jerked the barrels of her guns at Phyllis. 'You! Come here to me.'

Phyllis's eyes went wide. Her heart was hammering inside her. She couldn't move.

'Insolent child!' Vesta Colley strode over to Phyllis and, slipping one of the guns into her boot, she grabbed Phyllis roughly, pinioning her arm sharply behind her back and holding the young magician closely in front of her. 'You are going to serve me until your Time is done,' she hissed loudly into Phyllis's ear. 'Our kind should always stick by each other!'

'Let me go, please!' Phyllis implored.

Glory ran out of the fur collar and across Phyllis's shoulders and back into the collar again.

Daisy barked and barked as if she were about to burst. *'Arf! Arf! Arf! Arf! Arf! Arf! Arf!'*

Colley had lowered her other arm—the one holding the pistol—momentarily when she had grabbed hold of Phyllis. That one moment was enough for the quick reflexes of a trained policeman.

'Hold it right there, lady!' shouted Chief Inspector Barry Inglis, his silver pistol gleaming and aimed at Vesta Colley's arm.

'What?' spewed Colley, beginning to raise her gun at him.

All it took was an instant—an instant where Phyllis was fractionally out of his range. Barry Inglis squeezed the trigger, and there was a mighty explosion, louder than a thunderclap. The bullet shot through the air, trailing a cascading shower of brilliant sparks, and embedding itself in the arm of Vesta Colley.

She screamed, letting go of Phyllis and dropping her gun. She clutched at her arm. Her coat had caught fire from the flaming bullet.

Phyllis jumped away, and her heart almost stopped.

There, on the floor, lay Barry. His gun—his gun from the future—had exploded in his hand, and he had fallen, hitting his head hard.

He was not moving.

Taken by the blaze

Phyllis rushed to her friend lying on the floor. Will Shakespeare fell to his knees and placed a hand gently to Barry's heart.

'*Aaaaarrrrrrrgggggggghhhhhh!*' screamed Vesta Colley, trying to pat down the flames spreading on her coat as the pain from the bullet seared into her arm.

'*Skreeeeeeeeech!*' Glory flew from her collar, disappearing into a darkened corner.

Daisy ran to Phyllis's side and placed a paw on Barry's still leg.

Clement also acted quickly. He saw Vesta Colley's dropped weapon. He swooped on it and grabbed the heavy gun in both hands, aiming it at the burning woman.

'Help me!' she wailed. 'I am aflame! *Aaaaarrrrrggggghhhhhhh!*' Her arms spun around as though she were a windmill. The fire had now caught in the fur collar. Frantically, she tore off the coat and dropped it to the floor. It fell close to the small cloth bag she had earlier put there.

Inside this small cloth bag were enough reeds of high-explosive gunpowder to blow the roof clean off the Globe Theatre, along with most of the roofs of the surrounding neighbourhood.

'*My rings! My rings!*' Colley screamed wildly. '*They melt into my fingers!*'

'Chief Inspector?' Phyllis leant over Barry, but there was still no movement.

Clement's glasses had slid down his nose when he had stooped to grab the wheellock pistol. He pushed them back and, with trembling hands, he steadied his aim at the woman.

And he gasped loudly.

Despite the flames, Vesta Colley had whipped out her other pistol from her boot and was pointing it directly at Clement's head. Her face was contorted into an agony that made her almost unrecognisable. 'You wretched child,' she spat at him. 'You fool! You do not know how to fire such a weapon! I do!'

She looked down the barrel of the gun at Clement. His face went white as he realised that what she said was true. This was no game-type gun. There was something about the trigger on the wheellock pistol that wouldn't allow his finger to curl all the way around it.

'Kingdom come, here you GO!' shouted Colley.

She took her final aim at Clement, her good eye wide with fury.

Phyllis, still crouching by Barry, spun around. 'No!' she screamed. 'Don't do it!'

'Have mercy!' cried Shakespeare. 'He's only a lad!'

With a fierce, malevolent cackle, Vesta Colley squeezed the trigger.

BANG!

What happened next was bright, quick, sudden—so sudden that it took everyone's breath away.

There was a blazing flash in front of Colley's gun, and a huge puff of green smoke. The smoke billowed swiftly away to reveal a man . . .

. . . A tall, slender man with dark, glossy-black hair and a thin, neat moustache. A man dressed in a midnight-blue tuxedo.

'W.W.!' exclaimed Phyllis, jumping to her feet.

Wallace Wong, Conjuror of Wonder!, looked at his great-granddaughter, his eyes gleaming and throbbing with the green of the Transiter. 'Phyllis,' he greeted her quickly. He held out his closed hand and uncurled his fingers. The heavy bullet from Vesta Colley's pistol dropped from his palm, clattering onto the floor.

'The bullet catch!' Phyllis gasped. She had never seen the legendary trick performed before.

There was no time for proper greetings and introductions. Wallace Wong turned to Vesta

Colley. 'You and I, madam, have unfinished business!'

'Wong!' she spat. She looked at him, and then her eye fixed on Phyllis. 'That's why you look so familiar! You and he are—'

'Look!' shouted Clement. 'The baskets!'

The flames from the burning coat had spread along the floor and ignited the big pile of prop baskets that Phyllis, Daisy and Clement had been hiding behind. The fire had caught quickly, licking up all the way to the thatched ceiling of the backstage area, and crackling out across the dry under-roof of straw.

The small cloth bag containing the gunpowder was in the line of the creeping spread of the fire.

Daisy pawed Phyllis's leg. Phyllis grabbed her and slipped her into the change bag.

'Burn, house of dreams!' hissed Vesta Colley, the pain from her burnt gold-melting fingers and her wounded arm surging through her body. '*Burn and BLOW!*'

Out of the side of his mouth, Wallace asked Phyllis: 'What date is it today, great-granddaughter?'

'Twenty-ninth of June,' said Phyllis.

'And the year?'

'Sixteen thirteen.'

'Ah. The burning of the Globe,' he said sadly.

'It's unavoidable,' Phyllis said, and he nodded.

'The burning, yes,' said Wallace, 'but not *this*!' He'd seen, sticking out of the half-opened top of Vesta's small bag, some of the reeds of gunpowder. Like a panther he crouched and leapt and swept up the cloth bag of explosives, away from the flames. He shoved it under his jacket and said, 'At least we may be able to save *some* lives!'

Smoke was already billowing down from the thatched roof, falling in heavy, dark grey shafts and spreading out onto the stage.

A violent coughing came from the floor. Shakespeare looked up quickly. 'The Chief Inspector! He breathes!'

Barry Inglis was gasping and gagging, and his chest racked up and down as he tried to gulp in fresh oxygen.

'Quick!' cried Wallace Wong. 'Get him out! Take him to the stairs in the north tower—it's where I came from. And you too, Phyllis, and your friend here!'

Shakespeare grabbed Barry under both arms and hoisted him up. The Chief Inspector leant groggily against the Bard, still coughing heavily and blinking dazedly through the thickening smoke. 'What happened?' he choked. He winced as he felt his burnt hand. 'Oh, yeah, the pistol . . .'

'C'mon,' said Phyllis. 'We've got to scram!'

'Scram?' Shakespeare echoed, making a mental note of the word. 'Aye, let us scram with haste!'

'Let me help,' said Clement. He dropped the pistol, snatched up his backpack and ran over to Will and the Chief Inspector. Barry placed one arm heavily onto Clement's shoulders, and the other around Will's back. Together they dragged Barry away through the rear of the backstage area.

Suddenly Phyllis realised something. 'Colley! Where is she?'

Wallace Wong wheeled around and peered through the smoke and flames. The woman had vanished. 'The elusive larcenist!' he cried. 'She is as furtive as the eyebrow of the sloth . . .' He blinked, and said quickly to Phyllis, 'Oh, I know what I mean.'

The actors from the green room had come rushing backstage, along with Ralph the ruddy-faced stage manager. John Heminges raced in from the stage. 'Quickly!' he cried to the company. 'The fire is in the galleries outside, and the groundlings are rushing to escape! Go out and herd the audience safely away! Thou all know'st where the exits are better than they!'

The players threw off their wigs and cloaks and skirts and ran out into the auditorium.

Heminges caught sight of Wallace Wong. 'Who, sir, are you?'

'Do not mind me,' Wallace said. 'My visit will be brief. The people must be evacuated!'

'This is a dire predicament!' Heminges gushed, rushing to check that the green room was empty. 'Make haste to safety, for the entire Globe will fast be ablaze!' he shouted over his shoulder as he went.

Phyllis hugged her great-grandfather and he held her close for an instant.

'Why did you come?' she asked him, batting away the thickening smoke.

He put his hand on his white waistcoat, near where his heart was. 'You needed me,' he answered. 'I felt it.'

She looked into his glowing green eyes. 'We stopped her,' she told Wallace Wong. 'She didn't get what she came for, the foul papers of *Cardenio*.' She pointed to the box. 'They're still—*no!*'

As she spoke, she remembered that they weren't in the box, but in the pocket of Colley's coat, on the floor. The woollen coat was still burning, the flames bright and gold with dancing blue flickering edges, too intense to extinguish.

'*She* didn't get them,' murmured Wallace, 'but the conflagration did.'

Phyllis shouted into the air, 'You awful, awful—'

'Go, my dear,' Wallace urged, propelling her firmly to the door leading to the north tower's stairs. 'Before the smoke smothers the life from you!'

Phyllis hurried into the dense smoke. Inside her bag, Daisy was barking; soft, pleading yelps full of desperate fear.

Phyllis could feel her great-grandfather's hands firmly, reassuringly, on the backs of her shoulders as she stumbled along, out onto the stage and down into the groundlings' yard. She half-closed her eyes as they filled with stinging tears, and she started gasping for breath as the air became thinner and more burning in her throat.

'Get down low!' came W.W.'s voice beside her ear. 'And go straight ahead! Your friends are there already!'

She crouched and started running towards the doorway into the north tower. The flames out here had spread quickly, with lightning-like fury, along the dry under-roofs of the thatched galleries; the light rain that had fallen yesterday on the thatch above had not been enough to dampen the straw heavily, and the roof had no hope of dousing the fire.

People were rushing frantically through the exits, down the stairs of the towers and out towards the Thames. The crescendo of the crackling, crashing, crushing flames was almost deafening, and the late afternoon was filled with this dreadful blazing noise and with the shouts and cries of thousands of theatre-goers.

'Phyll!' came Clement's voice through the thick haze. 'Over here!'

She lurched onwards to the tower door, and he grabbed her and pulled her in.

The smoke was still dense in here, but so far the flames had not infiltrated the tower. Phyllis saw, through the thick blanket of the smoke, Barry standing upright, a piece of linen wrapped around his burnt hand, speaking to Will. 'Yes,' he was saying, 'we'll get ourselves away. You go and make sure everyone's safe.'

'That be all I can do,' said the Bard. 'We have surely lost the building.'

On the other side of the theatre, the heavy oak beams holding up the three tiers of the galleries came crashing down. The screams of the evacuating people tore into the air.

'I'm so sorry,' said Barry Inglis to Will.

'Farewell, Chief Inspector. Thank you for saving my work.'

Phyllis hadn't the heart to tell Will that this wasn't true.

Will turned to her and Clement. 'Farewell, young conjuror, and to you, brave one of a thousand faces. You played the red-bearded dwarf superbly.'

'Goodbye,' said Phyllis and Clement together.

Daisy poked her head out of the bag on Phyllis's shoulder and gave a spluttering yelp.

'And farewell to you, sweet vanishing pup,' Shakespeare added. 'Now I must to my duty!'

With a small bow, he hastened back into the auditorium.

In the backstage area of the fast-blackening and collapsing Globe, Wallace Wong reached down through the smoke to Vesta Colley's almost-burnt coat. Amazingly, a small part of one side of the coat had not yet been touched by the flames. He shoved his hand into the outer pocket and felt about for a moment. Then his eyes lit up, the greenness throbbing brighter. 'Ah, back at last,' he muttered, taking his Date Determinator from the garment. 'Rotten little thief,' he said, shaking his head. He pocketed the device and quickly made his way out.

Phyllis was peering up at the stairs leading to the top floor of the tower. The roof at the very top of this place had now caught well and truly alight, and a brilliant, crackling yellow filled the stairway.

She squinted, trying to find the outline of the Pocket on the stairs. Everything was hazy; the smoke was thickening and becoming blindingly smothering.

Then, through the dense haze, she saw a shimmer of green—a big almond-shaped outline, about two-thirds of the way up the stairs. 'It's there!' she exclaimed. 'This is where W.W. came from!'

'W.W.?' said Barry, confused.

'Come on,' she shouted over the noise of the fire. 'We've got to run, as fast as we can. Are you able, Chief Inspector?'

'Try and stop me,' he coughed.

She reached into her coat pocket, her fingers scrabbling around frantically. It was empty!

'Phyll!' gasped Clement. 'What's wrong?'

Her face drained as her hand crashed about in there. Her red glittery ball—the ball she used as her passport to get back to the basement—wasn't there!

Then she realised. She put her other hand in her other pocket and fished about. She almost cried with relief when she found the red ball in there.

Squeezing it in a *nothing will prise this out of my hand* grasp, she said, 'Okay, here we go. Clem, hold my coat; Chief Inspector, grab onto Clem's backpack.'

They did so.

'One, two, *three!*' Phyllis yelled.

Taking the steps two at a time, they raced upwards, through the smoke and the billowing, crashing destruction of the Globe Theatre, towards the mysterious pathway home.

No black and white

Wallace Wong didn't return with Phyllis, Daisy, Clem and Barry. Not that Time. In fact, it would be some Time before Phyllis would encounter her great-grandfather again in the flesh.

The Transit home was fast. At first the wind through the Andruseon Pocket had been hot and airless, carrying with it the intense, choking heat from the Globe Theatre. But the further they Transited, the cooler the wind became. By the time the four of them came stumbling-tumbling down the steps in the basement of the Wallace Wong Building, the temperature had levelled and settled. The fierceness of the final day of the Globe was nothing but a memory.

Barry Inglis made a quick exit, up to his apartment to get some ointment and fresh bandages for his hand. Before he went, he stopped in front of the basement elevator and looked down at Phyllis at the bottom of the stairs.

He stood there for several long moments, deep in thought.

Finally, Phyllis asked, 'Are you all right, Chief Inspector?'

'I *am* all right,' he said, his eyes glowing green as he looked at her. 'And you are brilliant. Brilliant and astonishing.'

She smiled up at him.

He did a small wriggle. 'Goodbye for now, Miss Wong. These pantaloons are chafing me something horrible. I . . . I need to rest . . .'

She kept smiling as she watched him entering the elevator. 'I've left the key in there,' she called. 'When you get out, just turn it and send the elevator back down here.'

'Will do,' Barry called back.

'See you, Baz!' Clement called when the doors to the contraption had closed and it was going judderingly up and the Chief Inspector was safely out of earshot.

Phyllis put her bag on one of the sofas and Daisy bounded out of it, a little groggy from the Transit. 'Here, Miss Daisy, have a munchie.' Phyllis gave her a treat, and the terrier sat there, sphinx-like, chewing away at it between her front paws.

Clement was busting to tell of his adventure to his mother, and especially to Evangeline Hipwinkle back at Thundermallow's. But, as Phyllis reminded him in no uncertain terms, he *had* given her the

380

absolute promise that he wouldn't breathe a word to anyone about what had happened.

'Oh, yeah,' he said. 'I did do the *crossing the aorta nineteen times* promise, didn't I?'

'You did. And you know you can't break that.'

He sighed. 'Yep. Still, you and I can talk about what happened whenever we want, can't we?'

'It's our secret,' Phyllis smiled.

Clem hitched his backpack over his shoulder. 'I'm starving. Ha, I feel like I haven't eaten in four hundred years! What's today?'

'Tuesday,' Phyllis answered.

'Yay! Mum does duck on Tuesdays!' He started up the stairs, then stopped, inspecting the top of the staircase warily. 'Hey, it's safe for me to go up here, right? I'm not gonna end up in Timbuktu or anything, running away from Genghis Khan?'

'You'll be fine,' she reassured him. 'You've got to have the gift to be a Transiter.'

'Yeah. Whatever.' He shrugged. 'And you've gotta have the gift to be an M.o.D.'

'A what?'

'A Master of Disguise. Y'know, on second thoughts, I think I'll go my own way.' He flashed her his wide grin, and his beaver teeth almost popped out. 'See ya, Phyllis Wong!'

'Ciao, Clem!'

She watched him come back down the stairs, then hurry round to the door he'd earlier discovered underneath them. In an instant, he was gone.

Phyllis went and sat heavily on the sofa next to Daisy. All at once she felt exhausted.

'I think I'll go see the Inspector,' she said to Daisy as she patted her gently. 'First thing tomorrow.'

'*Rr-gg-rr-gg-rr*,' said Daisy, making her gargling-with-marbles sound and giving Phyllis's hand a playful lick.

❋

The next morning, when Phyllis asked Constable Karin Olofsson at the front desk of Police Headquarters if she could see Barry, the Constable said sternly, 'Eggs can be dangerous, Phyllis Wong.'

Phyllis gave her a quizzical look.

'He should be more careful when he's frying his eggs. He should get a skillet with a heatproof handle. Have you seen the burn on his hand? I made him take the bandage off to show me.' She sighed. 'For a Chief Inspector, he sure needs a training course in home safety.'

'Oh,' said Phyllis. 'His burn. Yep, the world can be a dangerous place.'

Constable Olofsson gave Phyllis a *yes, that's why they invented heatproof handles* sort of look.

She picked up the phone and got through to Barry Inglis straightaway.

After a few words with him, she said to Phyllis, 'Go straight up. He said he was sort of expecting you.'

'Thanks, Constable.' Phyllis beamed at her and shot up the stairs.

'Ah,' Barry greeted her, getting out of his chair. 'Come on in. I was sort of—'

'Expecting me?'

'That I was. Have a seat.'

She sat in the chair across from his desk, and he went back to his chair by the window.

'How's the hand?' she asked.

'Ah. It'll be fine in no time. I can still use my fingers. Thank you for asking.'

Then they both spoke over the top of each other—Barry saying, 'Now, about what happened yesterday, if it *was* yesterday,' and Phyllis saying, 'I need you to promise me something.'

Barry leant back. His eyes were gleaming. 'You go ahead,' he told her.

'Well,' she said, 'I need you to promise me that no matter what happens to you, you'll never tell a living soul what happened.'

He clasped his hands across his shirt and studied her. 'Tell me, Miss Wong: what *did* happen?'

'Huh?'

'What did happen? Did I dream that I went back with you and young Clement to a theatre built hundreds of years ago? Or did it really occur, that we actually did visit that place?'

'Oh, it occurred, all right,' Phyllis said, a little indignant. 'Of course it did! How d'you think you got your hand burnt?'

'Of course it occurred,' said Barry Inglis. 'I know that; you know that. I have a very strange set of clothes hanging in my wardrobe that confirms it all. Pantaloons, for goodness sake! But if anyone ever, for some strange reason, got into my thoughts and discovered what really happened, why—I'd say it was a dream.'

'A dream,' Phyllis repeated, narrowing her eyes at him.

'People *accept* dreams, Miss Wong, as a way of explaining things. People are far less likely to accept amazing things that actually, really did happen. But dreams . . . ah, they're a different kettle of fish . . . Our friend Will himself said that there are more things in heaven and earth, Horatio, than are dreamt of in your philosophy . . .'

'Who's Horatio?' asked Phyllis.

'A character in *Hamlet*.' Barry twiddled his thumbs. 'What I'm trying to say is this: you and I know what happened, but if ever the world finds out about it, then I will maintain that it was all a dream. Otherwise it will do people's heads in.'

A slow grin emerged on Phyllis's face. 'I came here to ask you to keep it all a secret,' she said. 'But you've already decided to, haven't you?'

'A dream is best kept as a secret,' he answered. 'And this will be ours.'

Then Phyllis gasped loudly, and her mouth dropped open.

Chief Inspector Barry Inglis was smiling! A genuine, wide-across-his-face, dimple-in-the-cheek-making *smile*!

'Hey! You're—'

'Aherm.' He cleared his throat, and the smile disappeared. 'Before you go,' he said, putting on his Chief Inspector voice again, 'I want you to have this.'

He opened a drawer in his desk and took out a long envelope. This he slid across the desk to Phyllis.

'What is it?'

'Open it when you get home,' he said. 'And now, if you'll excuse me, I have a lot of paperwork to do. The House of Wendlebury's are up in arms that they're not going to be able to auction a certain "lost" play by the great William Shakespeare, and I have to examine all the correspondence between them and a certain woman who claimed she could produce it for them . . . seems they want to sue the britches off her. Not that I think they'll have much luck . . . they'd have to find her first!'

Phyllis took the envelope and stood. 'Thanks, Chief Inspector.'

'No, thank *you*, Miss Wong. Once again, because of you and your unique way of moving through your life, we have averted what could have been another major crime. At least in this century.'

'All in the line of duty,' Phyllis said. 'See you round some time.'

'I'm as certain of that as I am of the nose upon my face,' said Barry Inglis.

'Oh, one more thing.'

He raised an eyebrow at her.

'There's a bit of paper under your desk. It looks old.'

And, giving him her inscrutable smile, Phyllis Wong left the office.

Chief Inspector Barry Inglis leant down in his chair and picked up the scrap of light cream-coloured paper that had become dislodged from the page in the last First Folio he had seen. 'Hmm,' he hmmed, inspecting it thoughtfully. 'I was wondering where that'd got to . . .'

✳

When she arrived home, Phyllis went straight down to her basement.

She sat in a chair at the bottom of the stairs and took from her pocket the envelope Barry had given her. Carefully she tore open the end flap and pulled out what was inside.

They were pages, not thick but not thin either, and the paper was a high quality rag paper. On each page, written in ink in a scrolling, neat handwriting, were words from a speech.

Phyllis's heart beat quickly, and her hands began to quiver as she realised what she was holding: the only surviving samples from *Cardenio*. The part played by Barry Inglis at the premiere of the play in 1613.

Written in the Bard's own handwriting.

She read the words, and read them again. She held the pages close to her chest and rested her head against the high-backed chair. She stared at the ceiling of her basement for what seemed ages.

Then, realising it was time to go upstairs and take Daisy for her walk, she put the foul papers into a cupboard, safe alongside her magic tricks and her props and her Transiting journal and her little block of old type with the letter P on it and all the other secrets that belonged to Phyllis Wong— conjuror, Transiter and keeper of the mysteries of Time.

Endword

If you have read all that has come before this page, you will, like Phyllis herself, have made many new discoveries. Just as I did when I was writing this story.

Much of the information in *Phyllis Wong and the Return of the Conjuror* is based on historical facts and bits of information that have become 'lost' in time. We know, for example, that Mr Shakespeare wrote a play, *The History of Cardenio*, but it has sadly become lost. (People are still searching for it, and we can be hopeful that one day it may turn up— and that will be an exciting event!) We also know that none of Shakespeare's foul papers have survived, or, if they have, no one knows of their whereabouts.

Women were not allowed to perform on stage during Shakespeare's time, and would not be allowed to until after 1660, which is when the Puritans lost their power. Thankfully, the theatre has never reverted to such straitlaced traditions, and we can hope that it never will.

We also know that the neighbourhood around the Globe Theatre was a smelly one, because of the many tanneries in the district. Tanneries in those days used human excrement to help soften the leather, which accounts for Clement's reaction when he encounters the awful stench. He is a sensitive boy, and I am not at all surprised by how he took it.

What I love about history is that sometimes fact is far stranger than fiction. It is true, as Phyllis reads in the newspaper, that of all the hundreds of thousands of words that Shakespeare penned only six words written in his own handwriting still survive! That to me is a superb irony—the greatest writer we have ever seen is only represented in his own hand by six . . . count them! . . . *six* words.

Here and there I have taken some historical facts and changed them around a little, to make Phyllis's story more rich. The Globe Theatre was destroyed by fire. Historians believe that a different play by Shakespeare was being performed at the Globe when the tragic events took place there on June 29th, 1613. In Phyllis's story, it is the lost play premiering on that date.

Shakespeare was a prolific inventor of new words and phrases, and I have peppered the story with many of these words, phrases and sayings he wrote. Some of the chapter headings are phrases coined by Shakespeare, as are some of the things that the characters say. Ardent fans of the Bard may have fun finding these . . .

All the tricks performed by Phyllis have been performed for me by my favourite magician, to whom I've dedicated the story. Those card tricks that Phyllis does for Selena really are breathtaking.

Albert Einstein did indeed propose the theory that so influences, and alters, the world of Phyllis Wong. And 'Antigonish' was written by William Hughes Mearns. And stairs have been around for thousands of years. As will be stories of magic, and the magic of stories.

And sometimes, if you look quickly, fleetingly, out of the corner of your eye, you might find something that will one day change your life . . .

G. McS.
Sydney and Cawdor

The author

Find out more about Phyllis Wong at
phylliswong.com

Have you read Phyllis Wong's first mystery?

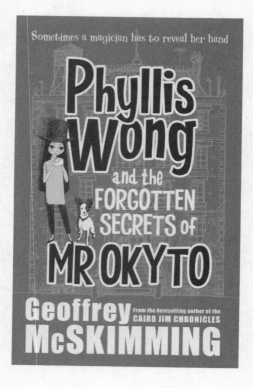

Find out how this junior sleuth with sleight
of hand tackles a series of seemingly
incomprehensible robberies.